CW00518105

RANDOM SKIES

VOLUME 1 NO. 1

QUORUM

SPEY SONDHEIM
Novelisation by Jim Cheshire

www.randomskies.com
www.speysondheim.com

Random Skies is a work of futuristic fiction set in a parallel universe. Names, characters, businesses, places, events, locales, and incidents are either the products of the author's imagination or used in a fictitious manner for narrative effect. Any resemblance, therefore, to actual persons, living or dead, or actual events is purely coincidental.

"...and finally in this hour, great news for lovers of the No Messin' Pizza chain who don't want to wait in the lines for their favourite family meals! No Messin's eight hundred and forty UK outlets have joined the government's EatSafe initiative, pledging to provide fast track lines for hungry diners who carry Global ID. A spokesman for the hugely popular restaurant brand told our reporter this: "Global ID is accepted everywhere, it's the easiest way to buy anything. If people want better value, better service and those all important discounts and deals on our range of fabulous products, then Global ID is the way to go. Clearly, the government's got it right on this one, so carry Global ID and 'EatSafe'. And that's No Messin'!"

No one was really aware of the sun finally setting. The sky had been a murky shade of purple all day, clouds shifting back and forth. It got darker as the rain thickened, pattering on the concrete and rubble in the old abandoned suburbs.

The beams of well-lit bulldozers crossed the front walls of an empty apartment block as they climbed the heaps. The arc lights fizzed around them and the night shift began.

Beyond the demolition, and closer in to central London, small fires burned in the shells of supermarkets and chain stores. Ragged figures threw shadows on the makeshift tin roofs. Above them, lone watchers in the mosques could see the glow of the city centre on the horizon and watch the police helicopters fanning out like hungry bees, losing themselves in the murk and the mist. Occasional stabs of laser and pencil spots gave them away. The bray of a bullhorn, the clatter of rotors.

A cleared zone, the width of a city block, backed up to the high security fencing where the army maintained curfew from mobile watchtowers that rose above the razor wire. Security patrols in body armour and thermal night vision goggles scanned the no man's land, preparing to fire on any target. There was nothing moving in the wasteland tonight.

Behind them, the lights of central London pulsed in the dull cloud of unnatural fog, a deliberate scene of normality. Mock neon crackled in the rain. Restaurants and clubs shone with multicolour holographic porticoes where the taxis pulled through and dropped their fares.

A Secorp passenger copter passed overhead. The side gunner watched the streets on a screen, waiting to pick up a heat signature with no

Global ID attached. They passed into a restricted zone, flying between the skyscrapers and letting Central Traffic Control bring them automatically to the helipad.

***

Cranton stood shivering on the pad watching the copter come down. He waited for the security detail to usher the guests across the rain soaked concrete of the roof. He straightened his tie, cursing the cold water running down his neck.

"Good evening, Sir. Did you have a good trip?"

The heavy set man in a thick black coat glanced through his military escort as he swept past.

"Who the hell are you?"

"Oh. Cranton, Sir. Head of Building Security. Ensuring you, er..."

But the guard had closed around the hurrying figure as they entered the building, forcing Cranton to one side.

"...enjoy your visit."

Three floors down, the guards posted themselves outside the double doors of the conference room. Inside, an impressive black glass horseshoe table swept around the room. The interior wall screen showed a floor to ceiling satellite map of Southern England, animated with points and lines of brightly lit communications traffic. The glass walls looked out over the smudgy landscape of illuminated skyscrapers and the dull mist that hung only a mile beyond.

"Good evening, General Rishek."

The greeting and handshake came from one of the dozen other expensively suited men already sat at the table, now guiding him to an empty chair.

Rishek shook hands.

"Gentlemen, I apologise for my late arrival. Some small delay in Zurich."

In the centre of the horseshoe sat a confident, well dressed, olive-skinned figure surrounded by paperwork. He waved away his aides, and waited til they had left the room.

The last man out was Cranton. He turned at the door and made an announcement to the room.

"Gentlemen, this building is now compliant with the GSC1 protocol and for the next hour this room is beyond the reach of the Internet."

Rishek slipped the GLiD out of his pocket and looked at the screen. It was all dark apart from a green diode in the top right corner that pulsed with a comforting regularity. It was his heartbeat, after all.

Cranton was followed out by two guards and the doors were locked.

Prime Minister Mohammed al-Degri allowed himself a small smile as he broke the silence.

"Yes, General Rishek. We were following your journey with interest today. It appears that even the Swiss are not immune to the shortages of manpower and equipment that the rest of us have been experiencing."

"Quite so, Prime Minister."

The glass walls had turned a smoky grey, hiding the lights of the city blocks and now gradually became interior walls showing portrait paintings.

"With no further ado, let us resolve this extensive and far-reaching investigation that we have spent so long preparing."

al-Degri indicated his piles of paperwork.

"I am not used to dealing with documents that are not electronic in nature. It has therefore been symbolic of our particular project that we have had to use so much 'unhackable' paper."

There were cold smiles around the room.

"Present here are delegates of the primary organisations who have attended the COBRA briefings. There are, of course, no minutes to this meeting, but so we are in accord..."

al-Degri motioned around the table.

"...Secorp Europe, employed by my government to lend their very extensive expertise and experience of cyber-terrorist activity to our own problem here in the UK. The Joint Intelligence Committee in conjunction with advisers from the private sector, notably the Cyber Security Institute and the technology company, Nightship Systems. The Armed Forces represented by NATO Northern Command. The UK Commissioner of the civilian police force. As would be expected from the transparent nature of our democracy, it is now imperative that we are ultimately able to keep the public informed and therefore, tonight the media is represented here by the Director General of the BBCE and the Chairmen of ITVE, SkyGlobal and the independent Metropolitan World Service.

I may remind the gentlemen of the media that, even during this consultation period, the UK government has already revised the laws governing the gathering and dissemination of personal data, indeed the very nature of what constitutes 'privacy' and the freedoms of movement, of political expression, and of speech itself. I accept that it has been a testing time for the definition of democracy, for the interpretations of the law and for the British public. As ever, your co-operation in presenting the narrative to your audience is not only appreciated but fundamental."

The screen behind al-Degri responded to his words, throwing images and newsreel from floor to ceiling.

"To summarise for you the main points of Operation Tin Man, the United Kingdom has long wrestled with illegal cyber activity. What began as piracy, hacking and online vandalism has become dangerous and subversive intrusion into the vital government systems that control our society. Systems of credit, identity, legal process and employment as well as the internal administration are all online constructs that cannot be compromised. It has become even more important now that Global Identity is fully integrated with the internet. The take-up of the sub-dermal microchip is only a step away from being a basic employment requirement for all citizens, rather than currently those professionals who require levels of security clearance. With careful explanation of the benefits of Global ID, the public are coming to trust the concept and, in the near future, we can move forward to promoting Global ID for everyone from birth to death.

"Clearly, this cannot happen without a watertight system of permanent, fully secure internet with no compromise, no cyber-terrorism and no downtime. We therefore initiated two programmes of investigation: National Security Through INfrastructure MANagement and secondly, Public Safety Through INfrastructure MANagement. Our goal has been to identify the predominant threats and neutralise their means of disruption, deploying new generations of government data centres with operating systems and hardware not otherwise available to the public. This would become a fresh start for all those accepting Global ID and a gradual phasing out of the voluntary system. Over time, the Internet will become fully and irrevocably controlled by government for the benefit of all and to the detriment of those who would seek to undermine our way of life.

"Under PS-TINMAN, Secorp have co-ordinated many drill scenarios in conjunction with the police forces of major cities to manage crisis situations in the event of internet failure. The media's mission to explain these drills to the public has done much to encourage the good natured acceptance of the disruption to daily life that they have inevitably brought. Problems of the potential loss of internet include no transport, no communications, no legal commerce - buying or selling - no access to buildings and businesses. Crisis management plans are well advanced and civilian and military training is under constant revision. The armed forces and the Police Commissioner have both expressed their approval of the intelligence gleaned from these operations and have worked closely with Secorp to harmonise contingency plans.

NS-TINMAN charged Secorp with protecting our new government systems from known and future criminal activity. The media have highlighted within the public consciousness the ongoing threat from hacking groups associated with the cybercriminal known as The User. Although the JIC have reported that we are not yet able to apprehend this individual or to break down his organisation, the very fact that he is able to consistently avoid detection is justification for the legal framework that we have put in place during Operation Tin Man.

I am pleased to report that the Cyber Security Institute has prepared recommendations for actions on the outcome of our drills and intelligence gathering. Particularly those that fall largely in line with the recent legislation passed through parliament to reform our definitions of free speech, freedom of assembly and access to transport and other resources. This, I can now confirm, has been passed through Cabinet and any further modifications will undergo further discussion, though perhaps in the next parliament and following a successful election result in the autumn."

al-Degri's confident smile fractured a little as he was met with blank looks.

"Our course of action therefore will be as follows..."

The screen highlighted the points as he spoke.

"A roll-out of the new datacentre technology will begin after due consultation with the service providers, employers and government departments. The Exchequer will approve the technology budget early in the next parliament and thereby determine how quickly it can be achieved.

"Public security drills will cease, until and unless a new situation develops. Although there will be relaxation of the perceived terror threat on the street, current measures regarding data gathering on those in public areas will continue in the background, subject to the government's legal constraints.

"The Cyber Security Institute could pinpoint no actual occasions when breaches of primary government systems in Whitehall were incidents of domestic terrorism by known hacking groups, or that significant data was stolen or compromised. Although it is unfortunate that the recent breaches remain unresolved, and lack of evidence points to the sophistication of hostile foreign agencies, the fact that nothing was gained is significant. Further work has been done to fortify the system and we suggest that our current arrangements are now robust and adequate until the new technology is ready to ship.

"A parliamentary unity group will debate the issue of Global ID and it is anticipated that within ten years, will pass into centrist policy, allowing future governments to propose a nationwide registration scheme.

"Finally, a new committee on radicalised cybercrime will be formed to offer new insights into the motivations and eventual nullification of threats from The User and his perceived associates, thus removing the domestic threat from the United Kingdom."

al-Degri noticed that no one around the table was moving. The tension seemed to be rising in the room. He blundered quickly on.

"Ultimately, gentlemen, and I am sure you will agree with the Cabinet's decision when you see the full report, that although the threat of cyber terrorism cannot be understated, at this point there is no evidence of the need for any overt action that might appear extreme in the eyes of a tolerant, though sometimes sceptical, public. I, for one, am pleased to suggest that this will be our last meeting outside Downing Street now that the results of our study show that national security is indeed comprehensive within Whitehall. The licences that we obtain from the United Nations for these 'black areas', beyond the reach of the internet, may have been necessary during this investigation, but can appear hypocritical when all Western governments are insisting that there is no longer any such thing as privacy. I am quite confident that the public will be behind a calm and logical approach to maintaining their own safety and well-being."

***

The Armed Response Unit used a hand-held hydraulic ram to cave in the reinforced steel door of the house. The collapsing weight of it nearly crushed the screaming man underneath as the squad poured in, helmet lights dancing beams across the damp walls and the repeated shouts of command confusing and paralysing the residents.

"Up against the wall! Up against the fucking wall! NOW!"

The door was moved out of the way and the young skinny man in a torn vest was hauled out, blood on his face and chest. His voice shook in near hysteria.

"Look, man, I'm sorry! I didn't know you were cops!"

He was flattened face first into the wall.

"Honest! I didn't know! You can't tell the difference between street gangs and..."

"Shut the fuck up!"

He felt a taser stick press into his cheek and his voice wavered.

"OK. OK! Take it easy!"

"I said shut up!"

He tried to move his eyes left and right to see if the women folk were complying. A couple of teenage girls were sobbing with fear.

"Where is it, you piece of shit?"

The cop wrenched an arm behind the man's back. He gave a short scream.

"Where the fuck is it? We know you've got it!"

"I ain't got nothing! Please, leave us alone!"

The sound of furniture crashing and the contents of drawers being emptied finally stopped. One of the six cops appeared in the doorway.

"Alright Chief, we've got it."

He held up a small bunch of tattered plastic banknotes.

The man caught sight of them and sighed as the taser stick pushed further into his face. A cold voice hissed in his ear.

"How many times do you bastards have to be told? Cash is illegal!"

The man wilted visibly.

"I know, I know. It's all they'd take for the food. It... was for food."

The taser stick pressed further til he couldn't talk.

"Well, you'll have to learn to eat what you're given. Now, you're in big fucking trouble."

***

"Prime Minister. If I may address the points..."

al-Degri waved a hand.

"Of course, Mister Abarlev. As head of the project for Secorp, your comments are invaluable."

Dovi Abarlev was a man bordering on overweight, his hair more white than silver and a face that showed confidence but no emotion. He waited until all eyes were on him. His accent heavily implied that English was not his only conversational language.

"Prime Minister. We have worked for some considerable time on the scenario of a cyber criminal attack that could bring down the systems that are vital to this country. Something far beyond the theft of personal details relating to Global Identification. We have presented to you the facts of the matter. We have researched the ability of the country to react to such an attack, and we have offered the solution."

Abarlev spread his hands in a slight gesture of disbelief as his precise Middle Eastern tones deepened with a note of warning.

"Yet, you wish to turn down the opportunity to act when all the pieces are in place. I appreciate that you are concerned with the forthcoming election and that your Cabinet is one of compromise and the appeasement of your supporters, but the issue is much wider and the window is much narrower than you realise."

al-Degri felt he could shut down this argument.

"I understand the issues well, Mister Abarlev. However, the legal solutions must be backed by purely political decisions, and that involves a process of discussion beyond a fact finding mission in an internet black area."

"I have to disagree, Prime Minister. The most important decisions in history have been made well away from the public debating arena. We would be beyond foolish to pass up this opportunity to move the government's own avowed agenda forward by ten years with just one operation."

al-Degri half laughed at the suggestion.

"Quite impossible at every level. You were fully aware that this was an investigative operation that would go first to Cabinet and then become a discussion document for the future. It is not up to us to make decisions about something as far reaching as Global ID on behalf of the legislature. Even if we could!"

Abarlev stood up and walked slowly up the line.

"A legal course of action takes time that we do not have. There are emergency powers that, in time of national threat, override the usual processes. Were there to be a catastrophic failure of vital systems - and there will be just such an event, I can assure you - then the same powers that are in this room right now will be called upon to manage the situation."

al-Degri pointed to the pile of dossiers on the table.

"But Mister Abarlev, I have the recommendations from the Chair of the Joint Intelligence Committee who is here today. Commander Thornelow himself has advised the Cabinet that there is no credible threat currently in play."

Eyes turned to Derry Thornelow, sitting motionless amidst the military uniforms. He turned only slightly, clearing his throat as he addressed the room.

"That's not entirely accurate, Prime Minister."

* * *

The army checkpoint on the approach to the railway station was unusually quiet. The arc lights lit the small compound as well as the road up ahead, but the sky was black and impenetrable above. Two squaddies stood in the drizzle, looking into the darkness, their rifles shouldered.

"Bloody hell. Where are they? Forty minutes late this time!"

The other one shook his head.

"Yeah. Forty minutes less guard duty for them, forty minutes less kip for us."

"Wait a minute..."

The sound of a big engine came through the darkness. One of the squaddies pointed a hand scanner in the direction and rows of IDs lit up the screen.

"At last... oh wait, no it isn't."

Appearing out of the mist, a truck painted in United Nations insignia drew up in front of the soldiers. The driver stuck his head out of the window.

"Get your CO."

The guard radioed in through his helmet mic while his mate approached the driver.

"We're waiting for a new guard detail from the barracks. You haven't spotted them on your way, have you?"

The driver started winding up the window.

"We're the new detail."

The checkpoint had already come to life, reinforced double gates opening into the commandeered goods yard and a second UN truck followed the first one through. From the tailgate, heavily armed soldiers in combat uniform jumped down and began forming into groups.

"Jesus Christ! Are we expecting another bloody war or something?"

An officer's voice shouted up the road.

"You men! Report back. You're returning to barracks."

***

Prime Minister al-Degri started to feel a little uncomfortable.

"So, gentlemen, what you are telling me is that you have garnered intelligence that is not contained within the report."

Thornelow sounded slightly imperious.

"It's too highly classified, Prime Minister."

"Then declassify it!"

"I'm sorry, that would not be in the best of interests."

Abarlev had appeared behind al-Degri's shoulder. He spoke more to the room than the Prime Minister.

"You see, my friends, things are a little more complicated, a little more advanced than appear in a pile of reports. We have built multiple scenarios for protecting the governance of this country at this vital time, and if we are to be successful - and we will be - then when that crisis comes we must seize the opportunity. It is our one recommendation, that we resolve all security issues simultaneously with mandatory acceptance of Global Identity for all citizens. It cannot be a phasing out of a voluntary system. It must be one blow."

al-Degri looked from one stack of files to another, his voice wavering.

"It may be your undocumented recommendation, Mister Abarlev, but it is certainly not your decision to make. We have several years of work to complete in the public arena, preparing the population to accept change. As of now, all we are prepared to do is ensure better implementation of existing law."

Finally, Abarlev addressed al-Degri directly.

"Prime Minister. We are, all of us, only in office for a brief time. But your position is the most precarious, with or without a general election. The media has been a good friend to your political ambition. Their sensitive reporting of the situation in America and the Pacific has done much to build your international reputation. However, the power of the media lies not so much in what it reports, but in what it is prepared to ignore."

Abarlev had moved around the table and stood beside Rishek.

"It was anticipated that your government would try to delay the inevitable, so it is unfortunate that time pressures us to move forward, with or without your co-operation."

Rishek held up a slim folder for Abarlev's outstretched hand. He took it, bringing it to al-Degri and dropping it on the desk in front of him.

"Another report for your paperwork."

***

Out in the evening countryside, in the sweep of spotlights mounted on helicopter rails, a scrapyard was taking in truckloads of iron railings, architectural steel and street furniture. A small crew on mini-diggers were picking through it.

In the near darkness of a converted container up by the perimeter, sat an unprepossessing youth in a grubby vest with a bandanna tied round his forehead. He was staring into the screen that rose up from a litter strewn desk. He tapped around on an old fashioned keyboard, stopping only to reach for a cardboard cup of cold coffee.

"What you got, Bug?"

He slurped the coffee.

"Bug? Come on, man. This carrier's gonna shut down in a few

minutes."

A disembodied voice appeared in front of the screen.

"Yeah, Hokey? I got fuck all here. Same old shit. Simulations over inner London and a beam back to the scarabs in Bedford. They never do anything else these days."

"Got any mist?"

"Big one over the City. Looks like a private bank. Nothing special."

Hokey was unimpressed.

"Hmm. More dark dealings to enrich themselves at the expense of the slaves."

"If you say so."

"Got anything else?"

"Nah. Bit more troop traffic than usual. Funny though, can't catch what they're saying. Sounds like Russian or something."

"Nice if it was a sub left over from the war."

"That's a long time ago. They'd have to be really good at holding their breath. Probably bouncing along the wires from the border near Finland or something."

Hokey finished the coffee.

"OK. I'm out of Hertz. Check in with you same time tomorrow."

"Ba-bah!"

Hokey punched out on the keyboard and the screen dimmed.

He got up from the desk, stretching and holding his aching back.

Outside in the yard the rain was coming back, shining through the lights and darkening the heaps of scrap left by the trucks.

He picked up his torch cutter's visor. Another night. Nothing new.

***

al-Degri looked with disdain at the first leaf in the folder. He had sometimes wondered if this day would come. He was used to the party whips using this sort of coercion on the backbenchers to ensure compliance, but now he knew how it felt.

He flicked through a couple of leaves and closed the folder.

"I see."

The room was silent. Only the representatives of the media were looking intently at the stony expression of the Prime Minister.

Abarlev spoke quietly and with a measured tone.

"If you take our proposals back to Cabinet and implement emergency powers, the actors in this room will have the covering mandate to do what must be done. The broadcast media have the task of selling your decision to the public, ensuring there is no panic, and controlling their understanding of the roll-out of the timetable. The rest will be our responsibility."

al-Degri jumped slightly in his chair.

"Responsibility? This is your idea of responsibility? When foreign agencies infiltrate a country to overthrow its democracy..."

He dropped the folder on the table and stood up.

"Are you all involved in this?"

There was silence. al-Degri looked to the representatives of the media.

"And you are their assassins?"

He walked a few paces then stopped.

"I want no part in your... coup."

Returning slowly to his place he picked up the folder.

"I will indeed be convening a Cabinet meeting at the first opportunity. This meeting is over."

As the doors closed, Abarlev saw the military escort fall in around al-Degri and guide him down the corridor.

Abarlev stood at the head of the table and addressed the expectant audience.

"Obviously, we knew the Prime Minister's speech in advance, but I don't think any of us imagined the speed of his capitulation."

There were one or two smiles.

"However, with or without official sanction and the cover of Operation Tin Man, the results would always have been the same. As of this moment, the timetable is live and your instructions will come directly from General Rishek under the codename of Random Sentry. For the security services, this will appear to be guidance from the United Nations, and for the media it will come through Reuter's Global News Agency."

Abarlev leaned across the table and pushed a meticulously stacked pile of folders so they spilt onto the floor.

"Nothing will be written down."

"*...and back to the main story this morning, in breaking news, the resignation of Mohammed al-Degri, the Prime Minister of Great Britain. Downing Street has confirmed, ahead of a planned broadcast tonight, that the leader of the Unity Government will step down just eight weeks away from a general election that was tipped to win an outright majority for his own party. So far, there have been no official reasons given for this turn of events that has shocked many in the government, though speculation is rife over possible health issues, following a well documented bout of illness last year. Prime Ministerial duties are currently being handled by Deputy Prime Minister Simon Fielding, a veteran of Cabinets and Shadow Cabinets over the last fifteen years. Tegwi Elkestu is outside Number Ten and we go over there to find out the latest developments, straight after this message...*"

Clayton Heath looked at himself one last time in the AppleSoft novelty mirror. He turned his head this way and that, checking his three quarter profile and the line of his hair cut. His suit was right, the overcoat in dark grey, the tie central in the cutaway V of his collar.

He let the door of the apartment close behind him and brushed his hand over the reader on the wall. He heard the reassuring sound of bolts sliding into the jamb and the quiet voice in his ear that told him the apartment's doors and windows were all secure.

Building technicians in corporation overalls had strewn their tools and ladders across the hall. They were changing the cameras again in the ceiling. Heath stepped around a large toolbox. He wondered what the upgrade was this time. They already had infrared and face recognition, the last upgrade was for x-ray and the latest GLiD protocol. What else could they do, now they can whisper to you as you walk past?

He waited in the foyer, looking at the full length screen filled with changing shots of Mohammed al-Degri. The newsreader stood out from the wall in crackly oversaturated hologram colours and mouthed the words of an imaginary autocue.

A few of the tenants were gathered round watching, and even the girl on the security desk was interested, constantly glancing up. Heath was fumbling for his GLiD to tune in the sound, in case something new had happened, when his navigator app cut in.

"Your taxi is car 731G and is two hundred and forty one metres from the main door arriving in eleven seconds."

At least it had stopped raining. It was hot and cloudy and the early morning light made the new all-weather trees shine with a slightly synthetic shade of blue and pink. The taxi drew up and the door unlocked.

It was the first time Heath had been on his own in a four man taxi. Plenty of leg room for long journeys and a neat little hot and cold buffet where drivers used to sit. The doors locked and the taxi slid silently forward while Heath poked around in the food trays and pocketed a couple of interesting breakfast items.

He took out the GLiD and the screen brightened into a grid of icons. As soon as he touched it the big display came up, hovering in front of the seat back. His Account Assistant faded up from the ether and grinned broadly, her eyes lighting up with good news.

"Hi Clayton! Congratulations. Your allowances have been renewed and upgraded. Do you want to see your new carbon credits for travel, energy and food? How about consumer resources?"

"No."

"Your new security clearance allows you to visit so many more exciting places! You can vacation on the Channel Islands, travelling by air! Or go virtual to Australia, Hong Kong and South America."

"No. Show me the latest news on al-Degri."

She talked through a little laugh.

"OK Clayton. Have a really great day!"

She disappeared and the screen cut back in with a newsfeed.

al-Degri was shown in casual clothes standing at the gateway to a field outside his country home. He looked out onto tranquil meadows with a distant pensive expression while his wife tended to the children nearby. Heath smiled. He recognised those poses.

The earnest, empty voice of the newsreader spoke over the top.

"Still no word from Downing Street until Mister al-Degri himself makes a formal press statement. The now former Prime Minister tendered his resignation to the King and briefed the sovereign on the implications of his decision before handing over to his Deputy, Simon Fielding. Foreign news sources are speculating that health issues and the pressure of recent events may have led to Mister al-Degri feeling unable to ride out this general election campaign, despite his huge personal popularity pointing to a comfortable win in the summer and reselection by returning MPs.

"Crowds have taken to the streets of London, confused and angry, demanding answers to why such a charismatic and progressive figure as Mohammed al-Degri should feel that this particular moment was the right time to go."

The report had switched to a close up of a jostling crowd being contained by the black clad squads of militarised police. Heath shook his head at the banner that was stripped along the bottom of the screen - Crowds Mourn al-Degri's Untimely Departure. The banner sat on a blurred out area behind which protesters could just about be seen holding placards. Heath remembered it from last year. It was a demonstration against the government's continuing policy of basic welfare payments. The placards would have read Work Not Welfare.

The taxi spoke through the GLiD into Heath's ear.

"Road closures in the New Metropolitan area. We are being directed out onto the One Three Five section of the M6 motorway and back into the city at Castle Bromwich. Your meeting time has been rescheduled."

"Oh, that's just great. The scenic route."

The taxi had turned at an open junction, watched by a traffic patrol, and then wound its way north along the neat blocks of rubble and the stumps of red brick walls. Over the crest of the hill and on down toward the section of old motorway, the underlying geography of the hills that were once furred over with towns and estates, now looked like the atrophied bones of a dead giant. No one was working among the ruins today. It was a silent deconstruction of an old world.

Out on the motorway, a smattering of dark limos slid alongside the military lane where big green army trucks followed the blue and white UN vehicles. Heath's taxi locked on to its fifty mile an hour speed limit and hummed along, an LED on the dashboard flashing in time with the overhead sensors.

His assistant was back.

"Would you like me to prioritise your email? You have one hundred and seventy four new items in eleven categories. I can read them to you."

Heath gave up on the newsfeed. Nothing else was breaking.

"Yeah. Go on then. I have a feeling this is going to take a while."

The taxi had barely turned back into the city when a new line of roadblocks were pulling the traffic into a filter lane. The big wagons were being inspected and bike couriers were fumbling for epapers and transit cards.

A red snake of carriages caught Heath's eye as they ran behind the factory units into a small station. He'd had enough in the taxi.

"Pull over, I'm going to take the train in. At least the bloody things have to run on time."

He left the taxi and joined the queues for the station turnstile. He gave it a minute until he was sure the security office had picked up the GLiD, then marched along the lines of people, looking straight ahead. He could feel the look of annoyance from these Ds and Es as he jumped the queue, but that was their problem. They should get a proper job.

Security could see him coming on their scanners and the guy with the hand-held gave him a curt nod as he came through. Heath took the steps over the footbridge toward the red bullet on the far track. All the while a small voice was talking in his ear.

"The route to the Metropolitan Building has been recalculated and your travel token has been transferred. This is the P3224 CitySpeed direct passenger conveyor to Old Snow Hill."

He slid sideways through the crowd of workers toward the front carriage where the doors only opened for GLiD carriers. The platform flowed with uneven streams of tetchy passengers, trying to get off or trying to get on.

As Heath reached the front carriage, his path was blocked by a small slight figure in a grey hooded jacket and jeans. The face under the hood had big eyes underscored with some kind of tattooed eyeliner and pale deathly white lips.

"Here, mate. Got any points?"

"No. Get out of the way."

The young girl just shuffled to her other foot, and tried to smile.

"Go on. You look like you can afford it. Just a few. I've got to get home."

Heath had heard all this before.

"Yeah right. Let Security help you out."

"Ah come on, mate. Well, how about some Nom Vouchers? I'm starving."

She wasn't as pushy as most and at least was trying to be appealing rather than aggressive. He remembered the breakfast snacks from the taxi and dug one out of his pocket.

"Here."

She took the wrapped package and immediately put it under her nose and sniffed.

"Ah cheers mate! Got any more? I haven't ate for days!"

Heath smiled at the cheek. He gave her the other one and she slipped them under the jacket and shrank back as the station announcement cut in.

"We apologise to travellers on the City Bullet to Old Snow Hill and all stations through Birmingham for the delays caused by today's security drills. Please work with the security assistants to access the designated carriages, showing identification, travel documents and station concourse permits as required. Follow their instruction to find your place in the carriages. The disruption to your journey will be minimised by your patience and compliance. Thank you."

The station screens were flashing up instructions. LINE UP, BOARD CARRIAGES, STAY CALM. They carried over into his GLiD, being repeated in his ear by the assistant.

The girl had gone when the door slid back and Heath was guided to his seat by the voice in his ear.

He sat watching the advertisements above the parcel rack while the rest of the train was being processed. They were silly 3D adverts for soft drinks or novelty technology. The holograms used their trompe l'oeil effect to throw cola over him or reach into his face.

As the train finally pulled away he looked out at the dismal faces of the shabby workers with ID bracelets or the old people with their welfare cards who had to wait for the next one, or the next one, or the next. He briefly caught the stare of big eyes and white elfin face up at the window before she was gone.

***

"...Sub-Editorial Domestic Team Suite, Meeting Room 6b, with Section Editor H.J. Toliver and Operational Director A. L. Verrick. Time: three minutes and fourteen seconds."

"OK. Got it."

Heath walked briskly up the acreage of concrete avenue to the Metropolitan building, following the herd of humanity on their way in. It was known locally as The Tombstone, rising forty floors above the Birmingham landscape in white concrete with its matching white one-way glass and a slight upward bow in the roofline that earned it the nickname.

Under the awning, armed guards watched him coming on the heads-up display. It showed the CCTV image of the avenue overlaid with arrows and markers that followed the Metropolitan workers up the steps, giving their GLiD numbers and names. Heath kept his chin up to be caught by the facial recognition cameras as he pushed through the revolving door.

The Metropolitan foyer was an impressive postwar statement of purpose. It was designed, like the Independent Metropolitan World Service itself, to reflect the authoritative voice and new information paradigm of always present, constantly updated rolling news. It rose several floors into the building and the vast space was a heaving multicoloured sea of holographic video, reaching down onto the floor. Virtual assistants sat in their booths on standby to offer information, make appointments and dispense drinks. Receptionists rose from their desks to welcome officials and guests, guiding them into comfortable carpeted spaces with perspex walls. Whatever privacy was conferred, the outside world of all-penetrating news information could be seen swirling overhead in a dozen overlapping scenes of saturated semitransparent colour.

Heath headed straight for the main trunk of elevators at the core of the building. His space aboard Lift 23 was already coordinated, an express to the third floor, shared only with a junior accountant and an auditor from the revenue.

Heath entered the meeting room where Harry Toliver and Verrick were in quiet conversation.

"Good morning. I took the quickest route into town. Sorry to keep you waiting."

Harry Toliver, a lean, smiling forty year old in a flowery tie and fashionably baggy white shirt, rose from his chair and extended a hand.

"No problem. We could see what you were doing. Crazy out there, no?"

"Yeah. Everybody's glued to this al-Degri business."

"Never a dull news day!"

They shook hands. They never did usually, but Heath knew today was different. Verrick stood up and shook his hand as well. He was a man not much older than Harry, but his smile made no pretence of warmth toward an employee he had only occasionally met and his voice was cold and low.

"Congratulations, Clayton. This promotion is well deserved. You've really made a difference out on that news floor. Some great reporting, great story telling. I've heard nothing but good things."

"Well, thank you Sir."

Harry clapped him round the shoulder.

"We're all proud of you, son! And I know..."

He feigned seriousness.

"... I absolutely know... that you won't let me down."

Heath gave him a bashful, you must be kidding look.

"Hey, Harry. I want this. I really do."

Verrick had been watching carefully, and pointedly refixed the smile as Heath turned back to him.

"Mister Verrick, I'm going to make something of this new role. Thank you for giving me the opportunity."

"I think you're going to prove to be... the man for the job."

Harry kept the game going, inviting Heath to sit at the table and watch a video that mushroomed up from the black projection plate in the middle of the table.

"Let's get straight down to business. Clayton, your investigation into unravelling the hacker networks has made a great series on Metro WSTV. Great research. Only you can take it to the next level. Literally!"

The projection came up with one of the virtual anchormen walking amongst a sinister group of hooded malcontents, their faces hidden but occasionally highlighted by the glow of their screens. They seemed to occupy forbidding rooms with nazi insignia, deaths-head motifs and the old union flag of Great Britain on the walls as if to inspire them as they stabbed at their lightboards with evil intent. Masked police were shown dragging the criminals from their desks and, as they entered the daylight of the outside world, the hackers' hoods were thrown off to show lily-white skin, blistered with spots and boils, rotting teeth and ugly shaved heads. They wriggled and writhed, snarling in the light of day, as the police manfully bundled them into a transport. No one had turned the video's sound on, they watched the pictures while they talked.

Verrick spoke with menacing quiet.

"You've worked on the case of The User more than anyone else on your newsteam."

"Yes, Sir."

"It's your pet project."

"I wanted to get underneath... to the root of his motivations. It seemed like the best clue to turning up his identity. Or at least, to start narrowing it down to a particular organisation."

The screen showed a satanic masked figure, a pose not dissimilar to the Goat of Mendes, but the face was in shadow with the curl of a question mark hiding the features. Just demonic eyes looking down at a graphic of urban chaos presided over by rumbling skies and the giant figure of The User. Heath shook his head and glanced toward Verrick.

"I've never really thought that graphic was helpful. Whoever he is, he won't be a conspicuous character. I think he's completely insane, but most likely a psychotic loner."

Verrick was unmoved.

"It fixes it in the public consciousness as a depiction of evil. Like a nightmare constantly in the back of their minds, threatening everything they do."

Harry leaned in to the conversation.

"Yeah. So that when the guy is finally caught, the weight of public opinion will totally negate any possible defence. He'll turn in his whole organisation for a few years less in jail."

"You still think there's a roomful of stolen documents out there, don't you?"

The video closed out and Harry stood up.

"Shall we go to up and join the editorial team?"

They headed out for the lifts and Heath couldn't resist slipping the GLiD out of his pocket to check the screen. He now had security privileges for the next section of the building, but there were no voices in his ear to give him directions, to tell him when his lift would arrive.

Verrick led the conversation as they walked.

"The government particularly needs to recover the full extent of the thefts from the national archives, the Ministry of Defence, Royal Air Force in particular, and the Special Intelligence Service. Petty intrusions into Whitehall departments, theft of Global Identities or snooping on public figures can be tolerated. It can sometimes even be beneficial. But operational data that could be useful to a hostile power is a different matter."

"I agree, Sir, but anything that important will already be scattered across the internet, broken down, encrypted and hidden. I mean, look at the Pentagon Papers from five years ago. We keep turning up new fragments, stuff that the MIs claim they never knew existed."

As they stood in the lift, Harry took his cue from Verrick.

"Clayton. Listen up. You've done great work down on the news floor, digging up stuff that a lot of people would have liked you to keep quiet about. You know, stuff about the war, the private armies in America, the banks and back-channel funding of KBRE and Halliburton South. But now you're moving upstairs, you're going to have just one story to work on. I want you to find The User. You will have the resources you need and my full backing to do it. But here's the thing. We all know that despite the best security money can buy, things leak. Shit, I can't even keep the office party a secret round here, and I'm the only one who knows about it! But the User organisation has little holes throughout the internet where information

20

can be compromised, stolen, subverted or just fucked with. You know that society's best defence is the Global ID. Once it becomes Universal ID, of course, it'll be watertight. There'll be no corrosive influence of the security deniers. Life will be so much simpler and so much happier for everyone."

They stepped out into wide well-lit corridors that Heath had only ever heard about. He'd come from the bear pit of the news floor, supplying titbits of news information, up into the clouds where all that heavily compartmentalised data was forged into broadcast footage.

"So, until the glitches in the ID system are under control, you need to work on your profile of The User in total secret. You report solely and directly to me and I sign off all your authorisations. Got that?"

"Yeah sure. But, won't it be obvious what I'm working on?"

They stood at the top of a short staircase, looking down at a well-ordered editorial floor, heavily staffed with teams working behind plexiglass baffles.

"No one asks questions up here. You'll be drawn into meetings for your input on a whole shitload of stuff for public consumption. You're the new golden boy of the newsroom now, remember? I'll be selling you every step of the way. Let's go meet people."

Verrick nodded his agreement, shook Harry by the hand, and backed away.

"Good luck, Mister Heath. I look forward to hearing about your progress."

Harry and Clayton moved from team to team. Introductions were made, GLiD networks were joined. The previously silent assistant in Heath's ear confirmed each new contact and suggested the level of shared interaction. Harry made up a new cover story for each team. Clayton would contribute to the shaping of news stories on the cashless banking system, the redevelopment of city suburbs or working conditions for maintenance technicians in the robot factories. Harry took Clayton into an editing suite where the team from graphics were working to create more footage of Mohammed al-Degri. A serious young man was pulling apart the video of that morning's bulletin when al-Degri was shown at his country home. They had separated up the layers where al-Degri's family had been added into the footage. The lush meadow background was removed to show the previous scene of a concerned Prime Minister rushing back from holiday to the site of a rail disaster in Kent.

Heath leaned over his shoulder.

"Might want to tighten up the crowd scene footage at Downing

Street. Someone's going to recognise that old demo."

The young technician pulled in a whole new scene where the crowd had swelled to a heaving sea of people. He panned across it to show its uniqueness.

"Yeah. It was a last minute decision to use a crowd. We had to take some library and cut it in. We've had time since to generate a whole sequence. They're all CG now."

The tech flipped between the wireframe mesh of the moving crowd and the rendered result. It looked suitably real.

"We've just got the footage cleared from the MI for his resignation broadcast. Have to work out some backgrounds."

The artist pulled in al-Degri standing at a lectern and looking like an international statesman addressing the nation on the eve of war. Behind him was a brightly lit green screen.

"It'll help when we get the sound to go with it, but it could be a Downing Street thing. Then again, might be in the New Commons."

He turned the lectern on and off a few times to show it was just a mesh.

Harry leaned in to Clayton.

"When the MI decide what they want to go with, this becomes the official version. They supply to the BBCE, SkyGlobal and whatnot for a simulcast."

"So, we do the dirty work and they have deniability if something goes wrong."

"Right. Lessons were learned in the past when awkward questions meant they had to 'lose' historically important video to cover the trail. No one believes those lame excuses anymore."

"Not since The User's BBCE leaks, anyway."

Harry was pleased.

"Now you're joining in! Let's go find you a desk."

3

When the applause finally died down, the slightly ungainly man with a floppy fringe and sad smile composed himself at the microphone again. Behind him, a row of secret servicemen and party officials scanned the room. He shuffled his shoulders inside the heat of his ill-fitting suit and addressed the expectant crowd.

"Do you know... how great it feels not to have to hide in the shadows any longer?"

The front ten rows roared their affirmation and furiously waved their smiley face flags. It was another minute before calm returned.

"Not to be afraid? Stigmatised? Not to be that gross caricature of the outdated reactionaries and the victim of their hate speech?"

The crowd whooped with approval, as if they knew only too well.

"Well, it's been a long road from trial to trust, from victimising one another to valuing one another and from discrimination to deliverance!"

He held up his arms to calm the ecstatic crowd.

"There was a time - a time I came from - when there were laws that persecuted you, and courts that judged you, on the colour of your skin, your religious belief, your gender, your sexuality and all the traits that defined an individual's natural state. And, one by one, I have seen them go. Those laws have been swept away, those courts have been silenced!"

A frisson of anarchy, driven by the image of silenced courts, instantly swept over the turbulent crowd.

"In the last twelve months we have seen breakthrough after breakthrough in the fields of medical science, redefining what is a mental disorder and what is a natural orientation. Also, the work of organisations and institutions who have lobbied for the laws to be changed, to finally free people to be themselves. Yes, it took a long time. Of course it did. The tireless work of schools and colleges to re-educate our children to accept each other and to embrace our differences required new generations to grow up in the light of new thinking. Of right thinking!"

The crowd's applause was falling into sync, urging him on to greater heights.

"The legalities are settled. The social stigma is lifted, and I am now able to stand before you, not just as an MP, but hopefully with the future endorsement of the people, as your next Prime Minister, and I can proudly say... I am a paedophile!"

The crowd went into frenzy, a bobbing flag-waving sea of approval, cheering their candidate with teary-eyed emotion. His voice rose with the grandeur of an apocalyptic prophet to compete with the applause.

"Yes, far from being a stereotype of evil, preying on the innocent, people everywhere who love children - who are drawn to them as innocents requiring guidance and understanding - can now stand up without fear, continuing on with their lives and ambitions, giving their gifts back to society and fulfilling their destiny! It's been a long road, not just for me but thousands upon thousands who have suffered cruel and unjust persecution! Today, yes I want your votes - I really want your votes - but more than that, I demand your respect as a human being!"

As the crowd boiled in an ocean of colour and ticker tape, the blank face of a newsreader appeared picture-in-picture and the whooping acceptance of the crowd ducked behind his voice.

"So, Sarion Dundas addresses the party faithful as he lobbies their MPs for votes. The leadership contest for the next government takes place after the upcoming general election. He is the first UK MP to benefit from the protection of paedophiles under the Hate Crimes Act.

Viewers are reminded that the one person one vote system, introduced by the New Democratic Socialists, requires all eligible voters to register and watch at least sixteen hours of party political broadcasts before casting their vote by television. The penalty for failing to log on or answer the questions at the end of each broadcast has been widened to include the withholding of internet free time and, more controversially, certain choices of food vouchers.

In other news, a move by the UK Compliance Group to offer mandatory re-education to those who oppose our system of government, came a step closer today. The British Psychiatric Association identified those who vehemently disagree with official government policies as suffering from Authoritative Cognitive Disorder. Although the degree of opposition has yet to be defined, it is expected to be covered under the same public protection laws that prevent the dissemination of conspiracy theories and views that challenge the findings of government bodies in both science and law."

"I don't care what they fuckin' say. He's still a nonce."

"Kez, shut your mouth!"

"World's going to shit!"

The crowd that had gathered in the light drizzle to watch the big screen news in the square started to disperse back to their bus stops. No one in that work shift had clapped and cheered through Dundas' speech. They watched without emotion, aware of the Police Crowd Units who stood in twos and threes around the pavement.

At the end of the bulletin, the people started their purposeful trot to the bus shelters. It didn't pay to dawdle or slouch. The eyes of the Crowd Unit officers were hidden beneath black visors, but the cameras around the square fed constant interpretations of human behaviour onto the heads-up displays. Faces were picked out and tracked, body language computed. Only the other officers in the square came up with the familiar pink outline of a GLiD and a scroll of information about their identity and occupation.

"Just don't say anything. We don't want to get pulled tonight."

The woman pushed Kez along, trying to keep her head down behind the group in front. No one spoke. There was just the echo of the tannoy announcing bus numbers and their routes.

***

A fresh sweep of limousines approached the gates of the Nightship compound. They'd already come through the manned perimeters and for the last two miles had been travelling in open countryside all owned by Nightship. The only sign of man was the odd redundant guard tower rising up through the trees and highlighted black against the murk of the evening sky. A prickle of cameras on every face of the towers now scanned the trees.

Through the chain link gates and twenty feet of razorwire-topped fencing, the inner core of Nightship beamed out in a blaze of lights and buildings. The vast test laboratories, the scarabs, were lit from beneath to cast their domed shiny shapes in contrast to the right angles of the big blocks.

The limousines were silently guided around the roads, barriers closing behind them until they were swallowed by the darkness of an underground parking garage.

"Good evening colleagues, customers and, of course most importantly... shareholders."

There was a rustle of quiet laughter around the lecture theatre.

"Welcome to Nightship Systems. My name is Abraham Whiting and I am the Senior Project Simulation Specialist here at Nightship. My job is to virtualise given scenarios where digital systems interact with the real world and evaluate the results so that when they go live they also go right!"

The crowd of boffins, technicians and government guests smirked at the simplification of his job.

"In tonight's seminar we will, as promised, for the first time ever, show you a live hook up to the government's entire countrywide server centre network. We intend to simulate the national defence protocols for isolating and defeating a potential cyber attack. We shall not be including certain vital government installations such as the MIs, the GCHQ and other listening posts, nor the Whitehall centre, despite this being the only node that has suffered from an intrusion."

He spread his hands wide as the audience took it in and he allowed himself a chuckle.

"Hey. I don't write this stuff. I just push the buttons."

***

The bulldozers had moved in for their night's work in the suburbs of South London. Crews were gathered around a foreman with a street map in a half built portakabin. He was having trouble making himself understood.

"Look. You take it all as I showed you but leave the building in 4335. They want nothing touched between the hospital and the railway line."

The drivers looked at each other before one shook his head and wearily offered an opinion.

"They should make their bloody minds up. Plans changing all the time. How come we always find out about this shit at the last minute? Nobody knows what's going on."

"Just make sure it's cleared by five thirty. We've got more containers coming in first thing and I don't want any spoil trucks waiting on you."

"Is that the road crew? Why are they resurfacing a road in a clearance zone?"

The foreman had heard enough.

"Hey look, I don't fucking know, right? I just do my job. You'd be best to keep your mouth shut and do your work. Don't ask questions and don't discuss your instructions. Got it? I can get plenty more like you if I have to."

The drivers went back to the map. Outside in the ruins a single cry like a wolf could be heard echoing in the distance above the rumble of diesel generators. A heavily armed security chopper swung by sweeping its pin spots toward any target that showed up on the thermal imagers.

***

On the Nightship campus, Abraham Whiting had his audience

26

prepared. They'd had the lecture, the credits, the compliance report and the necessary science. It was time for the show and he moved to the side of the stage where a camera over a console could beam his greying bearded face onto the back wall where it filled the twenty foot screen.

"One by one, I will connect to the government datacentres in mainland UK, and as they appear on the simulation, you will be able to access all kinds of data on your handheld devices."

He leaned into the screen and dabbed in the first keycodes. Meanwhile, the audience rustled and logged on to their GLiD carrier signal from Nightship. Five hundred faces in the subdued green of the exit signs glowed faintly with the changing patterns of their screens.

"I will remind you that we are reading the instructions from the multicore CPUs at each location and constructing their data within the simulation here. Nothing we do can harm the running of the datacentres themselves. OK, we have connections coming in."

Heads were raised to gaze into the open area between the dais and the front row of seats. A light appeared, hovering in mid air, blueish white and the size of a gala melon. In the air beside it, words appeared giving location, name and spec of the machines it represented. Another faded up from nothing a few feet away but somewhere higher up in the empty space. A snake of connections, beams of bending white light, shot between the two and the image stabilised with graphics denoting speeds and fibre connections in and out.

"We have Huntingdon and Cambridge. The connections will propagate exponentially and build the model."

Before Whiting had stopped speaking a dozen more coloured lights had appeared and the branches of light were already spreading between them. The model swayed like a tree, the lights oscillating in space to make room for more connections. The model brightened the darkness in a spectacular shimmering display of coloured text and pulsing connections that seemed to throb like a giant brain.

"Moving out to the coastal regions, we have Great Yarmouth coming in, Worthing, Bournemouth, Torquay..."

Within a few minutes the audience had abandoned their GLiDs and were mesmerised by the beautiful hologram that hung in the air like a living sculpture.

***

"I fucking hope you're getting this!"

"Holy shit! They're going for the whole country!"

Hokey scratched at his head, the itching was getting worse. He made a note to hack some of his hair off at the first opportunity.

"Bug? Is it the whole country?"

"Looks like it. I got Tinfoil on another carrier. He thinks something big is going down."

Hokey's screen, in the demolition jumble of the container, was old and failing. The on-screen graphic of the Nightship scarabs had whited out in the convergence of beams coming in from all over the country map.

"I can't see shit!"

"I've had to pull it into 3D. It's huge."

"What's Tinfoil say?"

"Says it's got to be a sim. I've seen it done in a region, but never across the whole set. Those are some wicked-ass connections, direct tunnels - nobody could get to the other end of them."

"Man, I'd love to know what they're doin' in there."

***

The light applause died away and Whiting could speak again.

"So, colleagues, we have a complete simulation of the national civilian datacentre network governing employment, banking, welfare, medicine, education, travel, security, agriculture, industry and all functions of the old regional and local council systems. Our goal tonight is to deliberately disrupt the connections between the datacentres and from the resultant collapse scenario, create a discussion about systemic weak points and the nature of intrusion. We will also observe how robust the system is at rebuilding its functionality. To reiterate, we have theoretical models, of course, but the mathematics will actually vary in the field. This is why we have created a complete virtualisation in this room that is functionally indistinguishable from what we believe would happen in the real world."

Whiting dabbed at a control strip that hovered in front of his console. The hologram seemed to come to life. Tiny points of light shooting between the nodes, running along the connections, with scrolling text in red and white rushing to keep up. Heads in the audience flicked between their GLiDs and the glittering light show that was growing to fill the theatre.

"These, colleagues, are Layer One encrypted protocols moving between the datacentres. They are swapping information, archiving data, updating records, carrying the lifeblood of human interaction in today's society. Be aware that this is only Layer One. To show every layer of human interaction in real-time would be massively beyond the scope of this simulation. It would also require a model that would be much bigger than we could project."

The audience were impressed enough. In a comfortable observation booth at the back, Nightship Director Lothar Friedland sat impassively with his special guests from Whitehall, the military and the media. He silently noted their enthusiasm for the show as they sipped their Champagne and nodded appreciatively with only a dim understanding of the proceedings.

***

"Right, Hoke, something just happened in there. You probably can't see, but they are reading petas of information from all over. It's pouring in. Tinfoil's on the carrier from his local centre. He can see what's going out but he can't follow it in at the other end. Looks like social security information, food shipments, CCTV reports, you name it. Those mothers are sucking in everything."

"It's gotta be a sim, right? But... the whole fucking country?"

"Yeah. That's not good."

The door to Hokey's container clanged back at the far end of the cold tin shed. The hard white light of the yard outside silhouetted a large figure in the doorway. Hokey turned as a big voice boomed.

"Hey! Hokey! Break's over! Get your arse back to work out here. We got trucks on the way in and I need you to drill out the fixings on the big steel."

"Oh, OK boss. I was just writing to my mother."

"I seriously doubt that. Let's go."

The figure retreated into the pool of light.

Hokey turned back to the screen.

"Bug? I'll be back to you in a few hours."

"Sure. I heard."

***

"So far, as we have seen, intrusion into a single datacentre is easily contained by the multiple firewalls at the gateway servers. Connection onto any encrypted data carrier is simply not possible. However, a major attack by an enemy, with the capabilities of say a hostile government, could theoretically result in denial of service between multiple nodes. This could choke time-critical transactions and lead to the collapse scenario we are testing here tonight. Of course, it's easy for us to simulate this massive denial of service attack, simply by blocking our incoming streams from the real datacentres. This will then be reflected in our holographic model."

29

Whiting glanced up into the control module at the side of the stage and nodded to the techs.

"OK. We will interrupt a random datastream."

He dabbed the control strip that hovered near his fingers.

Somewhere in the pulsing veins of the model a circular orb discoloured and blinked out. The writhing snakes of light cables that had been connected fell back and disappeared. New connections sprang out and tried to connect around the space with angry red warning signs and capital letter annotations.

"Note how the internet routes around the failure. There is adequate headroom in the system to allow alternate connections, at least in this case. Now we will hit ten datacentres simultaneously."

A few seconds later and a patch of darkness appeared in the hanging hologram. Like lightning the fingers of new connections scurried and busied themselves around the damaged area. The model seemed to be showing signs of restless discomfort. Meanwhile, the first node had brought itself back online and was reconnecting itself to the model.

"So far, we have seen a not uncommon occurrence of one datacentre going offline due to a technical difficulty. As you can see it quickly rebuilds itself without data loss once it comes back online. Several failing nodes could be caused by a more widespread problem, perhaps the result of grid failure county wide. This is much more serious, but over time can be restored. Now we will simulate, for the first time on such a scale, the result of multiple take downs across the country."

Whiting took a deep breath and as the eyes of the audience focused on the model, he launched the simulation.

For a few seconds there was nothing. He expected an implosion of the model, a few central nodes desperately sending out tentacles to locate any connecting port. Instead, some new graphic started to grow beside the nodes and a curious voice crackled in the space beside Whiting's console.

The front rows of the audience were first to spot that the growing graphic was an animated cartoon. A young woman leaned toward her colleague and pointed.

"It's a cat! Can you see it?"

As the graphic grew inside the model, spawning smaller versions of itself all around, the audience caught on, murmuring and smiling. Whiting's face fell. As the cute cartoon cat flexed and pawed, big pudgy 3D words came up underneath it that said MOUSER'S ON THE CASE!

The techs in the booth looked at each other in bafflement. The sound from their GLiDs was of an angry kitten, spitting and growling like a tiny demon.

The graphic was appearing all over the simulation, small at first but growing beside every node that was being affected. Nothing was going offline. The hologram held and seemed to grow a little brighter with the multiple cats and their growing mewls and comical growls.

Whiting found himself thinking aloud to the audience.

"It's a virus. It's a fucking virus. But that's impossible!"

Some of the attendees were furiously speaking to their GLiDs to ensure that their connections weren't compromised.

Whiting became aware that his head technician was speaking firmly in his ear from the booth.

"OK, Abe, we're going to cut the power to the sim. This is an intrusion."

"No! Wait. I need to know where it's coming from."

"Sorry, Abe. We've got to cut it out. We don't know that it's contained."

"Wait!"

Too late. The techs cut the main connection and the hologram disappeared in a blink. The restless crowd stared at the after picture of the giant sim burnt onto their retinas. The lights of the lecture theatre came slowly back up and Whiting felt very alone on the dais.

In the observation booth, Lothar Friedland could feel the quizzical looks of his guests and he turned to them with quiet confidence.

"An unexpected turn. Perhaps now you see what we have been facing all this time. I shall have a full report prepared for you on tonight's events along with our recommendations."

Friedland stood up, drawing his guests with him as they fumbled with their Champagne.

"Shall we repair to more comfortable surroundings?"

***

"Well, that's really crazy. Screwed up beyond belief."

"No way it was intentional, Bug. Telling you. They pulled the plug really quick."

"Reckon you could dig into it?"

"Yeah. Someone'll know something. Keep you posted."

"OK. Hoke's gonna be mad he missed this."

A fine rain fanned across the scrapyard where Hokey was out sorting cut metal into rail containers for weighing and shipping. He'd been on the laser drill all night, watching sparks through a black visor, and the

31

rain outside was a cool relief. The truck driver was helping him separate up some tangled road signage.

Hokey pointed at the lettering on a direction sign and called through the rain.

"Hey! I remember the M4!"

The driver nodded as he headed back to the cab.

"Yeah. Mways are all that are going to be left soon. They're ploughing in whole towns. It's like they never existed."

Hokey lost his grin.

"Yeah. Where you been working?"

The driver sat up high looking down with a grim face and jerked his thumb back toward the tangle of street furniture.

"I can't tell you that, can I? Work it out for yourself."

"Sure, man."

The driver hesitated, then motioned Hokey to come closer.

"Hey listen."

"Yeah?"

"Why would they build enclosures from the rail station up to a hospital? They seem to be doing this all over. Big fenced off pens."

"I don't know man."

"I saw them putting in turnstiles. Ten. Twenty of them, at least."

He suddenly thought better of it, slammed the door and fired up the engine.

4

"Dreemfeelds. They're my favourite places. They're your favourite places too. I know they are. You told me. You always want to be there. Relaxing with friends, meeting people, dancing, talking, maybe even falling in love. It's somewhere to come back to, over and over again. It'll always be here and all your friends will be waiting. You are in complete control. Where you go and what you do. Whether you want to walk in the rain or lie in the sun, you decide. Every day can be summer. On the beach, in the woods, at a restaurant, or just at home. The home of your choice. And the choices are now infinite. New to the Dreemfeelds. A country cottage in a forgotten lane, the sound of bees in a meadow and the murmur of a stream through the trees. A grand house with a ballroom and sweeping stair cases, marbled floors that lead to a terrace where the staff are serving drinks to your guests. Or maybe an uptown apartment overlooking the park, and a stroll away from the clubs and theatres in a city that lives by night. Amazing add-ons to your life experience. There is peace and tranquility in your Dreemfeelds. You feel good. You feel strong. You feel alive. You feel connected. It's a state of mind where all things are possible and every dreem is yours. Now."

Heath was barely in through security to the Metropolitan building before his assistant was back in his ear.

"Clayton, you have another red voicemail from Isobel Prine. Do you want to hear it? She's very persistent. If you like I can block her from the red channel."

"No. I'm here now. Put it through."

"OK Clayton."

The welcome tone played in his ear and Prine's voice cut through as though continuing from where she'd left off.

"...so I thought maybe he's just too good for his old buddies down on the killing floor. He's up there in the clouds with the people who really matter. You know, Clayton, when I think of the times I helped you out on research and presentation, all those angles, and your crummy use of English... Still, my shoulders are broad. I suppose they had to be for you to stand on them and slither up the side of the pyramid. Oh, I'm not bitter..."

"Stop!"

The voice died in his ear. Heath was smiling.

"Man, she's pissed off!"

He looked through the sea of activity in the foyer and the drift of workers and guests to the central elevator core.

"Locate Prine. How soon can you get me on a lift to the news floor?"

"Prine is logged in to desk one one seven on level six, tier two and is in that vicinity. Your place is now booked on elevator twenty three arriving in twelve seconds and departing in fifty seven seconds."

"Wow. This upgrade is good!"

Heath wondered as he got in the lift whether any of the sulky faces and lack of eye contact around the entrance to elevator twenty three was due to his new rank. He was taking somebody's pre-booked place and now they had to wait. He'd been there many times himself as a junior. The same vacant stare trying not to look bothered by some senior stranger pulling rank, then hanging around listening to his GLiD and waiting for a re-book.

He spotted Prine from way across the sea of workstations on the news floor. She was wearing the whitest shirt she could find and remonstrating vigorously with a colleague. She looked like she was guiding aircraft in to land. Heath tried to sneak up behind her, but the Prine radar was finely tuned to the notifications of her GLiD and she waved away her target to watch Heath zig-zag over to her position. She put her hands on her hips.

"About dam time!"

"Don't stand like that. You look like a pair of scissors."

She grimaced.

"I see they didn't upgrade your sense of humour."

Heath had been her mentor when she started on the news floor three years ago. She'd come straight from Metropolitan College to the Birmingham tombstone and apart from developing an open love-hate-abuse relationship with the unresponsive Heath, she hadn't changed much. She'd gone from the girlish high maintenance long student hair to a shorter, more aggressive style that framed her face and accentuated her look of piercing enquiry. She'd also learned to swear and shout to confirm her place in the pecking order of the news floor. But she always had humour and the annoying academic neatness of a straight A student.

"Thanks for your voicemail, Prine."

"Yeah? Which one? Two days you've been ignoring me. I suppose you told that bitch Mimi to autoblock me?"

"No. Not at all. They've just been keeping me very busy."

"Have you still got Mimi?"

"Yeah. But she can be upgraded."

"Privilege. The richer you get, the less value things have."

Prine sat at her desk and Heath arranged himself on the corner.

"I thought you hated Mimi."

Isobel shrugged.

"Yeah. I hate everybody these days. It's getting harder and harder down here, and then an arse-kisser like you gets bumped upstairs. I'm left babysitting the half wits who couldn't write a shopping list."

"Your day will come."

She looked at Heath without gratitude.

"Is that it? My day will come?"

He nodded.

"Hey look, Clayton. I can't wait for days to come. How about something now? You're at all the right meetings, you see it all put together. You can point me in the direction of a nice little data mine."

"Not really. You guys supply the street data. We just turn it into news, remember?"

"Yeah right. But you see the spin. Everybody here knows that the real news comes from the MIs and the end result is faker than a politician's smile."

She ran a finger under an imaginary catch line.

"The Metropolitan World Service. Where Facts Are Fiction."

"Yeah. You don't want to talk like that, Isobel."

"So, give me something I can work on. We could have lunch, you could tell me about the al-Degri business. I bet you know what really happened. There must be a hundred side-shoots off that I could work on."

"Not really. That's not my department."

"So, what is?"

"You know better than to ask. But I'll tell you this much. When some major story breaks, watch the first forty eight hours of reports before the official narrative is put together and then repeated over and over. If you want to look at al-Degri, go back over all the rumours and opinions that got corrected soon after, and then chase down the origins."

"And I thought you'd tell me something I didn't already know."

"Well, that's my cutting edge, slightly subversive advice for today."

Isobel wasn't impressed. She waved a hand at the block of yellow light that hovered an inch off her desk.

"D'you know how to fix this lightboard? I can't feel a dam thing."

"Nope. We have a kennel full of evolutionary throwbacks to come and stand up the kit. Phone Tech."

"Already have. Nothing. The sooner they're replaced by robots the better."

"I heard they're coming for all of us."

Isobel washed her hand through the lightboard but nothing was happening.

"Aah, bullshit!"

"Have you tried turning it off and turning it back on again?"

"Haha, not funny. Look, Heath. I don't think you're a complete arsehole, OK? So I'm sending you a key to my dippo with as much space as you need. Just give me something."

Heath slid off the desk and straightened his jacket.

"Hey you look, Isobel. There's no way I can do that. Even if the diplomatic bags were truly private, we're not on the same team, not even in the same department. It's a space for people collaborating on official projects, not for leaking editorial content."

Prine looked disappointed.

"Well, that didn't stop you getting bagfuls of juice for your pet projects from your ex. And, she wasn't on the same team or the same department or even... oh yeah that's right! She worked for a different company in a different town!"

"She was advising the Metropolitan."

"Oh please! She works for a government think tank. She was your girlfriend. There was stuff going on there."

"Sorry, Isobel. Really. I can't do it. Things have moved on."

She looked as winsome as anger would let her.

"No. You've moved on, and I've changed my mind. You actually are an arsehole."

**

Bruno, one of the engineers from Technical, was in full lecture mode to the dozen or so new college recruits in the conference room when Heath slid in, twenty minutes late, and tried to look discreet. He quietly sat alongside the security officer, the Divisional Human Resources Manager and one of the departmental legal team. They looked an uninspiring bunch, but the fresh faced college graduates were enrapt in Bruno's introduction.

Bruno wore the company shirt and tie with a sense of insolence. Like Techs everywhere he felt apart from the company philosophy. His trade was that of a disposable journeyman, but he was expected to be fanatically loyal to the hierarchy, innovating on their behalf and supercharging systems that his employers didn't even understand. Like most Techs, he gave little away of his opinions and appeared remote and withdrawn.

He was holding up his own GLiD to demonstrate.

"Your security implants are now active, paired with your handset and managed by the Human Resources Department here at the Metropolitan. You will have noticed on the screen that the unit is registering your pulse, and if you load the personnel medical file, it gives you a whole load of other information about your breathing, stress levels, blood sugar and just about everything else you need to know to prove to yourself that you're still alive. It's synced to your medical history and the doctor's file from your Metro Health Check so medications, vaccine notifications, referrals and internet diagnosis are always active and ready to be checked at any moment. Pretty important these days, as I'm sure you will agree."

The recruits watched their pulses pip with a light green diode at the top of the screen.

"However, it's more important than just an electronic medical card. The implants underneath your hairline and in your hand, that were little more than security tags at college, now triangulate with the Global Identification Unit to place audio in three dimensional space, allowing you to have your new virtual assistant talk directly in your ear. It will also take phone calls and record sounds around you. The handset still functions as a security measure. The apps on the unit will lock up if it is further away than the distance between your outstretched hand and your head, so your data can't be compromised by someone else. You will soon learn to keep the GLiD unit close to you at all times. If you do become inadvertently separated, the GPS capabilities of your implants and your unit can actively help GI Tech to put you back in touch again."

Bruno paused briefly as they refained focus.

"You have no doubt seen the manual movies and know that the Global Identification handset is your telephone, computer, mailbox, diary, wallet, identity card, travel ticket and a thousand other things. Like every other machine nowadays, it has passive RFID that can transmit its identity to any other machine within proximity. Acts like a radar on the 'internet of things'. Nice feature if you want to find the nearest coffee machine! But none of this is as fundamental as your permanent connection to the internet. I cannot stress this enough, but you may not be disconnected from the internet at any time. Not that you'd want to be, of course. As Legal have already told you, your contract of employment is based on the use of the Global Identification handset and the permanent connection, twenty four hours a day, to the internet. Long gone are the days when you might be somewhere with no signal. Everywhere your travel permit allows you to go is covered by the internet.

"What if the unit goes wrong, you may ask? What if you drop it out of a twentieth storey window or under the wheels of a taxi? Well, it's pretty robust, built to take knocks, no moving parts, but beyond that, the unit is self diagnostic. Should any component exhibit signs of imminent failure, it reports back to the GI Tech labs and you will be called in. If it fails altogether and the Metropolitan GPS can't grab your chip location from the internet, then you're probably dead. Also, it doesn't happen often, but just in case you are ever tempted to try and tinker with the inner workings, or modify the unit in any way, then don't. Never, ever, compromise your GLiD account. Everything will stop. Insurances, travel permits, food vouchers. The lot. You will not be able to transact, conduct business or move anywhere. The Global Identification handset is company property and the ramifications of wilfully altering the core program or compromising the GLiD's functionality do not bear thinking about. Remember, the implants you have are much more sophisticated than those that are currently implanted into the prison population, children, the elderly and the vulnerable. You can still be identified, traced and monitored. With the graduation to the Metropolitan GLiD, you have been handed real responsibility balanced with all the ramifications of failing to comply with company policy."

None of the recruits dared move, giving Bruno an effective pay-off on his final page of script.

"So, with all that responsibility, what's in it for you? As you will have read in the company manuals, apart from providing all the tools for you to do your job more efficiently and completely than anyone else in your profession, you have an extensive travel permit shaped by certificates that you are granted. You also have excellent food scheme and recreational passes based on your personal carbon allowance. For the icing on the cake, yes... the rumours are true."

Bruno waited for his half smile to be mirrored in the faces of the relaxing recruits.

"The Metropolitan has the most generous corporate account with Dreemfeelds, bar none. Your allowance is basically unlimited during your own time, and the use of Dreemfeelds Decks in any UK city is complimentary for all employees of The Metropolitan. So, if you don't want to log in from home for a solo flight, you can go multi-player in a Deck with your friends list. From tonight, when you log in, you will be offered the chance to join hundreds of new and exclusive groups. You will be able to share your own Dreemfeelds with each other and to enjoy your breaks from work in hundreds of brand new worlds. These can be modified and augmented as you please and to suit all budgets."

The recruits looked pleased with themselves.

"Very, very nice. No?"

***

Heath had missed his opening slot when, as a representative of the junior editorial team, he had been tasked with selling the Metropolitan career path to the new recruits. He liked the touch of freedom that his upgrade had given him, to cancel or delay meetings with the lower grades. He could cite company business and never have to explain himself.

The induction group broke for lunch and over an extensive buffet in an adjoining suite they watched the activities of the news floor on the wall screen as the recruits eagerly questioned their new colleagues.

A skinny youngster, with bright yellow blond hair and a collar that seemed so tight it interfered with the function of his Adam's apple, had cornered Heath.

"I took extra qualifications in finance and banking, so I could join the Economics team. I'm going to be a Business Editor."

Heath said nothing, but seriously doubted that this kid would ever get further than Statistics and Data Research. Mimi was telling Heath quietly about Zachary Kloter's grades and college profile. He seemed to be an honest idiot with an over-exaggerated sense of his abilities. Kloter pressed on.

"I remember you were on the team that covered the financial collapse just before the war. It must have been an extraordinary moment to be reporting on the passing of a cash-based economic era."

The question was semiserious and Heath felt compelled to engage.

"As a historical moment, I suppose. Bear in mind that the overwhelming majority of global transactions in all sectors were already based on digital money."

"But you were right on top of the collapse when it started. You almost saw it coming."

Heath shifted from one foot to the other.

"Well, once there is a strain on the system, like the risk of national debt becoming unrepayable, people look to secure their capital against sequestration by the banks. It's a logical next step to move money out of the system and into physical cash. Of course, when there's not enough, the system can implode."

Kloter's eyes flashed.

"You were right on the front line of the street riots during the Big Bank Holiday. Did you feel that society itself might be imploding?"

"Not really. The army were right behind the government, and literally right behind us. Most people hadn't used cash for years so when the Bank of England recalled all physical money it was only the dodgy tax evaders and illegal businesses that really suffered."

"But that wasn't the people's argument, was it? They seemed to miss the lack of choice. They woke up and suddenly decided they wanted to control their own money."

Heath had heard enough and wanted to shut down the conversation.

"People have never controlled their own money. All money belongs to the banks. It was just loaned to them. People own nothing."

Kloter felt the sharpness and straightened up.

"I see. So you had little sympathy for the movement to use existing cash as an alternative barter system?"

"No sympathy whatever. Thinking they could get away with it was crazy. Bank notes had RFID chips in them for years. After the recall deadline, holding cash was a self-incriminating act. Today it's theft of bank property. Anyone with cash now will simply be disappeared."

Heath was getting a meeting call in his ear from Mimi. Harry wanted him in a conference booth in Editorial.

"I have to go."

Heath headed for the door, instructing Mimi to reschedule his address to the new journalists for later in the afternoon.

***

The two men sat in the glass cubicle watching the video feed hover in the middle of the table. Heath caught the multiple views of the CCTV system playing side by side and appeared dazzled by the shifting hologram that grew and flowed in front of him. He shook his head slowly.

"I'm not that familiar with core computing. Is this thing doing what it's supposed to?"

Harry pointed Heath's attention back to the footage.

"Watch. Here."

Heath saw the expression on a bearded man's face change from cool control to cold confusion. He heard him mutter "It's a virus. It's a fucking virus..."

The screen closed up on the cartoon cat and froze as the lettering appeared underneath.

40

"Mouser's on the case?"

"Freeze!"

The playback stopped on Harry's command and they sat looking at the still frame.

"That, Clayton my boy, is an intrusion. A serious fucking intrusion."

Heath shifted in his seat.

"OK. What's the story?"

"Nightship Systems are the government's preferred advisory body for digital systems. They were testing shutdown scenarios during a cyber attack, simulating the country's datacentre activity, when this shows up. It's a virus, all right, but it seems to prevent the servers from shutting down during an external attack. You'd have to rip the plugs from the wall to quit these servers."

Heath looked baffled.

"So, isn't that a good thing? This must be a safeguard of some kind. Looks kind of crazy, but it works."

"Look at it, Clayton. Mouser's on the case. What does that tell you?"

"I don't know. That somebody likes cats?"

Harry slapped the table.

"Oh come on! Look at it. Mouser. It's even got his name in there. USER."

He threw his hands in the air.

"It's the MO of the USER! Or some shit like that!"

Heath wasn't so sure.

"Harry, OK, that's a stretch in my view, but why would The User produce a virus to protect government datacentres from attack? This guy's anarchist. His MO has always been to steal identities or bring down government systems. Why would this show up here and how could a virus be carried into a third party simulation?"

Harry was smiling now.

"Clayton, now you're talking. All questions that you are going to answer, my boy. You have filed more examples of systemic abuse by The User than anyone else I know. You are literally writing the book on this guy. I want you to follow this up, work with Nightship and get us an angle on this. You're right. There is something unusual about this. It may be the break you've needed. Something different. A mistake. A miscalculation. I don't know! It's top secret right now, only a few people outside Nightship, who weren't there on the night, know this happened and until we get some answers, it's more heavily embargoed than the Royal Dreemfeelds. You get me?"

Heath sighed.

"Yeah. I get you. How long have I got?"

Harry looked conciliatory for a moment.

"Not long. A week. Most."

"Who's screaming?"

Harry pointed at the ceiling.

"The top. The very top. You're the man, Clayton. You're the man."

***

"I started in computer tech back in the day, but switched to journalism to join The Metropolitan. I came from a background of plastic keyboards and 'touch screen'. Monitors were big blocks of plastic that showed a picture made of pixels. Remember those? No, maybe not. We had hard drives in those days to store information. A long, long way away from the quantum light drives of today, stored in the cloud, with unlimited space that you just pull out of the ether. Hard drives were spinning metal disks with just a few terabytes of storage. They were physically connected to your computer. Unthinkable today."

The recruits smiled with wonder as Clayton paced around at the front of the conference room and waited for the back-up footage of old journalists in front of their ancient workstations to play out and fade.

"I got all the tech stories to cover in the early days. After the war we had loads of new kit that had never been seen before. Hard light was brand new. It blew us all away to see pictures appear in mid air, to be able to walk around them and hear 'em. That's when the rules changed. We moved into creating footage by merging two or three video streams and ending up with a whole new reality. A whole new way of telling a story. It was the real start of modern journalism."

Heath pointed vaguely in the direction of an attentive face.

"So, in answer to your original question, I was brought into the news floor team when they were trying to make sense of the data they were gathering on the activities of dissidents. People who were resisting the need for homeland security measures in the wake of the eastern hostilities. We had links to the secret services and great latitude from the government to access whatever information we needed to identify the activities and operations of our homegrown terrorists. Sure, the MIs were in charge of the operational information, but we worked hand in glove to direct the narrative towards the public. In the middle of all that, I came across many thousands of communications from an entity called The User. A more crazy, demented, psychotic and dangerous individual, I could not imagine. From a sick sense of humour to an overtly fascist worldview, there was nothing that this

42

guy wouldn't do. He'd post full dox of serving policemen, politicians and corporate directors online. He'd crash the welfare services, the broadcast media streams and even find a way to bring down the military drone service that protected the country. He became the public enemy, and in so many ways, my nemesis."

The room was rapt with attention. The demonic graphic of the Goat of Mendes had appeared in front of the screen and glowered at the recruits.

"The User is today's bogey man. Whether he's responsible for every ill in society or not, whether he will be able to bring this country's services to its knees in pursuit of his insane goals, it is our job to face the threat head on."

In the brief silence of the room, Heath had a vision of a crazy cartoon cat pawing at the air with playful abandon.

Something didn't fit at all.

5

"Thank you Kevan. Well, the result was not as clear cut as some were suggesting, and the polls certainly pointed to a close contest, but this morning Britain has a new Prime Minister. And, it's just weeks before he has to go to the polls again in order to seek an MP's mandate again, for the next five years. The often controversial figure of Sarion Dundas has beaten the three other more traditional candidates to become one of the most powerful figures on the world stage. During his years in parliament he has risen from an advisory role with the Home Secretary to prominent positions on committees for defence and security. Recently, he has held a Cabinet position under Mohammed al-Degri. Dundas was in charge of the UK's far reaching programmes of restructuring and internal developments since the end of the war.

"In a moment of high drama for the nation, Mister Dundas used the leadership campaign to reveal that he is a latent, non-practising paedophile. Despite calls from across the party spectrum to deselect Mister Dundas, pending a reconsideration of the new laws protecting sexual preference, the grass roots of the party clearly felt that it was not an issue that would detract from the experience and capabilities that he would bring to the job. Some have applauded the dangerous gamble of coming out in public, while others saw it as inevitable after years of speculation and rumour surrounding the forty three year old unmarried white male.

"It is, however, a ground breaking moment in British politics which is not lost on the recently reformed Paedophile Information Exchange. The once banned organisation is already lobbying for a reappraisal of historical allegations against politicians and public figures dating back to the last century.

"Mister Dundas is expected to address the nation from Downing Street in a press conference scheduled for later today.

"Back to you and the team in the studio, Kevan."

The Swiss countryside moved through its seasons oblivious to the rest of the world. Skies of deep blue lay behind white shapes of passing cloud. The sun lit the green valleys that poured down from the glittering snow peaks of cliff and rocky mountain.

Past patchworks of agriculture and high fields of sunflowers, the country lanes and their petrified wooden field fencing wound lazily toward the lake. A large town ran along the shore, bisected by a twin track railway that disappeared amongst ancient church steeples and the high gabled roofs of black and white guest houses. Life continued at its orderly pace, with a sense of unchanging tradition and the inevitability of history.

Across the water, on an imposing rock promontory, stood a château, backdropped by the livid green of a pine forest. The woods backed up the mountain to its cliff edge and from there up into the clear skies where only eagles circled in the chill air. In the manicured grounds and gardens an occasional shadow of uniformed guards passed along the gravel paths.

The crenellations and alcoves in the solid architecture of the château were blackened with age. Its towers were worn with the storms and winter pollution of the lake, accumulated over the centuries. Small rectangular windows in the many turrets gave nothing away and only the rusty red of tiled tower roofs hinted at warmth and habitation.

Those windows had the finest views across the lake to the town and then beyond into the rolling green of the spring fields. In the sumptuous wood-panelled dining room the afternoon light fell across a long table where food had been eaten and the diners had now left to sit in the adjoining antechamber.

"I listened to his inaugural broadcast on the radio. If the people can be persuaded that it is business as usual, then we do indeed have a chance at bringing about the necessary change."

The old man was engulfed by the high wing-backed black chair from where he addressed his guests.

"Finally, the power resides, within this room, to reshape the world that we have made. Britain must not appear to be untouched by world events. Suffering yes, but still in control and leading the way to the future."

Derry Thornelow shifted slightly in his seat.

"We have engineered a situation from which we could not credibly retreat. By putting our man in position we have certainly played our hand."

The old man waved it away calmly.

"Oh, it has to be now in Britain. We accept that the war did not achieve all of its aims, not always going as expected. Many scenarios were created to deal with the unexpected. You wrote many of the set pieces yourself. Masterly acts of theatre which undoubtedly brought business to a conclusion long before the prize itself was destroyed in the process. But today our crisis window will be brief and we will have one decisive push to redefine the function of the human

45

population on planet earth. Otherwise we will be clearing up this mess for another century."

Another guest, sweating slightly in a voluminous grey suit and dabbing at his jowls with a handkerchief, was startled into action.

"There is no question of failure. We have invested everything in the... reconstruction."

The old man smiled.

"The Bank For International Settlements was formed for just the investment that it has now made. It holds the purse strings not just of the central banking system, but by inference of the security services, their military operatives and the major corporations that supply them. It is a time to be brave. To be audacious. Destiny walks beside us all."

"Annuit coeptis!"

The old man leaned round in his chair but didn't have to see the figure at the door. He smiled thinly.

"Dovi! Come and join us."

Abarlev took his seat in the semicircle of dark leather furniture that followed the contour of the tower wall. He nodded a greeting as he did so to the deputy director of the CIA, to Thornelow, the bank governors and the young CEO of the Zura Corporation.

The old man waited until a smartly uniformed flunky had settled a small drinks tray before Abarlev and retreated into the depths of the château.

"All eyes are on London, Dovi. We have been watching the developments."

"It has not been easy. We are relying on the speed of events to push the program forward. If there is enough new headline stories each day the analysis will be short and always inconclusive. We can generate any number of social interest pieces, more civil unrest perhaps, just to keep the level of distraction high."

The banker leaned in.

"What if the public start to question the lack of action by the authorities to stamp out the unrest? Crowd control weaponry is formidable nowadays."

"Well, what could they do? Besides, we have operations waiting in the wings to justify an escalation of chaos."

Derry Thornelow leaned across to the nervous banker.

"Remember the stadium bomb in London back at the start of the war? It wiped the news media clean of the Shanghai operation for months. Once the virus had taken hold and the Chinese censored all reporting of it, our job was done. Official stories were in position to be parroted by every licensed outlet on the internet. It's really just a matter of timing."

"Good God. Yes."

The banker managed a weak smile. The old man picked up on Thornelow's calm confidence.

"How advanced are the logistical plans for displacement and processing of the population once the grid goes down?"

"The manoeuvres have been signed off by NATO, the British Armed Forces and now, of course, by the government."

To Thornelow's right sat a United States four star general, the Supreme Allied Commander for Europe. He felt the need to cut in to the conversation.

"The Military Council have approved the necessity of controlling displaced civilians. It remains only to be rubber stamped by the North Atlantic Council itself. And, that covers the worldwide legalities..."

Thornelow turned away slightly from the General, body language that was not lost on the old man.

Thornelow spoke up again with an airy sense of control.

"Of course, we have to bear in mind that this is nothing like the scale of the United States operation undertaken by FEMA. We have no need to operate concentration camps, we simply fence off inner city areas and they become self-contained. The program of removing feeder towns to further concentrate the population has been most effective."

The banker was back with his nervous questions.

"What if desperation sets in? Animals become nervous in captivity."

Abarlev leaned forward in his chair to address the banker directly.

"As I'm sure you know, Mister Schakt, former Prime Minister al-Degri embarked upon a very generous welfare program for the many, er... inactive economic units in British society. We intend to introduce a 'vote catching' welfare bonanza before the shutdown, which will allow people a window in which to stock up on essential items that will see them through the shutdown period. The old model of society breaking down after three days without supplies will be adequately addressed. People will count themselves lucky and therefore be amenable to the authority's suggestions to resolve the crisis."

"I see. I hope you're right."

The old man turned to the young CEO of the Zura Corporation.

"Do you like what you hear, Mister Hanser?"

Hanser waited a few moments for attention.

"I do, indeed. I have been fascinated by the moves behind the scene in Whitehall to prepare the political system for an evolutionary step forward. I feel most confident in investing in the new Britain and working with the City of London."

The carefully prepared words seemed cautious and unrevealing, coming as they did from such a young man. Unexpected, given that he was dressed in his fashionable clothing, his white blond hair touching his ears with a hint of narcissism. But, his thin frame was scored with a humourless expression and his English was flavoured with a strong German accent.

"I, of course, would like to be clear that the new Zura that I am developing in the English Midlands will have the same sovereign status as the City of London and perhaps other extra national entities in the UK, such as, perhaps, Nightship Systems for example."

The old man saw the meeting going off topic and stepped in sharply.

"The operation of the Crown and its legal framework are a very different matter than those of national governments awarding contracts and charters. Concessions and rights derive from the Crown, therefore if the Crown were to exclude itself from the foundation of those rights and concessions, they would logically become instantly invalid. Therefore the Crown is supranational."

Hanser could see that there was no negotiation, and jabbed with the only retort he had.

"I see. Like the arrangement with the United States of America."

The Supreme Allied Commander for Europe shifted sharply in his seat.

***

Across the lake in the town, church bells were chiming six o'clock. Although the working day was ending, the streets were curiously alive with children and their parents. Most were dressed in an array of carnival costumes with elements of medieval tunics and quartered jerkins in red and blue. Some had hats with bells and ancient thumb sticks that seemed at odds with their mobile phones and cameras.

As colourful horse drawn floats passed the waving lines, the crowd followed along behind and they processed out of the town to the accompaniment of accordion and brass bands.

Out in the field stood a twenty foot pyre, stacked all around with seasoned wood and topped by the giant effigy of a grinning snowman. The children gathered obediently at the guide ropes, gazing up at the bonfire but concentrating on their hot pastries and other street food from the carnival vendors.

A master of ceremonies emerged like a green-clad sprite from between the ranks of local aldermen. The town officials carried giant cowbells that clanked in time with their step. The sprite held his radio mic so that it was masked by his staff and he prowled the lines of laughing children, smiling like a devil as he welcomed the town to the rite of spring.

Horsemen in traditional costumes had ringed the outer perimeter of the festival field. Their torches were dancing dots of light against the deepening blue of the sky. The cajoling figure of Robin Goodfellow gurned and gesticulated to the expectant crowd who clapped and cheered his extravagant ode to spring. He retrieved a torch from an advancing horseman who had left his mount and slowly processed through a parting in the crowd. He danced a complete circle around the bonfire as the crowd urged him on, the children shouting with delight.

Finally, he touched it to the base of the giant mound and transferred the fire to its target.

***

From the window in the château the growing bonfire outshone the lights of the town. The old man stood watching, flanked by his guests holding their shot glasses and taking in the scene.

"It is good to see Swiss traditions spreading to the towns again. It helps to anchor people in their identity when all around is uncertainty. Celebrating the end of winter should be a joyous occasion. I see the torch is lit, Dovi! Are you ready to illuminate the world?"

Abarlev smiled.

"I will simply play my part. But there is indeed a feeling that from this pivotal moment, the world will be following a new light."

The general seemed less impressed.

"Pivotal moment. Hmm. As long as your new datacentres come up within the time frame. The forces in the field can only contain a situation without orders for a few days before they have to make their own decisions."

"Global ID servers are already in position at the datacentres. They have only to be brought online by Nightship in the correct sequence. The grid will then be controlled from The City. Your orders will reflect that."

The general grumbled.

"A lot of things seem to go wrong with computers."

"That's why we have alternate plans and suitable... fall guys, for want of a better expression, who can distract the public's attention."

Thornelow stood next to the General and offered a thought.

"We have a highly disposable Prime Minister, you know."

"I hate that guy."

"He is a useful pawn. He is *our* useful pawn. Beside that, we have numerous scenarios at ground level for tieing in the event to groups of anarchists and bogey men that will do the public's thinking for them. We write the plays, so we can stay several steps ahead of the audience."

The general was happier with the inference.

"Yeah. Strategy and tactics, developed over centuries of warfare."

"Know thine enemy, General."

The old man was quietly pleased.

"We have spent the afternoon playing out the scenes in our production. Where there was disagreement we have found concord and doubt has become clarity. While the post-war world is still in chaos we have a chance if we hold our nerve and play our roles effectively."

Across the lake, the bonfire had grown into a writhing beacon of flame against the evening sky. As the flames began to obscure the giant figure of the snowman, fireworks built into the head exploded in a ball of white light and a clap of sound. It briefly lit the field and its cheering crowd. The sound rolled across the lake to the observers in the château.

The old man smiled.

"Ah. Once lit, the sooner the head explodes, the better the summer will be."

"Prime Minister elect, Sarion Dundas has paid tribute to the legacy of his predecessor, Mohammed al-Degri, in a speech to the City of London at last night's Lord Mayor's banquet. He underscored his support for the cornerstone policies of al-Degri's tenure in Downing Street and pledged to immediately bring forward and implement the remaining stages of the government's welfare reforms. This means fast-tracking increased allowances for food, rent guarantees and entertainment for hundreds of thousands of people who have yet to be offered employment through the Private Company Direct Retraining programme. Those in state-controlled employment, including the administration, security sector and the military will also benefit from increased allowances for their Global ID grades.

"The Shadow Minister for Internal Affairs, Keisha Lamontaigne, played down the multi-billion giveaway claiming it was "a cynical stunt to buy votes in a hastily cobbled election campaign that would end in disaster for either the government or the economy".

"The Treasury conceded that as yet there has been no breakdown of the figures from within the government to explain how the move will be funded.

"In other news, following a security scare at one of the biggest datacentres in Southern England, the government's Watford Digital Exchange, United Nations troops have been stationed on the site to augment the regular Army as they manage perimeter security. Two days ago a group of masked anarchists broke through the perimeter in an attempt to damage and disable vital systems. During the pitched battle with armed security, one guard died and three others were airlifted to hospital with serious gunshot injuries. Plans have been approved to deploy more troops throughout the country at vital installations to prevent attacks that could compromise food distribution or paralyse commercial activity. Although the attack was unsuccessful, the nine masked anarchists caught on camera are the subject of a countrywide manhunt involving thirty six regional forces."

Whiting stood in front of Friedland's desk like a naughty schoolboy and had to watch as Friedland let the report scroll up through the air in front of him. He had to listen to his own voice narrating and watch the mirror image of his charts and diagrams play to Friedland's disinterested eyes.

Whiting was particularly furious that he had not been allowed to have his team with him. His report was deemed to be too highly classified to have input from his own experts, and most humiliatingly, he wasn't even allowed the civility of a seat in Friedland's opulent office.

The report was finally coming to an end with Whiting's shaky conclusions.

"The attack, if indeed we are to call it that, shows a baffling contradiction of genius and naivety. While the execution of the intrusion is so well-hidden that we were able to import it into the simulation with the profile of the chipset, the pay-off is an unsophisticated, childlike and deliberately outdated graphic. While the intrusion itself is effective at cycling between shutdown and start-up routines when a given quantity of nodes become unreachable, the purpose of an external agent deliberately implementing this remains motiveless. It is my recommendation that a coding team disassemble the full coreware of an affected server node to discover, what I suspect will be, a simple solution to removing the code."

Friedland had seen enough and stopped the report. It froze and hung in mid air.

"I know you're playing it down, Abraham. I understand that. It happened on your watch. But the implications of a nationwide, integral virus, morphing between servers with impunity is, well... beyond a simple solution."

Whiting was building a case in his head, but Friedland had made up his mind.

"Abraham, I have already acted on your recommendation of appointing a team to take this apart and discover its origin. We will resolve this issue within a week, a new simulation will be run and it will not fail."

Whiting couldn't help but interrupt.

"A week? You're talking about deconstructing millions of lines of code, and we don't even know where we need to start. It'll take a week just to section up a datamap."

Friedland looked down at the frozen image in the air.

"It's already underway. We have a new team."

Whiting was stunned.

"Am I not involved in this?"

"Not at this current time."

"Can I ask who is more qualified to handle this than me?"

"You may not. Your input to date is under review as part of the investigation."

Whiting felt a crawling sensation in his stomach.

"Am I still under contract?"

"Yes."

"For how long?"

Friedland had tired of the chase.

"That depends on the review."

***

"Is that too tight?"

"Nah. It's OK."

"Next!"

The construction worker in the blue overall and yellow hard hat stepped out of the line, testing the lightweight metal bracelet around his wrist. It felt strong enough but was unlikely to interfere with manual work. He joined the rest of the detail in the back of the open truck and they started out through the gates of the army base into the clearance zone. Another truck started to follow them out.

In the front cab the chief engineers were going over their section of map.

"The old city services reach twelve miles maximum into the country. It gives us enough infrastructure to commission the primary substation, then build some accommodation and engine sheds. It's a few miles further on to the town."

"What did the survey say we can expect? Any geological issues or landscape anomalies?"

The other engineer found himself shouting over the roar of the engine.

"No. It was farmland! Mostly flat, but some rises in the process of being cleared. One of the reasons the client wanted to redevelop the town was the surrounding rural area. It gives a perfect perimeter with close services, but great security."

"When do I find out who the client is?"

The engineer considered for a moment.

"Well, I suppose you'll know as soon as their architects arrive. It's the German aerospace company, Zura. It looks like it's going to be some sort of headquarters. Big development."

"Another multinational. Same story up north. I was on the team putting in the perimeters around York. Looks like this is the way the whole country's going."

He lifted his arm so the sleeve of his heavy duty jacket fell back to reveal the bracelet.

"They might as well just stick us all in handcuffs!"

Whiting had been sitting in his living room for an hour. His herbal tea was cold in the cup.

He'd spent a little while just gazing through the open door into the tiny conservatory that cantilevered out six stories above the quad. He grew flowers, strange hybrids he bred himself in that little glass laboratory. All year round there were seeds and pots at different stages of germination and growth. He'd always been fascinated by Nature's codework. Perhaps he could have been a horticulturist? He started to see the privilege of his hobby being taken away from him if his contract was renegotiated. His little apartment with its kitchen, shower room and living space suddenly seemed precious even if he didn't own it. It just came with the job.

His gaze finally rested on the workstation. A flat slab of wood effect plastic with the dark glass pane in the centre. That was his way out into the world. Through the internet.

His GLiD rested on the desk beside him, the screen scrolling with information and pictures. He'd turned his PA to silent. She'd only interrupt his thoughts if a more senior manager wanted to communicate.

A symbol of the Nightship Bulletin System came up periodically in the feed and his finger started to hover over the screen. Eventually, he bit.

"Give me a board and a screen."

A lightboard appeared beneath his fingers and the dark rectangle of the screen cut a hole in his vision. The Nightship logo emerged, grew and dissolved.

"Load the most recent cabinets."

Columns of information flowed in, colour coded, pocked with symbols and annotations.

"The whole of the month."

The screen jogged a bit but not much.

"Hmm. One simulation in a month."

His insecurity grew as he reviewed his last work. If he was the paranoid type, he might believe that he'd been given that sim to set him up, or to separate him from the herd. But of course, it wasn't. That would make no sense. It was just his seniority and experience that isolated him. His discomfort was the long drop from the remote, aloof grandee to the excruciating embarrassment of looking like a fool in front of his peers, not to mention Nightship's corporate guests. The GLiD screen on the desk kept on scrolling with the bulletin notices, showing how the working life at Nightship carried on. It developed, it ran... like clockwork. Night and day. Whiting felt friendless and alone. A decision came to him.

He looked at the lightboard for a moment, then placed his fingers on the move bars at the top of each section and rearranged the blocks of keys to his liking. He looked back to the screen and highlighted the main simulation project.

"Do I still have access to my back-up of the core files?"

"Yes."

"Log me in."

"You're now logged in."

A floating pyramid of file structures grew into the screen. It looked simple, but it belied the vast depths of information that lay beyond. His report had covered the what and the when. The who and the how were buried deep within the layers of code.

He rotated the pyramid with hand gestures and zoomed into the graphic.

"Give me the nodes in order as they came online."

A list appeared. He scanned it up and down.

"Give me the first node to refuse a disconnection request."

The list reordered.

"Bletchley. Ironic. And just down the road."

He zoomed in further into the pyramid model and further layers of complexity came into view.

"Load the coreware for Bletchley. Outer cabs."

A froth of file columns started to replace the spider's web of the hierarchy. He glanced at the top corner of the screen. One of two hundred and thirty four.

"Give me diags."

A multicoloured 3D cube began revolving in front of his fingers. It was going to be a long night.

***

A patrol swung by and joined up with the trucks as they moved through the clearance zone. Lines of houses in once green avenues were now just the geometric patterns of floor plans. There were stumps of walls and piles of rubble, loosely separated into their material components. The construction crew were now wearing face masks, watching the rise and roll of the hills that were once hidden by towns. Every few miles a pile of rusting cars teetered in the brick ruins, stacked by a giant uncaring hand and awaiting removal. One of the crew tried to break the doleful silence, gesturing to his mate as he

55

turned to shout over the vehicle noise.

"My family came from around here! Somewhere around here anyway!"

The mention of family drove the silence deeper. So many had died in the chaos of the war and the epidemic that no family had escaped intact. Medical services were overwhelmed by the casualties, whole streets abandoned in towns across the country as remaining children and relatives grouped together. Then afterwards came the relocations to the big population areas. At least there, the trains could bring in food and there was a functioning housing system with services and rudimentary jobs. So much had happened that the old way of life seemed like a golden age.

"I came down here from Stafford. Don't know how much of that's left. I never went back."

The conversation dried and they watched the army patrols instead, scanning left and right from their gun mounted trucks. Nothing was moving today amongst the rubble.

The checkpoints out on the open road came every few miles. Each time the trucks waited while a soldier walked around consulting a hand-held scanner. He viewed streams of data about the truck, its occupants and the GLiD outline of their designated driver. Thermal images, metal detection and the search for illegal electronics were documented and stored. The soldiers looked weary and tired, impatiently waving them through the barriers.

The countryside was losing its manicured grids of farmland. The hedges had grown high and wild and only when it gave way to wooden fencing was there a glimpse of thigh-high undergrowth and new saplings sprouting at random in the fields. Food production had been concentrated around the farms where unravelling coils of six foot razor wire wound between makeshift guard towers and electrified fencing. Tiny figures in the distance could be seen patrolling.

At the final checkpoint, the trucks were directed off the main road and onto a thin, broken track lined with trees. When they finally pulled into a field, they were met by a small convoy of personnel carriers and jeeps, a catering truck and a group of soldiers who were still clearing the field around a large green army tent.

The chief engineers climbed out of the cab, stretching and grimacing at the lack of facilities. A wandering squaddie was hailed.

"Hey, where's all our gear?"

"Nothing turned up yet, mate."

A Brigadier stepped in between them.

"That's right. We're still waiting for the prefabs. And your equipment will start arriving tomorrow."

The engineer was uncomfortable and hungry.

"Are you telling me this is it?"

The Brigadier looked stony.

"That's right. Not even any toilets, so you'll have to piss in the hedge with the rest of us. OK?"

***

Whiting rubbed his face, smoothing his hands down his beard and trying to refocus his eyes on objects around the room. He was seeing sub routines, cache locks, loops and arrays everywhere he looked. His mind was drifting with the full expectation of what he was seeing. Nothing unusual, nothing out of place. He was going about it all wrong.

He looked back over a table of notes he'd compiled from the internet while in rooms full of technical reviewers, statmen and programmers. They all came up with the same tried and worthless approaches. Only one piece of advice stuck in his mind. You might have to go dark. He dismissed that as a kamikaze move, a career finishing gesture of desperation. He had never left the permissions area of his internet allowance, not even in the early days of the Dreemfeelds when the speakeasies offered access to anything his mind could imagine. His fear of discovery, public shaming and destroyed career kept him afraid and compliant. Now, with his future uncertain, he was indeed peering into the darkness.

He slept for an hour or so, lying on his bed with the heating pumped up and visions of spiky red code and their containers playing on his mind. When he awoke, he was thinking of Friedland. His traumatic conversation with him was repeating in his mind. Here was a man who believed he didn't need to know anything about the nature of the business he was managing. He seemed to feel that knowing anything would actually be detrimental to decision making. How could he imagine that a new simulation could be built and run in a week? It was impossible.

Whiting stared at the ceiling in the halflight and remembered.

"A week? You're talking about deconstructing millions of lines of code, and we don't even know where we need to start. It'll take a week just to section up a datamap."

Friedland looked down at the frozen image in the air.

"It's already underway. We have a new team."

Whiting was suddenly fully awake.

"It's already underway. We have a new team."

Whiting swung his feet off the bed and headed back to his desk.

"It's already underway..."

It could only be underway if they knew it was there all along. Now he definitely had to find it.

***

The construction crew had been up since dawn surveying from the top of the hill down toward the campsite and from there to the main road. It was a chill April morning and the tea and sandwiches from the side of the truck had done little to ease the discomfort of last night in the prefab huts. The chief engineer looked up from the tablet in his hand toward the sound of engines in the lane. The army had carved out a length of the overgrown hedge. Low-loaders, carrying giant pipes, were easing into the field to join the rapidly expanding encampment of army personnel.

The Brigadier came and stood at the engineers' shoulder.

"Your stuff's on its way. Make sure you stick to the territory marked on the maps. Everything else is out of bounds."

The engineer nodded toward the trucks.

"Why are you laying drainage pipes in a no-man's land?"

"We're expecting a lot of rain."

"They're four feet wide!"

The Brigadier thought for a second.

"We're expecting a lot of rain... in the next thirty years."

One of the construction crew called across the field.

"Chief! It's on its way!"

On the main road in the distance, a long line of trucks could be seen, escorted front and back by a security detail with flashing lights.

The Brigadier started to walk away, talking over his shoulder as he went.

"Now be a good lad and get your fences up. We've got a busy schedule."

***

The day was turning to evening before Whiting stood at the door of his little conservatory and looked down across the courtyard. Second day shift was underway and managers such as himself were either at work or socialising in the campus restaurants and bars. He still had two days before his next project assignment would have begun and the GLiD was noticeably quiet about it.

A small janitor bot was bumping from wall to wall in the courtyard, meticulously brushing up the windblown detritus that came in from the woods. It would come back time and time again, never tiring of its tedium. He watched it for a while and had a thought.

Whiting sat back at the desk and pulled up the diagnostic screens again. One of the oldest tools was janitor software, used in debugging. It scanned every line of working code, cleaning up poor syntax and removing snippets that had been left over or forgotten. It could also run in the background, gleaning titbits of broken code and holding them for inspection by an editor who could manually delete them.

Whiting hovered his finger over the software to highlight the icon.

"Janitor, have you got anything in the inspection cache?"

"Yes."

"Display."

Whiting was immediately disappointed. It was a hodge-podge of meaningless symbols, truncated lines of notes and a bunch of random coloured tiles. Just what he'd expect to see. The only line that was truly unique was a programmer's comment, a line with symbols at either end that tell the program itself to ignore the line while running. It was used to tell other programmers about the following blocks of code.

This one read: /* CAT 5 - RETRO L8-ACT ON DISC */

Whiting smiled. This must be really old code. Nobody used Cat 5 cabling anymore, and there would be no need to mention it in the software. But old coreware code got reused for many years without getting edited down, so it was nothing unusual to find thousands of lines of dead commands.

His smile faded and he went to lie on the bed once more.

Late in the night his assistant, who he had named Phaedra, was still talking quietly into his ear, relaying email and making suggestions for suitable replies. He slept. Phaedra detected it and went quiet.

The next time he awoke, it was in a half dream somewhere in the early hours of darkness. In the dream he had an idea, so compelling that he didn't want to wake fully and forget the thread. He fumbled in a hazy stupor over to his desk where the janitor software was still frozen in the air. He wanted to speak, but thought he might lose the idea, so he dragged the lightboard closer to him and his fingers followed the concept playing in his mind. He hit enter.

The janitor software backed out to the root layer of the code and on Whiting's command began collating and ordering the cached comments scattered throughout the program. Huge tracts of redundant code jogged up the screen to accompany each comment. When the flood stopped, Whiting organised the code into running order, separated out the CAT 5 comments and hid the code that went with it.

He was left with a line of comments, identical apart from a repeating sequence of letters before the word ACT. He traced them down from the top. B1, O1, L1, S1, T1, R1, O1, D1, E1 and then the sequence repeated suffixed by 2 and then 3 on down the scrolling list.

Whiting started to come fully awake.

"Bolstrode! What the fuck is a Bolstrode?"

***

A mile and a half of fifteen foot high galvanised steel fencing flowed up onto the low rise of the hill where vegetation had been cleared by bulldozer. A stream of trucks had worn the lane into a mud bath, crushing the hedges and demolishing trees at will. The double wall of steel fencing sat over a trench packed with electrical cables that were connected to the spider's web of razor wire threaded between the two. The crew moved efficiently along the staked out route, first digging out the trench, laying the pipework and cables, then a piling rig followed hammering down the twenty foot steel posts into the earth. The crews behind guided in the panels and moved along. The countryside seemed to be disappearing within mud and steel as the gangs worked into a floodlit night, completing their two mile sections to join up with another team on the horizon.

The prefabs had been moved up the hill from where the crews on a break could look right the way down to the main road. In the other direction they could see back toward the next crew coming along the ridge to meet them. The scale of the compound was becoming clear. The engineers had calculated that from this outer fencing, there was a mile of no man's land before the outer perimeters of the corporation stronghold and then a two mile drive to the town. The architects had been over and authorised the latest maps on the engineers' tablets. They showed the same topology but the old place names had been replaced with grid sectors for the new city of Zura.

At the end of their three day shift the crews were out looking for the trucks back home. The substation was online, providing power to the lights along the fence. It fed the thermal cameras in the watchtowers and the electrification of the six foot web between them. Finally, the notices were being riveted onto the panels. It was a logo of skull and crossbones. Underneath in small capitals, for those who would ever get close enough to read: DO NOT APPROACH. DANGER OF

DEATH.

As the crews boarded the lorries, counted on board by another squaddie with a handset, the chief engineer scanned the area one more time. What had been countryside was now a wasteland of concrete, steel and mud. He watched the army engineers outside the compound fencing, marking off fifty yards of ground with stakes and tape. He guessed it was to do with the hut full of carelessly tarpaulined crates with APBM360 stencilled on the sides. He knew from his own days of service with the army that they were a particular sort of landmine, a vicious device that when triggered rose out of the ground and detonated at waist height. They could destroy an advancing mob before they ever reached that fence.

As the truck pulled out through the new gates across the A road he started to see how the whole world was splitting in two.

***

"An aborted start-up company at a college facility owned by then privately owned Microsoft. Specialising in security, intrusion detection and anti-virus applications."

"Who started the company?"

"College records are sealed."

"Why was it aborted?"

"There is no further information available."

Phaedra waited for another question.

Whiting sensed a brick wall and sat back looking into the screen of collected information.

"Dam!"

Friedland was looking at the same screen in his office. He heard Whiting's interjection and looked up at the Security Manager standing at his desk.

"Where does he go from there?"

"Nowhere. He gives up at this point. Since then he's slept a while, eaten, started writing an email to you, but abandoned it. He may not know where to go with it. He won't do anything illegal."

"OK. We might have to help him again. We give it twenty four hours and next time he's asleep, we'll bend him a little in the right direction. That's all."

The Security Manager nodded and left. Friedland waited til the door had slid shut and pulled up a new screen.

"Get me a tunnel out. I want Board Level Encryption."

He chose the addressee as they scrolled up his screen and the connection was authorised. The tunnel hopped between cameras to find its target. There were shots of corridors, meeting rooms and the executive suites of the Metropolitan World Service. Eventually, the image settled and a figure slid into view.

"Andrew? We have an individual of interest in one of our teams."

Verrick's face gave nothing away.

"I see. Are there conclusive connections to a certain narrative?"

"Not yet. We shall be monitoring over the next twenty four hours."

Verrick thought about twenty four hours. Time was getting short.

"Is this individual of interest pursuing an unauthorised course?"

"No. The individual is very cautious."

"Let me know of developments within the day."

"I will."

Verrick cut the connection. Friedland's screen showed the Nightship logo. His mouth had overridden his mind. Could he set Whiting up within the day?

7

"Dr Kramer, the BPRC has published a new paper on the underlying causes of the terrorist mentality. How is this a progression from previous studies that have shown alienation and social dissonance to have been the leading factors in promoting terroristic tendencies?"

"Well, in this latest study, we are able to show that the terroristic tendencies, as you put it, may be triggered by social factors, but the root causes lie in the individuals' preponderance for living in a fantasy world, if you will. This seems to begin in childhood. For many, many years the supposition has been that we should encourage small children to play in an imaginary world, perhaps even have imaginary friends, and to basically make things up. We have led them to think that this is the way to behave."

"But isn't that natural to children, to use play as a way to learn how the world works?"

"No. We don't believe so. Encouraging children to believe that fantasy is an acceptable mindset encourages them to pursue quite often meaningless self-serving activities and often dangerous critical ideas that are opposed to the good of society."

"What do you mean by 'meaningless activities'?"

"Well, we have correlated information from many sources to profile the activities of terrorists and other criminals during their re-education and many of them pursued their dangerous fantasies, at one time or another, through very imperfectly realised acts of writing, or what passes for music or the visual medium."

"So, basically, you're focusing on the arts? Isn't that a very passive way of expressing their thoughts and feelings, though? In the old days, prisons, for instance, encouraged this sort of creativity as a stepping stone toward rehabilitation."

"Well, first of all, it is not a passive way of doing anything. For instance, the jarring dissonance of what used to be called acceptable music was a tool to agitate crowds of people and encourage their worst instincts as an unthinking mass that could be used to voice the so-called musician's own perverse theories on society and government. This, really, was nothing less than terrorising the public. To give another example, we are all aware of how the dissemination of literature that is, say, critical of society's governing mechanisms actually helps to transfer the neurotic anxieties of the writer to people who would otherwise never entertain such nonsensical ideas. Dangerous notions that are wrought with fallacies, spewing hatred

for the state and therefore, by association, all humankind, can never be seen as progressive, enlightening or entertaining. It is the result of a damaged mind."

"You mentioned visual media. Are artists terroristic by nature?"

"Perhaps the most dangerous of all. History shows us that artists have been celebrated over the centuries for their instability and delusion. What we must now realise is that their mostly ugly compositions and pointless creations were the result of untreated mental illness."

"Where do we draw the line between, for instance, design ideas that progress technology and architecture and what the report considers to be mental illness?"

"Well, clearly the state must always dictate its requirements for technology and architecture, giving a set of parameters within which the workers will operate. Where there is a clear need for treatment is in the non-requisitioned activities of individuals who have not been authorised by the state. These people are wasting their own time and the state's resources and therefore clearly exhibit signs of a treatable neurosis."

"Since the art galleries were closed and public music events have dwindled to nothing, do you see the conclusions of your paper to be justified in re-educating individuals away from acts of self-creativity?"

"Art galleries or not, the conclusions are inescapable. The self-creative urge in all its manifestations is undoubtedly a mental illness that the state is obligated to treat. It will be controlled and one day eliminated."

"Thank you, Dr Elias Kramer of the British Psychotherapy and Re-education Council."

"Did you get my key?"

"You know I got your key."

Prine had to walk quickly to keep up with Heath as he snaked through the human traffic in the Metropolitan foyer.

"Well, you just don't seem to be using it."

Heath said nothing and Prine persisted.

"Hey, it's a serious proposition when a girl gives a man her key! The least you could do is take me seriously."

Heath took Isobel's arm and guided her into a small empty oval meeting capsule. He sat her on the chair opposite his and as the bustle of the foyer continued frantically outside the perspex walls, the volume automatically died back to only a murmur.

"Isobel. Listen to me. I take my job seriously and like you I want to make progress here. Passing information back down the line is a security issue and is illegal. The fact that you're even here asking me is now on your record."

"I was just showing initiative."

"No, you weren't. You were trying to break the rules."

Isobel gave him the disappointed look. How could he be so straight with her when his career had been carved out with cut corners and minor bends of the rules. She got up to go.

"I bet you'd help me if I was one of your buddy buddies playing football in the Dreemfeelds!"

"I don't have buddy buddies. Besides, I reject your inflammatory sexist implication. Men and women have equal status in my personal and professional life."

"Status! Don't make me laugh. We're equal to men, alright. Which means we don't have any dam status at all!"

Heath stood up, holding a hand out in defence.

"Don't blame me for the equality laws. Hey look, you're right. You're showing initiative. How about you research on a newsgroup for me as soon as I get something suitable scheduled."

"Big deal."

"You might even get to lead it."

"Keep talking."

"Well, OK, I can tell you I'm going to be looking at a weird new situation that's come up at one of the top tech companies..."

"Which one?"

"Come on! I can't talk about that. But there's going to be background to pin down and connections to dig up."

"Hey, if I'm going to lead the team, I want to be your wingman. No pinning and digging."

"Jesus, I only said might. Nothing is settled yet. I'm working on other stuff right now. Let me come back to you with an outline. I'd have to clear a team first and get a plan approved."

Heath ushered her out of the pod and back into the flow of people. She pointed a threatening finger.

"I want something soon, Heath! Don't put me off!"

"No, boss."

***

Heath was starting to enjoy his promotion. A minor project role in a subsection of the editing floor wasn't the height of modern video journalism, but it could be counted as a solid step on the path to full section editorship somewhere a couple of floors above. Granted, the levels of secrecy, paranoia and the politics of compartmentalisation were ramped up to a much higher level than the more relaxed integration of the news floor. He felt only a twinge of regret at stonewalling his old colleagues. They knew only too well that, in this game, you stood on your contemporaries' shoulders to scrabble up the pile to a better place. That they cut all communication with him was understandable. Only Prine had kept the old banter going. Hers were the only messages from the news floor that stole across his GLiD and hinted at personal regard. Heath had gladly accepted that you had to be blank and unemotional to get on. You really had no friends in the migratory business of chasing your career upstream. He was now spending time looking for new colleagues to clamber over.

Heath had been assigned a couple of highly recommended Asian compositors and a library technician to start fleshing out his cover story for the Nightship incident. Harry wanted it kept totally confidential and had even quietly given Heath some computing time and disk space with a bogus ID to gather and store the results. The cover story was entirely down to Heath. Harry didn't even want to know about it.

The team sat around Heath's desk in sullen silence. He made them wait while he checked his GLiD and gave Mimi some routine tasks to keep her busy. He enjoyed the kick of being the man with his teams. He put Mimi on silent and dropped the GLiD on the desk, leaning forward in his chair to focus his meeting.

"OK guys, this is the theme of our project."

He brought up a three sixty degree screen in the middle of his desk and the group leaned in, swiping out notes and pictures from the hologram as they came up. They turned them around in their hands, closed them out or picked new ones while Heath spoke.

"We're looking at the tech companies that came up after the war. Rise of the Robots, that kind of thing. I know, that's nothing new in itself, been done a thousand times, but we're going to look at the funding and financing of some of the big ones. We're going to look at the advances that came out of the war itself. The big one, obviously..."

Heath gestured at the hovering ball of light.

"... is 3D hard light holography. Been around for forty years as a military secret, finally wheeled out to be used on the Russian Chinese front. From there, released to industry as a consumer technology. Now it's literally everywhere. But I want to look again at the funding.

66

Black ops budgets, maybe, for what they used to call the military industrial complex? The first private companies to break it out, set up the lines and bring it to market. How did they do that in such a short time? Who made available the trillions that have never been recouped because the war left virtually every country on the planet with just a fraction of their populations? It can't have been planned as a purely commercial enterprise, but it was deemed a necessary advance for society."

Heath dug into the hologram and pushed up a folder of documents to be grabbed.

"Slightly more traceable story here. Wham! War ends and within the year electric battery technology is on the market that produces enough power and efficiency to turn oil into a minor industrial commodity. Suddenly oil and power companies are one! The military and the law come together to control availability so that rogue organisations can't challenge the world authorities. That doesn't happen by accident. We're following the money. And then there's this..."

Heath scooted his GLiD across the desk.

"... been around fifty years as a tool to help you. Now it is you."

He held up a hand and then pointed to his head.

"It's wired into you. Everyone who has one is something more than human. Again, the war. Pushed it beyond being an electronic identity paper. You and me can't do nothing without it. And we're the privileged ones. Hundreds of thousands more want nothing more to do with it than phoning their friends and logging into the Dreemfeelds. To them, taking the chip to join the rest of society is the mark of the beast. Total slavery. But it's been creeping up on them over the years. When that day comes, who's going to be paying that bill and seeing a return on their investment? To turn humanity on and off at will."

The techs had heard it all before and though unimpressed, tried to look interested. The librarian was looking down at the floor.

Heath leaned back and smiled.

"Yeah. A somewhat sensational take, I know. These things are little more than glorified net connections with RFID under your skin, but Heng's Global ID is the biggest software and tech company in the world. Bar none. Bigger than AppleSoft for Christ's sake. Their customers are actually part of their own supply chain. Think about that."

Mimi awoke and started whispering in Heath's ear.

67

"Your corporate event is brought forward one hour. Departure from this building at eleven thirty seven. Compliments of the Board of Directors."

Heath felt a skip of his heart. When diary announcements came with compliments from the Board of Directors, they were more like campaign medals. His promotion had come with compliments, too. A standard approval, but this was pure hospitality. He felt good.

"OK guys, you have briefing papers and a schedule now being uploaded to you. I want some first visuals to look at tomorrow morning and enough library to be able to discard ninety five percent and still have too much. Any questions?"

The team said nothing. Heath knew this was so far beneath their capabilities, and his status was so low on this floor, that they tolerated him with silent contempt.

"OK. Fine. Let's see what you can do."

There was brief eye contact and a nod of compliance and they were gone. Heath had been there himself. It was nothing personal. Their meeting record would show that they had absorbed and accepted the brief and their results would be excellent. Insubordination was much harder to quantify in a report when it was based on silence.

Mimi had no further information on his early departure for the company event, but it was all good. Heath rubbed his hand along the edge of his white synthetic marble desk. He was really starting to enjoy his job.

***

The taxi took Heath through the centre of the city. As part of the Metropolitan fleet, the long, sleek and well stocked limo was barely halted in its quiet journey. The shuttle trams full of shift workers and their shabby untouchable cousins, the prospective shift workers, slowed up for the Metropolitan taxi to glide past. The few pedestrians were either road crews of maintenance workers and cleaners, or queues for the next shuttle out. Enforcement Officers watched in pairs from the crossroads, their motorbikes parked up together, scanners and taser sticks at the ready.

The metal shuttered shop fronts gave way to noise and colour when the taxi turned down an underpass and headed into some foot traffic. Here, the fast food frontages, manned by holographic greeters, throbbed with clashing colours and grotesque cartoon characters shrieking their slogans to entice passing trade to part with their food credits. The synthetic singing tones of a gravel-voiced hobbit barked out the familiar slogans of the No Messin' Pizza chain only to be replaced by the banshee wail of a mock Chinese garden with hovering, ghostly faces crooning the benefits of their noodle bowls. Heath only craned round to look as they passed a Dreemfeeld Deck, just a doorway with the intertwined logo, blue smoky neon and a glimpse of yellow white light through the frosted glass. Around it hung dark figures, clustered like flies around rotten food. They'd be there to buy and sell allowances to desperate people or just to rob the plain stupid.

Militarised security at the dark end of the underpass pushed the shambling citizens out of the way to allow the taxi through. They entered an underground parking garage, the gates came down bringing with it a calm geometric order and silence.

The lifts were quiet and spacious, like upholstered rooms sliding silently up to the reception area of the New World Hotel. Here, very different populations were gathered in lunch groups, lounges and conference rooms. These were an international elite, a business class of owners and employers, top professionals who brokered the lives of those who could only walk the streets.

Mimi guided Heath out past the dining rooms to the open plan lounges where real bar staff brought trays of drinks and food of choice. The wealthy could sit in the open, showing off their opulence and status to each other. The bigger the table and sofa areas, the more other people had to detour around them, so the better they were. Fat, laughing owners with their surgically altered wives and escorts, basked in the sight of their overflowing tables that cost more for a snack meal than their employees would earn in a year. Nervous lawyers and accountants sat sweating in their suits between the smug guests who lapped up the privilege.

Mimi had Heath approach one of the glass elevators on the outer wall and, as he stepped in, a soothing voice welcomed him by name. He watched the city flatten out beneath him as the lift took him up above the rooftops and the low rise dormitories. In the dank grey of the sky he could see right into the mist at the edge of the city centre where the barricades rose abruptly. Beyond, the demolition kicked in, disappearing into the milky whiteness of cloud. He tried to see the few trees amongst the concrete that might have been his part of town, but there were only helicopters, hovering like black insects in the indeterminate cloud. He guessed that the best views were to be had at night.

The elevator announced him into the Metropolitan Suite and Heath stepped out into a world he'd seen but never been invited to join. A few of the guests even turned to look at the young, sharply dressed man who nervously straightened his jacket and unconsciously looked from side to side to find a familiar face or a waiter with a drink.

"Clayton! Come and meet some people."

Harry had appeared at his elbow, almost unrecognisable in his formal dinner suit, twinkling with rings and studs.

"Er... wow, Harry! You didn't tell me it was black tie."

"Nah, don't worry about this. It's for something later on."

Heath was here as an example of the working sub-editorial journalist fielding technical questions from the advertisers and shareholders. Even the raw recruits that Heath had been guiding a few days back would know that the Metropolitan's lifeblood was circulated by the endless rounds of executive parties and dinners in their numerous luxury environments in Birmingham, London and Manchester. To have been invited to attend was a chalk mark on the CV that did no one any harm. Those who hadn't been there, and never bothered to check the records, wouldn't know whose hand had been shaken and where eye contact had been made. It was a great bluffing point at interviews.

Heath was so pleased to be there he let Mimi have free reign with his business profile and whenever he approached a group in passing, his GLiD transmitted to any open ports, his identity, contact details and role. Executives who shadowed their bosses might look briefly to see if the subject could carry off the identikit bluster of his electronic profile in person.

All top CEOs were known names, they were required learning in Heath's profession. Usually, short, rotund figures, moisturised with sweat and eye-watering perfumes, orbited by exotic, vaguely unreal concubines and all surrounded by their minders. Heath had to shake the hand of a dozen personal assistants who stood before their bosses like food tasters, sampling the unknown. He took no notice of their names, Mimi would be storing all their conversation for later.

Harry had guided Clayton into a seated area where the sweet lull of a real string quartet was gently simmering beneath the conversation.

In a large circle of gold and black oriental seating sat a Chinese delegation, the outer players in western style charcoal business suits and an inner core in the red, gold and black traditional costume adopted by the Heng Corporation.

An immaculately dressed female in figure-hugging grey suit and a structured coiffure that Isobel Prine would have killed for, stood in front of Harry and Clayton. She bowed slightly to them both and looked into Clayton's eyes.

"Mister Heath. I have heard a great deal about you. Would you join us for a moment?"

"Thank you. I will."

Mimi had already whispered to Heath the identity and role of Miss Soto. No one at this level of the Heng Corporation was either a secretary or a minion. They were powerful and trusted executives of the biggest post-war Corporation in the East. Heath knew that the information they gave the media to disseminate was not to be interpreted, merely forwarded.

Heath gave a smile of thanks to Harry, assuming that Miss Soto was to be a gift contact for future pieces. He could already see an expansion of his entertaining budget, travel allowances and maybe even an upgraded accommodation now that his star was rising.

Harry made a little gesture of departure.

"Look, Clayton, I have to go talk to the Germans. Let Miss Soto tell you about the, er... new installation upgrade that Heng is bringing to Southern England."

"Sure, Harry. Don't have too much fun."

"Right."

Harry made his excuses and left the Heng group as Miss Soto beckoned Heath to sit with her and take a glass of Champagne from the waiter who materialised at his elbow. She waited til he had sipped from the glass.

"What do you know of Heng Corporation, Mister Heath?"

"Well, it's a giant multinational corporation headquartered in the New Republic of China. Interests in everything from mining, iron and steel, minerals, fabrication, building and manufacturing. Plants across the globe producing everything from aircraft to... the tinfoil around the neck of a Champagne bottle. Basically, one of the post-war world's largest ironmongers!"

"Heng Corporation is involved in much more than just mining and manufacturing."

"Well, I guess you mean shipping, armaments, aerospace, exploration, pharmaceuticals?"

"Is that your research, Mister Heath, or is your assistant giving you clues?"

Heath tried to deflect the dry comment.

"Well, Heng Corporation also manufacture the Global ID handsets, so maybe I should be asking you that."

"Perhaps you should."

71

He felt a little uncomfortable with her unrelenting gaze and pointed past her with the Champagne glass at the inner core of guests in their traditional dress.

"Are they members of the Heng family?"

"Of course, you know they are."

"But I don't know why such important members of the family would be in the UK attending what is little more than an elaborate press briefing."

"The new Southern development will be our largest presence in the UK. Over twenty square miles of corporate structure and one hundred thousand employees. After Britain's role in the... restructuring of China, this represents, for us, a very significant inroad to the new Western business model, as well as a major investment for the UK itself. It is not all diplomacy, Mister Heath."

"I understand. The corporation city model originated in China, of course."

"Perhaps. Though in the past the Metropolitan news media has often confused western corporations building Chinese work cities with the operation of the state prisons."

"The laogai?"

"Precisely. A relic of another time. But even since the end of the war, your media portray eastern work cities as prisons keeping people in and your western operations as protecting people from the outside."

"Have you seen what it's like outside?"

"As it is all over Europe and the western world, Mister Heath, and regrettably also in China. Having less mouths to feed might seem to concentrate economic sense, but the reality is a hopeless lack of manpower to build for the future or even maintain what the world already has. The only answer is to scale back population centres and return the land to Nature. Don't you agree?"

Heath shifted in the seat. The Champagne was having a dizzying effect and collided with his own memories of the world that collapsed only a few years before.

"I don't think economics can be blamed for everything, Miss Soto."

"It has underpinned all three world wars. The funding of extremist groups to take over weak and failing democracies. The building of a great terror to galvanise the people and a spark to ignite the war. The pattern is the same each time and the result is always the transfer of economic ownership to a new entity. All the while, the media follow a script to maintain the lie to the people and to protect the state from the truth."

72

"You should have been a politician!"

"The truth would serve no political purpose, Mister Heath."

Heath put down his Champagne glass and waved away the waiter as he approached.

"Miss Soto, if the media is such a conspiracy of lies and deception, why are the Heng Corporation even here? Surely, Heng could start their own media service and tell it like it is?"

Miss Soto smiled sweetly.

"But Mister Heath, don't you know? Heng Corporation are now the largest independent shareholder of the Metropolitan World Service."

***

Harry caught up with Heath as he stood looking at his own reflection in a water fountain near the bar.

"How'd it go, Clayton?"

"Hard to say, Harry. I may have just pissed off the largest independent shareholder of the Metropolitan World Service."

"Really? You're on form. But did you ask the right questions about their new metropolis in Surrey?"

"Maybe not. I think I likened it to a state prison."

Harry guided him away again by the shoulder.

"Well, I look forward to reading the transcript of that little meeting! Perhaps you need to relax for a while. Come and have some lunch."

Heath was slightly stunned by the tables of food laid out in the dining room. The buffet was just a statement, not the full menu. Guests could order anything they wanted and it would duly be brought. The sight of real food was something people like Heath rarely saw, and never got to choose. Food was pictures on a screen, glossy and steaming or oversaturated colours with subliminals to tickle the taste buds. Punters didn't see it til they'd bought it and by then they were too hungry to be critical. Heath always ordered through his account and, from what he now saw here, the usual menu was strictly limited.

He picked at real fruit, tiny vol au vents and crêpes before Harry scooped him up and took him toward a private booth.

"Let's go before you start scratching around the farmyard."

The booth was set out like a miniature dining room, elegant panelled walls, silverware and crystal that glinted in the subdued lighting.

Andrew Verrick was seated in a dining chair, talking quietly to a young woman who leaned in at his side.

"Andrew! Here's Clayton. Just been pressing the flesh with the PR team from Heng. I think they liked him."

Verrick nodded in their direction and Harry took it as the cue to sit.

73

Heath was still disorientated from the Champagne and gladly took the outstretched chair.

A waiter appeared and Verrick indicated that he and the girl had already ordered. Harry started coming up with lobsters and crisp salads and stuff Heath had never heard of. When the waiter finally turned an enquiring eye, Heath had no appetite and little imagination for ordering anything.

"Er... Chicken. Please."

"Sir?"

"Whatever the house recommends."

Harry immediately stepped in.

"I think that means your famous Bresse chicken in the Volmer Kronap."

"Of course, Sir. And with it...?"

"The Chretien potage and English Stilton I think. Am I right, Clayton?"

"Sure. Sure Harry."

"And a bottle of the Champagne served at the Heng reception."

The waiter disappeared and Verrick unfolded himself from the conversation with his guest.

"Clayton. This is Cerise. She is one of our most talented hostesses. You really should have made her acquaintance earlier in the day."

Heath was ignoring Mimi's potted biography and staring at Cerise as she looked at him face on. She was undoubtedly human, but had submitted to so much work that she looked like an android. Her face had been altered to widen the eyes, streamline her nose and push her cheekbones so high that she had a permanent smile that reminded Heath of a porpoise. Far from being the restructured face of a crash victim, this was a sign of high status. Androids looked indistinguishable from humans, so humans had to look slightly unreal. She wouldn't have liked to be mistaken for someone who worked in a factory or modelled clothes.

"Hello Clayton."

Her voice had a dreamy, far away quality of one whose brain operated in an artificially low gear.

"Hi. It's a great show. I'm very impressed."

She giggled slightly and looked at Verrick for reassurance. Harry took control of the conversation.

"You know, Andrew, Clayton didn't take any shots from Heng's people. Said what he thought. I liked that. I think they'll respect him."

"I doubt they'll ever take me seriously again."

Verrick stirred.

"They're a predictable team. That's why they see through our..."

He waved at the decor.

"... window dressing. You're new to them, Clayton. They don't know you. It'll take them time to understand your style and your motivations."

"How is that going to help us, Sir?"

"I want you to get close to Miss Soto and her team. Involve them in your work on cyber terrorism. Make them a model development for controlling our... British problem."

Heath was baffled.

"How am I going to approach that, Sir?"

"I'll have some data forwarded to you in the next couple of days, strictly confidential of course. The important thing is that you have a direct contact."

The talk drifted into the arrival of food and Heath pushed the chicken around and drank a little more Champagne.

He caught Harry and Verrick discussing the new Prime Minister and how he was the only logical choice.

What had seemed sensational to the public and to a lesser extent Heath, was a minor topic to the executives who'd controlled the great media splash and its hours of exuberant coverage.

Heath had wondered why Simon Fielding had not been shoed into the job as Prime Minister. Harry was smiling.

"Did you ever see him at a rally? At a constituency meeting?"

"Nope. That's my point. He was always the deskbound anchor man. A Whitehall fixture. But I guess he must have come from somewhere."

Harry and Verrick were looking at each other, sharing a secret. Harry grinned.

"Want to know something? Implausible. Too crazy to consider?"

"Sure."

"Only found this out myself before the vote."

Verrick leaned across the table to deliver the punchline.

"Fielding doesn't exist. It's part of an... initiative between the government and the media. He was a constructed idea."

"Yeah, but..."

"Think about it. The percentage of people who have ever got within spitting distance of an MP is small enough to control what they see and what they experience. The rest believe what they're shown on television."

Heath felt like he was caught in a joke.

"Well, that's the best dam hologram I've ever seen!"

Verrick sat back.

"I'm surprised there weren't rumours down on the floor."

"No. None. Maybe we're so used to everything else being comped that we missed the big one."

"Outside of the Cabinet, the MIs and the team who run it, there's no reason for the world to know. People assume he's attended meetings, because it was reported. They assume he has a wife and family because they see them on the screen. If he was in the room now, you'd swear he was real."

Heath tried to adjust his mind as only one who has fabricated many truths can do. Was nothing impossible now?

"Amazing. One question. Why am I in on the secret?"

Verrick smiled thinly.

"It was my decision. I want you to think a little deeper about the world you now find yourself in. What's real and what may just be a mirage to keep you distracted. Yes, of course it's a secret, but... Fielding is going to be retired shortly. The project is considered a great success."

There was something about the occasion, and the Champagne and the company, that had Heath drifting out of his usual mindset. Nothing was familiar anymore. Maybe he was up in the career clouds where he had dreamed he would be, or maybe it was a childhood terror of the unfamiliar. The food was awful. Expensive and awful. All expenses paid and awful. That made him snigger into his meal as Harry and Verrick talked earnestly about Fielding, and then Heng, and finally catching his wandering attention with talk of The User. He wanted to join in but suddenly felt very drunk and unsure if he could form words, let alone stand up and stagger out to the toilet.

He half remembered a kind of lumbering dance with Cerise. It was suddenly just happening, no logical reason. Her face looked distorted and grotesque so close to his own, the eyes cold but the smile fixed. It was a whirling dance of dozens of guests, laughing and lumbering through their moves with partners that Heath began to think were holograms, or androids. He felt the sweat prickle on his forehead and his breathing was shallow and sharp.

Somewhere in the miasma of the night that came creeping over him, he was in a guest suite lying naked on the bed as Cerise looked over him. Her eyes were wide and her snakelike body moved left and right in the low pale pink of the hidden lights. At the same time, his memory tricked him into a drunken conversation with Verrick, buried in the private booths of an exclusive bar. But Verrick was looking past him and talking to an unseen figure. It made little sense, but there was a mention of airmen and soldiers, sons and daughters working far away somewhere they couldn't be reached and might not return for a long time. Heath wanted to talk about the internet, the golden rule that nowhere is unreachable, but he was ignored. It was a crazy story about somewhere far beyond the internet, a place of danger and yet great promise. Heath assumed they meant China. His concentration was interrupted by Cerise, whose smile widened into a cry while her eyes were full of concern. It was a hellish night with the continuous background sussuration of the GLiD in his ears, telling him of things he needed to understand and the facts and figures of his brief, his job and his purpose.

It was somewhere in the minutes before dawn when he awoke in a Metropolitan hospitality suite bedroom, motivated by the need to pee, but battered by the distorted visions of the night before. He was alone.

As he staggered to the bathroom, a spasm of pain drilled through his head. He felt his skull with his fingers and automatically recoiled to the bed where the GLiD had originally been placed beside him. The pain seemed to subside a little and the LEDs on the screen unlocked from red to green.

A residual horror gripped his mind. Naked, trapped, mind distorted with weird unfathomable stories, sick to his stomach and not altogether sure what the ritual of the last eighteen hours had been.

8

"It's been nine years since the outbreak of the most devastating disease ever to sweep across this planet. The H61K virus, commonly called The Afghan Flu has killed more people in the world than can probably ever be counted. So many died in the first year that there simply weren't enough national institutions and assets to maintain the functioning systems of government. In turn, this led countries with high populations into anarchy and then a war for resources.

"During the chaos, the World Health Organisation called for global governance to unify the planet's effort to overcome this disease and manage the huge death toll. In turn, they faced extreme hostility and angry accusations from rogue states that the H61K virus was a man-made disaster. It was designed, they say, to overwhelm national sovereignties and impose an unelected technocratic world order on the survivors.

"Reporting of the aftermath has tried to tell a different story. The countries hit hardest, some of the most populous in the world - China, Russia, India, Brazil, Japan and the USA - are still locked into a state of emergency. United Nations troops have sectioned those countries in conjunction with their governing agencies to co-ordinate and control the rebuilding of national infrastructures and contain the nuclear contamination of water supplies.

"Europe fought its own war against the virus, along with the millions of refugees and the collapsing bureaucracy of a failed superstate bankrupted by its commitment to NATO's war.

"That war introduced to the world the cybernetic soldier. A man in a mechanised uniform commanding hundreds of thousands of unmanned autonomous machines that wiped out defending armies and, to this day, patrol the wastelands of the East.

"As the sun rises on this new world, the surviving populations exhibit the surreal behaviour of people in denial. They placidly accept the news from abroad that the most devastated countries are rebuilding their identities and culture with cheery optimism and gratitude for their new place in the world.

"People have learned how to queue in silence for their food and their medicine, rations that are dispensed through the identity of their mobile phones and their bank accounts. No one questions how the great multinational banks and corporations were unscathed by the war and emerged like saviours to administer their conditional largesse to a broken population.

"It seems improper for people to question too deeply the world's wider situation when their own existence is concentrated solely on the day to come. And in case any concerned citizen should feel moved to demand more, the civil authorities are tasked with an uncompromising enforcement of the law in order to maintain cohesion and prevent anarchy amongst an otherwise compliant population.

Only when conditions improve will there be a reintroduction of the privilege to travel, an allocation of resources to host public gatherings and the right to choose one's own employment..."

The carrier went down without warning, leaving the screen stuck on a still frame of bleached black and white. It showed the hollow-eyed faces of displaced workers queueing behind the gates in a chain link fence.

Hokey slapped the edge of the desktop in his annoyance and dislodged a collection of gathered objects that slid onto the rest of the crap covering the floor.

"Oh shit! Come on, not now!"

He waited for a minute, scratching at the side of his head in the dull glow of the screen and wondering if there was any way he wouldn't have to watch the whole movie again when the carrier came back up.

He pushed the window to one side to see his messages decrypting on the other carrier. Usual kind of stuff. Can he get two twelve volt DC motors? Can he get the fixing armatures for two twelve volt DC motors? What does he want for any quantity of ball bearings? There was a short message from Bug about ten minutes previously. It just said: 'Get on the wire.'

"Dam!"

Hokey tapped a request into his keyboard and the screen showed his machine's search for any available carrier. It found a local taxi that was sucking up GPS information from a connection to a PowerTrans military super satellite. He highlighted it and locked onto the back. The signal was excellent. He muttered to himself.

"Why weren't you around earlier, asshole?"

He scrolled down to Bug's proxy and sent him a key. Moments later the line popped a few times and the revolving avatar of skulls crawling with insects heralded the connection.

"Hey, Hoke, glad you're there. You're going to want to see this."

"Something new?"

"Something weird, is what it is. We've been watching the Nightship beams ever since that major sim and one of the peers just came up with a nice little outgoing comm channel."

"Oooh. Big boys who don't know how the security works?"

"No, no. I did say weird. It looks like a Field Engineer pretending to tone out a line and then trying to cover his tracks onto the dark stuff. He's making a right fuck up of it, so if that's what it is, then Nightship are now employing the most incompetent Field Engineers since the days of BT."

"What do you think? Security?"

"Nah. That's what's weird. He's asking the craziest questions to anybody he can find. I'm kind of hoping we may have ourselves a whistleblower."

Hokey leaned in to the screen.

"Really? Shee-it! That would be so cool! Who's handling him?"

"Well. Right now he's found The_Gnome, which is far from ideal. He can get too careless with his connection. And if he starts behaving like a total dick, he'll scare off whoever it is stumbling around at Nightship. I'm going to keep an eye on how he's doing, probably make the trip up to Jacky's yard. I'll send you an update."

"OK. Oh Bug! Have you got a full link to that new movie on the Boogie Woogie Flu? Lost it ten minutes into a stream."

"That User thing? Yeah, somewhere."

"Cheers."

***

Whiting was crouched in a booth on the lower floors of the archive room and nervously jabbing at the lightboard that lit his face from below in a Halloween yellow. He watched the tracer window that hovered in front of the screen and dragged the little lightning bolt into a new shape. The word 'searching' appeared and then a line of dots which the lightning contorted around. He set a time limit of 100 milliseconds.

"OK. Umm... are you still there?"

A dry voice came back to him.

"Just about. Do you really have to throw that thing around so much? Re-routes through four or five servers is just as safe as, like... twenty."

"I have to be very careful, my friend. I can cancel the VM and lose this entire conversation, but the trail would still lead back to my machine."

"Is it really your machine?"

"Er... yeah, of course."

"Then why haven't you secured the camera feed?"

"Camera feed? There's no camera feed."

There was a sigh.

"Then who am I looking at, fuzzy face?"

Whiting reeled back, but the voice went on.

"OK, OK, don't shit yourself. It's no big deal. I can fix it for you."

"What? There is no camera!"

"Seriously? All the Tri-Eye screens have a totally insecure back cam built into the feed. Do you seriously not know that? And you're an engineer? Oh wait..."

There was a little shout of laughter and a girlish ooh.

"Well, good evening Mister Abraham Olias Whiting, Senior Project Simulation Specialist at Nightship Systems UK!"

Whiting was almost out of his chair with the shock. He alternated between making a flimsy excuse about testing security and capitulating because he knew that the game was up. He was, without doubt, caught in the hands of a stranger.

The laughing voice was showing signs of enjoyment.

"Don't go away now. What can we do for you that the ol' deadly Nightship can't provide, eh? According to your dox that go with your picture, you're quite the big man. So, quit looking so worried, I'm not exactly going to be shopping you to the Electric Chuckle Brigade, am I?"

Whiting had nowhere to go and the defeat in his voice was evident.

"Hey look, I just want some information without having to go through channels. I'm not exactly planning to start a revolution."

"Oh. Pity. Well, let's see, you've been asking around for some juice on a little caper called Bolstrode. Not exactly a huge secret, but you could have found out from your own people without having to soil your lily-white hands on the darknet. Unless..."

"Unless what?"

"Well, you know... you might be on the naughty chair. No Dreemfeelds til you've done your homework."

"OK. I'll be straight with you. I'm on a special project and I'm doing some background that the rest of the team will be expected to discover during a simulation. It's just a little idea of my own."

"Special project?"

"Yah!"

"Rest of the team will be expected to discover..?"

"Uh-huh."

There was another little sigh.

"You know, Aby baby, you are really bad at this. I should just send this whole video feed to the board of Nightship and let them get you some treatment for your frankly pathetic lies."

Whiting had almost had enough of the humiliation. His stress levels made his voice sound a little more wooden.

"Do you actually have the information I need?"

There was a brief laugh.

"Hah! I think even my chihuahua, Mister Puddles, has the information you need."

"OK. What will it cost me for you to give it to me?"

"Don't go frosty, Abe. I'm just yankin'."

"I gathered that."

"OK. Here it is. Information for information. I'll start. The Bolstrode of which you speak was indeed a college start up and the records have been sealed since the war along with a gazillion others. By the magic of intrusion, the names and dates have been doing the rounds for... ooh years by the look of it."

"And...?"

"Here it is. The team members consisted of two very, very choice programmers called Kelvin Reid and Samantha Wilshire. Their marketing boy was..."

"Wilshire!"

Whiting was out of his chair again.

"Yeah, Abe. Samantha Jane Wilshire. Friend of yours?"

"Yes, I've known her for some years. She's a consultant at the Cyber Security Institute. We get on the same conference lists. Usually same tables. Whiting and Wilshire. Alphabetical."

"Cosy."

"I didn't know she'd been in a college start-up"

"Well, it wasn't much to get excited about. Lasted just long enough to upset the security services who stole the work and classified it. Some college scandal finally buried the whole operation. There's gratitude, I suppose. Reid went to work for Intel and Wilshire went on to Cyber Security after a while."

"Stole the work and classified it..."

"Yeah. Teach them pesky kids to try and change the world. OK, that's pretty much what you asked for. Now, your turn."

"What?"

"Now you give me some information. That's how the deal works, Abe."

Whiting's mouth went dry.

"What do you want to know?"

"Oooh. Umm. Let's see. I know. What was the giant datasim you ran three nights ago when the whole country lit up like Christmas? Hmm?"

Whiting's throat was drier than his mouth, and his voice wavered.

"Datasim?"

"Yeah. I think you know the one. Came online at precisely..."

"OK. Yes. It was a... actually, how do you know about that?"

"You guys in your compounds need to get out into the real world more often. Really, it's a fun place out here! Now never mind how I know, just tell."

Whiting was defeated.

"It was a simulation of a cyber attack on the country's datacentres by a hostile government."

"Fascinating. Who in the name of righteous fuck could give you the authorisation to tap every datacentre in the country simultaneously?"

"Well, I don't know exactly. I just knew that the brief was approved at board level. Who they dealt with I don't know, but I was given full access for over a month during the prep."

"Someone thought very highly of you, Mister Whiting. And that's government level shit. Which makes me wonder why you are definitely, *definitely* on the naughty chair."

"Er, the presentation went wrong. This virus appeared in the sim."

"Oooh. Silly me. Now I get it!"

"Look. I need to wipe this machine and encrypt the GLiD stream. But, I may need to talk to you again."

"OK, cool down. Take it easy. If you need info I can get it. Same deal. Oh, but don't bounce around so many servers, it's actually more obvious than it looks."

The outgoing line dropped, the display blanked and Whiting was left looking at the residual image of a screen in his blinking eyeballs. He sat there for a short while in the semi-darkness.

"Samantha Wilshire."

***

"Way to go, man. What did we get on this Bolstrode shit?"

"Well, eliminating all the dross and just looking at everything with a source, there is a picture in there of what's going on."

Bug tapped in a share request and the transfer started.

"Tinfoil says it was an intrusion detector that matched up server connection performance with unscheduled downtime. Basically, if too many connections were being bounced, it assumed deliberate denial of service and blocked any future requests on the network."

"How did it know when to kick in?"

"I dunno. Didn't ask. Maybe analyse the traffic, or aggregate the performance of the previous month or so and decide on a fair number?"

"Wait up. That's like the Quorum algo on the old P2P."

"Yeah. Suppose."

"So what happens. Just requests hanging?"

"Yeah. And there's this cartoon cat playing whack-a-mole, apparently!"

"Oh right. A signature."

"Yeah. Stupid tag, but the genius seemed to be in hiding it."

"Like you said. Coreware."

"Yeah. Whiting told me that they're able to download the entire fucking core of every datacentre server..."

"Wow. That's big!"

"... yeah, and run it all up in the air in real time. This Bolstrode thing was in there when they ran it."

"Is that really likely?"

"No."

"What then?"

"Somebody knew it was there. Nightship. Their firmware people. The chip writers. Somebody. It wouldn't be missed. When you know where to look it's not that well hidden."

"But Whiting knew where to look..."

"That's the puzzle. He reckons he just fell over it, after he had an idea. Sounds like bullshit to me."

"Someone's playing games."

"Yeah. Whack-a-mole."

"What next?"

"We have full dox on Whiting, GLiD sigs and whatnot too, his security is pathetic, so with little effort we can follow him around without him noticing. We just need to see where he goes next."

"Gnome, you done well. I've got the full download now. Keep me in the frame til I get there. Tinfoil's on his way in, as well. I think he kinda feels responsible!"

"Sure."

"Oh, and Hokey sends you greets."

"Wanker."

"Haha! Later man!"

***

At first, Whiting thought he had time to plan. Knowing that there was someone to confide in, a stepping stone to the next level of this problem, had seemed like a break. But time was never on his side. Every new jigsaw puzzle piece was shortening the decisions he could make in the game.

He'd been out only once after the botched attempt to anonymise his call to the darknet. He hung out with his tech team when they were on downtime in the refectory. They were pretty sure that there was no alternative team working on the data from the failed sim. The whole disaster had been mothballed on orders from the board and all documentation was now sealed until further notice. They were on a different project now, something to do with population movements and the migration of Global ID.

Whiting headed back to his quarters and got caught on the way by a Security and Compliance officer. He'd been ignoring the emails all day. The guy wanted to make sure that Whiting was aware that someone using his group's authorisation had been on a strictly unauthorised line out of the archives and then wiped the machine's VM to try and cover his tracks.

Whiting nodded like a duck, looking this way and that down the corridor.

"Yah. OK. I'll look into it. Kind of busy right now, but I'll come back to you."

"Well, all right. As it was from your team I copied you in on the personnel request for a Global ID in the area."

"Right, and...?"

"Seems to be some hold up on that information right now."

"Too bad."

" Going to need some answers by tonight."

"Sure. No problem."

Whiting had trotted off down the corridor back to his rooms and let the door slide shut behind him. He leaned against the wall in the dark, breathing heavily and knowing that the nightmare was only just beginning.

"By tonight..."

He could probably make just one more call out and, if he was being watched, would never finish it. He drew up an email to Samantha Wilshire, and as the words poured onto the screen his mind started restructuring the events and the facts that mingled with the paranoia, until they started to make sense. The email became long and complicated and finally looked like the ranting of a man who believed he was being set up for something. He couldn't send it. She didn't know him well enough to know he hadn't flipped. He had to go to her. In person.

As he deleted the draft, he knew where that one last call was going to go to. It chilled him to think that his next move would incriminate him completely, end his career and lose him everything. But if Compliance went through his histories anytime soon, they'd dig up everything he knew about Bolstrode and the call out to the darknet. He'd already lost everything.

***

Friedland walked the last few paces through the tunnel and out onto a running track that bordered the football pitch. A cold wind was rolling through the abandoned stadium causing him to hug his hands in the pockets of his overcoat that was pulled close in to his body. He walked across the track to the edge of the overgrown pitch and saw the group of figures standing in the centre circle, watching him approach.

The wind made a faint, ghostly moaning sigh as it swept into the covered stands, a rustling between the rows of fading coloured seats and, from somewhere, the echo of a slamming door was reflected in tiny echoes

Friedland stood in the centre circle with the three men from the Ministry of Information. Like himself, they wore dark suits with the addition of bulky overcoats that no doubt hid a small arsenal of weapons and electronics. One held a thin briefcase. They all shook hands with the visitor.

"Mister Friedland. Thank you for contacting us."

Friedland glanced up at the stadium.

"Do you always do business in these dramatic locations?"

"Short notice, Mister Friedland. Your request was for off-the-record. We can always get a GSC1 for this venue, so yes, this kind of business comes here."

"I see. I'll come straight to the point. As outlined by our liaison team at Nightship, we have a direct trail to a terrorist cell that you might find to be of interest."

Friedland took his GLiD from his pocket, briefly noticing the blank screen and the rapidly pipping green diode at the top.

"We were monitoring one of our employees who was out of bounds and discovered that he was connecting to a powerful mainframe. It's old, probably pre-war, a long dead business identity up to the west of Birmingham. But that would represent quite a population of insurgents."

The man with the briefcase had opened it and held it up. Friedland handed his GLiD over to an operative who placed it in a cradle on the computer in the case. The screen in the lid confirmed that the public key was accepted and they downloaded the full location report and security files from Friedland's GLiD. It took seconds and the GLiD was handed back.

"Sometimes the old fashioned ways are the best."

The man closed the case.

"It's even difficult for us to maintain watertight security, Mister Friedland. The bigger the operation, the more holes can be poked through it. You were involved in Tin Man."

"We consulted on it with the Cyber Security Institute."

"Then you know why the system needs to be massively simplified to work. This employee. I take it you were allowing the external connection to go through?"

Friedland's face stayed blank.

"Of course. We don't have so many security holes at Nightship."

The conversation faltered.

The man with the case raised it fractionally in front of him.

"Thank you for your input, Mister Friedland. Any other activity you'd like to pass on, don't hesitate. We may be in touch."

Friedland nodded and turned back the way he had come.

The wind in the abandoned stadium was picking up. Litter that had blown through the tunnels was being picked up in a vortex and blown around the rubble in the dug outs.

Friedland never looked back, but he knew they'd be standing in the centre circle til he had long left the stadium.

***

"OK, Aby. So how much exactly do you know about frying your dog tags?"

"I've read the court cases so I know it can be done."

"So you know the options, too. How much are you willing to pay?"

Whiting hesitated for a moment.

"I don't know whether I have anything you want."

"Don't be so bashful. You could leave a back door open for me when you leave. Come on, you don't owe these scum anything. I could make a few distractions while they're looking for you."

Whiting's pride was collapsing under the veiled blackmail.

"You people really are something. This planet's falling to pieces and you can't wait to get in there and smash up something else."

The_Gnome's attitude changed sharply.

"You just don't get it, do you? They stitched you up, boy, and you still feel the need to cling on and defend them. Guess what, the war never ended, and it won't end until everybody that's left alive is a microchipped animal and we're all living in compounds run by fascists like Nightship."

Whiting sneered at the tirade.

"Not that tired crap again! It makes no sense. Corporations need customers not prisoners! It's paranoid bullshit to justify anarchy and destruction."

"So, report it to the thought police. I'm out of here."

Whiting panicked.

"Wait! OK. Look. Nothing's perfect. We all have... issues to deal with. I don't know how I got myself into this, but I have to find a way out. Can you help me? Please?"

"You're a fucking stooge, Whiting. They're sacrificing you as part of their own crazy ritual. I'll help you, but I want a back door into Nightship, and I don't mean some fake-ass VM in a broom closet. Got me?"

"Got you."

Now. Are you willing to pay?"

Whiting slumped a little in the seat.

"Yes."

"Then let us discuss what's on offer, like gentlemen."

***

By the time Friedland was returning to Bedford in the black limo the late afternoon sky was turning dark red again, darkened by the streaks of cloud that fanned out from the horizon. He turned away from the view as a message tone drew his attention to the screen and a slowly circling Nightship logo appeared.

"What have you got?"

The face of his trusted Security Manager appeared.

"Whiting's on a line out. Less hops but the same location. I'm replicating the whole VM. It'll hold up in court anytime."

"What's the gist?"

"Whiting's thinking of running. He's going over some kind of cover for it. Wants to alter his ID."

"Well, that's twenty five years in prison straight away. Has he been given options?"

"Yes, Sir. But he doesn't like them. He won't take physical intrusion, but the soft alternative isn't going down well, either."

"He needs to make up his mind quickly."

"We have the option to intervene and apply to alter the credentials ourselves."

"Not even Whiting is that gullible. Let's see how far he's prepared to go on his own. Can you send me a live feed?"

"Yes Sir."

"Do it, and get me a full transcript that Legal can understand as soon as it's over."

"Patching it through."

A new speaker icon appeared in front of the screen and Whiting's shaky voice was beamed into the car as Friedland relaxed back into his seat.

"Yes, yes! I've seen it and I've told you there is no way I am making holes in my head!"

"I guarantee you it doesn't hurt. Trust the program to numb the area and when it guides you in, you just hit the spot. Just like when you're at the quack!"

"Yeah, but even if the pain barrier numbs your whole head, as soon as you drill out the chip it'll stop working!"

"Yeah, well, that's when you know it's been successful! Job done. Jesus, it's only a tiny little hole. And let's face it, small program, direct, simple and instant. It don't bleed much and you can pretend it's just a big zit til it goes away!"

"Not going to happen. Get it out of here. It's got to be software only."

The_Gnome could be heard giving his characteristic sigh.

"Well, OK. But I'm telling you that the 'You Know The Drill' tutorial video has saved more lives than penicillin! And it's available right away."

"It's barbaric! I've decided I want software only."

"OK. Well the safest alternative, as I said, is a little app called Free Your Mind."

"Hey, this isn't the thing that freaked out those conscripts in America?"

"Er, no... that was an early botch job called False Plates. Stupid idea really, it tried to make physical changes to mask their vital signs and basically blew their minds. Not recommended at any level. Free Your Mind has the advantage of leaving your chips untouched and redirecting your GLiD towards a library of proxy machines, changing your ID on the fly."

"How many of these proxy machines do I get?"

"You don't *get* any machines. They're cloned GLiDs out on the internet. What do you think the cyber attacks are really about, man? They're stealing IDs, thousands at a time so they can be reissued onto the net. You get time on an available ID and when it times out you get the next available one."

"Time out? Can't I get just one ID?"

"For a smart guy you're pretty dumb."

"Yeah well, this is not my field."

"OK. You don't want one ID. You want many, it keeps you hidden. Even if you're picked up on a trace, you'll have changed ID before they can send out a team to find you."

"Won't there be a database of these false IDs?"

"That's the clever part. Your new ID is a random morph of your own information and the clone. There are endless combinations. That's why it's called Free Your Mind. Interested?"

"Wait a minute..."

"Hey, come on."

"I got another question. This cloning thing is fine for information over the internet, but police hand scanners read the GLiD direct. They'll know it's me."

"Well that makes sense, don't it, seeing as you can't change your face?"

"What if there's a call out on me?"

"Just use small stations with Enforcement Officers. They don't have cop clearance so they don't get the wanted ads. Where you can't avoid cops, stay in a crowd. Oh and stay off main roads with scanners on the gantries."

"There are cameras everywhere!"

"They're not fucking perfect. When you get out, lose the beard and wear shades. Look, read the help that comes with the download. This app is used everyday by thousands of people. The only time you're really screwed is if you get in the mist, unlikely but obvious."

"What the hell's the mist?"

"Jesus Christ, don't you know anything? An internet free zone? Somewhere that has UN clearance for some big deal secret meeting. Anyway, without the net, you're you whether you like it or not."

Whiting was silent for a few seconds, just the sound of a long hesitant exhale.

"OK. I'll do it. I agree to your terms."

Friedland had been holding a holo-remote as he lounged in the soft back seat of the limo. He'd been turning the volume up and down to hear Whiting's breathy tones. He cancelled the feed and the vehicle returned to its near silent hum as the sun came one last time through the clouds that were closing in. He let the remote go and it vanished.

9

"As UN troops push further north, an end is in sight for the fighting in the Peak District according to the Ministry of Homeland Resources.

A spokesman for the Ministry briefed reporters on the final push to cut off supplies to the insurgents from Manchester and Sheffield. They have caused chaos in the region, destroying rail lines and bringing down communications. Their actions have forced convoys to take much needed supplies of food and medicine by sea and air to the residents trapped in the cities.

"Since the town of Matlock was liberated by UN forces last week, the rebels have been increasingly isolated as troops have poured up the M1 to the East and the M6 to the West, surrounding the towns of Buxton and Macclesfield and pushing forward to Manchester.

"Prime Minister Sarion Dundas has reconfirmed support for his predecessor's light touch approach to resolving the sectarianism that has gripped the north of England in particular. The army's approach has been one of containment and attrition rather than direct confrontation in an attempt to defuse violence and reduce casualties. The Prime Minister has, however, authorised the deployment of further crowd control equipment to the area in anticipation of the aftermath of this campaign. A controversial drone program has been used over cities to drop the harmless soporific control agent, Sordax. There are plans for it to be redeployed over the area, using larger quantities targeted at insurgent strongholds. The use of barrier weapons has not been approved at this time. It is thought that the estimated numbers of innocent women and children, caught up in the movements of the rebels, is considered too high to risk deployment.

"The insurgents, crucially, have dwindling supplies of ammunition and their command structure is breaking down as separate groups launch their own attacks on troop positions. Reporters for the Metropolitan, who have been embedded with the front line troops for over six months, have described the scenes in the Peak District as desperate.

"This report from Jasmina Hamid..."

"Since the crucial drive to take Matlock and re-establish positions here on the edge of the Peak District National Park, these troops haven't made any further ground. It's a deliberately cautious approach to minimise casualties on both sides and try to bring a speedy end to the conflict. The problem though is snipers. Here,

somewhere between the towns of Bakewell and Newhaven, some eight hundred troops are waiting for an all-clear from a mechanised division of ATRs, the All Terrain Robots. They were deployed here to go forward and identify positions and armaments that the insurgents have set up to attack us. By day, the risk of sniper fire is increasingly real as the rebels are contained by the troops. Under cover of darkness, we have been slowly moving forward, mapping the terrain thanks to equipment on the ground and from the air. As bodies are recovered from the woodland on an almost daily basis, it is surely just a matter of time before the insurgents simply give up. Once this area is secured and Manchester is once again under the full control of the government, the troops will move further north, where the situation is currently less certain."
"More on that plan as it develops."

Heath leaned forward, elbows on the desk, and looked at his reflection in the plexiglass screen of his office walls. Lights in other areas of the floorspace were dimmed, leaving his work area standing out brightly. It was a little cube of activity in the dead of night. His shirt sleeves were rolled up, tie discarded and his face was glum and sleepy. But at least he'd finished the piece. It was no thanks to his 'teams', who were getting the idea from somewhere that he was not the golden boy that Toliver and the other seniors had been telling them. It wasn't that his research came in late or his graphics didn't appear, but he was definitely made aware that he was not priority on the floor. On his way around the groups, he caught the gist of pieces that were being worked on. New GLiD instruction videos were being readied for public service broadcast on an industrial scale. For some reason, there was a major flap about the countrywide rescheduling of new rail timetables that were being rushed into service. Something, he felt, was about to go down. But he knew the protocol when eavesdropping on another team. He asked no questions and appeared to see nothing.

Heath ended up scripting his new piece by himself and submitting it back to the copy writers for review. He sat in the semidarkness and read back some introductory notes. The first part of a new breakdown on cyber terrorist activity that 'promises to be the investigation that will finally unmask the figure of The User and break the hacker underworld wide open.' Beneath it were the latest cases of intrusion, of theft and damage from all over the country. He cross-referenced their modes of attack, their perceived opportunities and their goals.

Where he'd been struggling was in joining the dots. On the one hand was the media's own image of the desperate outsider, hell bent on destruction, lacking in funds, resources and access. On the other was the record of precise, almost surgical intrusion into systems of government and their key corporate connections.

He was saving the Nightship intrusion for a future piece. As Harry had told him, it needed some serious shaping and Heath would find himself on his way to Nightship in search of answers. His new travel and access credentials would allow him into places he'd never been before. He felt a frisson of unease. The more he went over the details of Nightship's open report, the less likely this seemed to be the work of a disenfranchised outsider. Could The User have been given an opening by someone in a privileged position?

He let the concluding section of his report roll up the screen and speak the words back to him.

"We stand at a crossroad where the ideological refugee and the dissident meet the machinery of state. The struggle we see in the wastelands of our post-national borders between the old world chaos and the new world order are just one front in a wider war. How do we resolve this great divide, where the philosophy of unity is head to head with the politics of division?

"The very thinking and reasoning of life on this planet is contained in the digital constructs of our cybernetic systems. Money, property, identity, knowledge are all governed from within this ephemeral space. The robots that build other robots that build the factories for yet other robots to manufacture our products are simply taking orders from the internet. The machines we sent out to protect our freedoms against the aggression of the eastern axis, now keep us safe at home. At the ame time they are patrolling the fringes of civilisation to ensure that the world will never know war again. The squaring of the circle can only be fully accomplished when the power of the many become the force of one, when dissent is melded into common agreement.

"After all that we have been through, the voice of protest today is just one man alone. He is known to you and me as The User. He is not the demon of your dreams, but a product of our age. He is one of us, a face in the crowd. Not a hero, or a warrior, but an ordinary person. He may be someone close to you. You may be looking at him now."

Heath froze it and pulled up his notes from the producer. He'd got in most of the required soundbites and just a few of his own observations. His twenty four minutes revolved around twenty one minutes of official handout and three minutes of his own work. The rush of idents, product placement and credits filled the remainder.

He went and stood in the gap between the screens that baffled the noise of the floor when the day shift was in full flow. Even his work area had been placed right on the edge of the floor plan, like an afterthought to shoehorn in one more worker. No wonder no one took him seriously.

He'd had enough for the night. It had all been a strangely unsatisfying experience since leaving the news floor.

***

A personnel carrier wound quickly through the London streets following the four motorcycle escorts and tailed by a short security convoy. Litter cartwheeled down the empty pavements in the wake of the military vehicles. The convoy passed a loitering guard unit at the entrance to an underground station. The security gates were pulled most of the way across. There'd be no evening commute, just an inspection every hour.

The convoy found its way through another checkpoint at the archway leading through to an anonymised government building. It backed onto the Thames where the gunboats crossed and recrossed the river.

Commander Thornelow had the attention of the war room. Before him, in blocks of seating were his team leaders, representatives from the UN, Government Data Systems, the civil police and the MIs. He spoke into the construction of holographic screens where the maps and diagrams of the UK mainland shifted before him.

"This summary is drawn from the reports of all agencies who have contributed to Random Sentry.

"We have substantially concluded our program of clearing and consolidating outlying populations into secure areas. From here, upgraded rail links can safely transport proposed numbers to processing centres. Stations are manned and operational with staff given full United Nations oversight according to the resolutions and proposals that have been agreed. We anticipate that, once there is an operational necessity for the movement of populations, a period of seventy two hours without services will be enough to ensure minimal resistance from the public on their way to the relocation centres.

"The centres themselves are now all online. Perimeters have been secured and zones allocated for red and blue groups. Each of these groups have dormitory facilities with post-medical recovery and education. Once an individual has been inducted into the scheme, post-processing will allocate them to their new population centre and

95

they will be transported. Detention areas and holding bays to deal with unexpected behaviours are compliant with the minimum conditions as outlined by the Global Convention on Human Rights. However, it is to be noted that since the terrorist action will have constituted an attack on the country, we will be operating on a war footing. This means that we will be entitled to interpret any levels of resistance in the way that individual locations and circumstances see fit, to ensure the continuity of operations.

"It is anticipated that there will be very little or no resistance from those already within the designated town boundaries. This step is merely the culmination of a project that has been planned and prepared for many years. The greater part of the planning has been the psychological preparation of the wider public for this moment. Years of redefining, and in some cases removing altogether, their cultural and social values have certainly helped. We have been able to redraw legal and political boundaries. There is unity and consensus on education, employment and civil rights which have shaped a pliant and docile population with simple needs and aspirations. The psychology of the mass media and the further education movement has triumphed over the attempts from breakaway dissident groups to present a contrary narrative. The public will gladly join the greater project for the promise of security and the enhanced benefits of their membership.

"The greatest concerns are not the vast majority of displaced people but, as a result of their reallocation, layers of previous administration will be rendered redundant. Council leaders, certain civil police groups, members of local government. In order to maintain confidentiality until the critical moment, they must be aware of nothing and remain in a position of operational authority. These actors will then be removed immediately the action begins, in fact as the primary procedure, and under cover of the chaos on the streets. They will be taken to a place of safety and detained until the threat of any counter-revolutionary measures have been dealt with."

Thornelow motioned to a figure in uniform who sat flanked by military staff.

"This action will be taken by the authorities of the European and world courts, under the guidance of General Rishek. He will have at his disposal, deployments of the Special Air Service and international contractors from the private arena."

Rishek sat stock still until the glances of attention had passed back to the screens.

"This has been our final large scale briefing. Everyone concerned with the upper directorship of Random Sentry now has enough operational information to function purely on orders received. Your upward chain of command will be directly through the office of Joint Intelligence. One of the drills that you participate in, during the next hours, will go live and will represent the defining moment of our entry into a new world."

***

A whole side of the building up from the shuttle stops was showing the big game, while the crowds shifted uncomfortably in the near darkness of late afternoon. To anyone who cared, the figures on the football field were not the best example of 3D generated content, the close-ups especially had a cartoon-like quality with their lack of detail. But actually nobody did care. It was their team and it had been edited into an exciting duel of incident and truly impossible athletic feats. The crowd stared and gave a weak cheer when the ball hit the back of the net which ballooned out from the building in a thunderous roar of artificial crowd noise. These matches had no real beginning or end, they were a pageant of acrobatics and colourful advertisements in between the multiple views and replays. Attention wandered immediately a shuttle bus came towards the interchange and everyone shuffled a little closer to the barriers.

The football highlights cut out as the breaking news logo of the Metropolitan network exploded out from the building and the grim face of a male construct appeared.

"Good afternoon. In breaking news at this hour, extra troops have been stationed at main rail network concourses throughout the country. They have been deployed to deal with the possibility of interruption to the automated travel turnstile system. The head of MI5's Domestic Terrorism Unit has raised the threat level to 'severe' following a series of failed attacks on government installations and national infrastructure in the previous twelve months. A spokesman said that lives lost in terror attacks by armed gunmen on the nation's datacentres, would be dwarfed by the potential loss of life on underground trains and in packed stations due to terrorist activity. Anti-terrorist officers discovered plans to cause havoc on the trains and buses, endangering the lives of the public and bringing life in the cities to a potential halt. As it is, those travellers without Global ID can expect long delays at the verification terminals while officials check travel permits individually in an attempt to keep people safe under difficult conditions.

"Members of the public are asked to help the authorities by showing patience, having ID and permits at the ready and being prepared to board trains at the request of rail staff quickly and without delay. This state of emergency is ongoing and according to MI5, will be lifted only when it is considered safe to do so. More on this story as it comes in."

A slew of logos and advertising trails flashed on and off the screen as the crowd shifted uneasily at the news.

"They diverted us up to Wolverhampton the last time. Had to wait two hours for a connection back into town. Bloody ridiculous. Kept us all in the dark, and then it all just went away. Never heard another thing."

A woman behind the complainer piped up.

"Better to be safe than sorry. Best just to follow what they say, they know what they're doing."

No one seemed to agree with that and the growing disquiet led to an Enforcement Officer breaking from his group at the front and patrolling down the line.

As he passed by, with his face hidden behind a smoky black visor, the original complainant's mate spoke up quietly to the woman behind.

"They'll have us all fitted with clockwork like him soon. Then you won't have to think about anything."

"No they won't!"

The man spoke with a smile to discomfort her more.

"Oh yeah? I've heard that it's coming. Once they chip you, they can make you think what they want."

She tutted and looked around.

"Heard it all before. They can turn you off and you fall down dead. It's bloody stupid! Scaremongering is what you're doing."

"Nah. Straight up! That's why they never talk about it. They can't. Minds are a blank."

A voice from behind chimed in.

"My old neighbour's girl went to university after the war. Took the chip, and when she got a job, they made her go full Global ID. They never saw her again. She just stayed away."

The woman was getting agitated now.

"Probably glad to get out of this shithole."

There was a ripple of laughter.

"Why don't you take it then? It's free if you've got a job."

"I would... but I get migraines, see. Might make me go epileptic, doctor says."

"Well it's coming, whether you want it or not."

The original commenter craned forward to watch the line slowly move.

"Over my dead body, pal."

***

The border guard yanked on the roller shutter and the back of the truck opened up to reveal its contents.

"Says here, five thousand coffin liners."

The driver looked over the guard's scanner as it totted up the RFID tags on each black plastic box, all stacked inside each other, row upon row in the back of the long, low loader.

"Still tickles me how they always call them liners. They should just call them what they are. Emergency coffins to fit family of four."

The driver shrugged.

"Don't ask me, pal. I'm not even supposed to know what I'm carrying."

"Yeah, I know. We ain't needed these for years. Hope there ain't going to be another outbreak of the snuffles. Are we storing them on the base?"

"What does it say on the transport ticket?"

The guard tapped at the destination section and waited for the new orders to come in.

"Looks like you're going on to the station goods yard. With a full load!"

The driver shrugged.

"It's all the same to me."

He helped resecure the roller shutter and headed back to his cab, leaving the squaddie to look out across the miles of fencing either side of the road, The gray rain swept hills that hid the razor wire and guard towers of the city border.

As the truck rumbled on to its next checkpoint, the squaddie was left alone in the bluff breeze of the roadside, wishing he was back in the hut brewing tea. Funny they were storing local emergency coffins at the goods yard. Not a sensible place to retrieve and distribute if they were ever needed. Unless something happened at the station itself, of course.

The GLiD in a side pocket on his arm gave a short tone and the synthetic voice of a sergeant crackled in his ear.

"Shift change at 18:15 hours. Report to guardroom 4B. All personnel to then remain in position. Leave cancelled until otherwise notified."

The squaddie slowly shook his head.

99

"Not again! What are they up to now?"

***

"Elton has left the building!"

"Who exactly is Elton?"

Harry dropped the hologram and it evaporated into the air. He shifted in his chair to smile at Verrick.

"Oh. He was just a singer back in the old days. Very big business though, played to thousands in Las Vegas. They used to say 'Elton has left the building' when he'd finished up to send the crowd home."

"Yes, I vaguely remember that."

"Well, Heath's done. Left the building and gone home. Looks like he's all but completed the assignment."

"Good. I hope he's done it right."

"Sure. Sure he has. He doesn't care what he has to write if it'll buy him sex in a Dreemfeeld with some whore."

Verrick paused for a moment and then spoke into the air.

"Encryption E-level 1. No interruptions until I say."

Harry sat up as straight as his chair would allow. To be invited to the Director's suites high in the Metropolitan building was always an honour, but an encryption level meeting was something considered altogether more important.

This suite was a stark statement in off-white scumbled walls and Japanese screens. A lacquered cabinet in gold and black stood on gilded legs against one wall. In between the pierced screens a low seating area surrounded a square table top that hovered inches off the floor on hidden supports.

Verrick had presented Harry with a tiny shot glass of colourless liquid that rested on a transparent coaster beside him.

"Harry, as a senior editorial... guru, your ear is very much to the ground. You know when there are rumblings that foreshadow future events."

"Well, Andrew, I think I understand the market forces that drive the way forward, if that's what you mean."

"Yes, I suppose they are market forces. Your background in economics draws interesting parallels. But, when events occur, there is a need at all levels to make sense of the changes that are everywhere around us. Sometimes, people need to crystallise their thoughts around a figure, an event, that has the common purpose of unifying and resolving the... pain and hardship of change. Do you follow me?"

"Well, all the senior editorial management know that an event of

100

some kind is imminent. We can see it in the flow of information from the MIs. Maybe you're talking about scapegoats?"

"I'm talking about cataclysmic shocks that turn pain and suffering into great hope for the future. Great hope supercharges religion, bolsters the unity so craved by politicians, and produces opportunity for progress."

"That sounds more like a human sacrifice."

"We are tasked with producing a... reason for the way things are. You and I are tasked with a mission to explain. Can you help me, with that, Harry?"

Harry took the shot glass and positioned himself on the seat. He turned on the smile.

"I think I've already been doing that, haven't I, Andrew?"

Verrick was expressionless.

"Like I said, your ear is very much to the ground."

Harry took the shot and relaxed a little.

Verrick allowed him a few moments.

"Harry, in the absence of any firm intelligence from the MIs, we are in the position of having to produce an alternative storyline for public consumption. We are tasked with both calming and focusing the public's attention on the need for affirmative action. That is, decisive action on dealing with, and resolving the blame for, the theft of thousands of Global IDs."

Harry nodded, perhaps a little too quickly.

"Right. Which is why I had to bring Clayton Heath into Editorial."

"Yes. Exactly. Except that we don't have the time for him to stumble his inept and futile way through the tangle of facts and fables that constitute a pet theory. I had hoped that, with the help of a colleague, we might have been able to push Heath in the direction of a suitable candidate to be presented as The User. But time is, as ever, against us and we have to play several hands at the same time."

"Right. We can't use a construct."

"Not under these circumstances. There needs to be a credible investigation, backed by unimpeachable sources with first hand witness testimony. With a situation so close to home, there needs to be a real predator amongst the real victims. It's not like the depopulation of some African country that no one's ever heard of and will never visit. Everything can be fictitious. The entire operation can exist within the information matrix of the internet. In this case, questions will be asked."

"Do I pull Heath from the project?"

Verrick was up and talking over his shoulder as he poured more shots. "Well, there's no time for him to go to Nightship now. He won't be in a position to get connected. So, dependent on the moves of our number one target, Heath must come into play as the alternative. I want to see how far he has reached in his dabblings and how you can help to, shall we say, reorientate the storyline. You have a free hand in adding anything to his biography that would be useful to an investigation team, which I will appoint at the due time. Understand me?"

Harry felt a mild choke of implication in his answer.

"Yes. Yes, of course... Andrew."

"Good."

Verrick held up his shot glass and drank. Harry's discomfort found its way out in repeating himself.

"So, do I pull Heath from the project?"

"Quite the opposite. Give him an absolute free reign. Let him feel the power of freedom to enquire. No limits, and no editorial censure beyond the script. We will simply call him in at the appropriate moment."

Harry stared at his shot glass as he took it from Verrick. The fakery and illusion upon which his career had been built was breaking through the walls of his reality and starting to wrap its cold, dispassionate arms around his heart. He was powerless to resist, and from here on, he was complicit.

He raised the shot glass, watching the liquid tremble in his unsteady fingers.

10

"To: Samantha Wilshire,
From: Abraham Whiting
May I start by saying thank you for issuing me with a key to send you
this email. I confess that I was not entirely honest in my original
message and that the reason for encryption will become obvious to
you. I am naturally expected to submit my key to the Nightship
authorities as indeed you will have to submit yours to CSI, but the
nature of this message is such that I fully intend to avoid this course
of action. I sincerely hope that you will consider the same after
reading this.
You will remember that in my video calls I was asking you to provide
background legal information on the security arrangements for code
submissions that are run by government servers. I referenced the
holographic national security simulation that we ran at Nightship
last week. Representatives of the Cyber Security Institute were
present in their official capacity as suppliers of technology to the
government. You will, no doubt, have seen the open report as
prepared and disseminated by Nightship following the unexpected
failure of the simulation. However, that report was selective in both
its analysis and history of the event and I must tell you, that if you
had been there on the night, I feel that you would have witnessed
something of great interest to yourself and perhaps of vital interest to
the CSI.
The failure of the simulation was caused by an injection of code from
a long discontinued anti-intrusion program with the codename of
Bolstrode. I know that you will recognise that name as I believe you
were one of the developers back in your college days when Bolstrode
was also to be your company identity. I believe it to be either the
same program or a revised version. I found the code grafted into the
coreware of government servers and effectively 'hotwired' by
shutdown requests. I have researched, as far as possible, the origins
and many revisions of the coreware involved and I have come to
conclusions that have potentially devastating consequences.
However it may have got there, your program could not have gone
unnoticed over any considerable length of time. This is despite the
common practice of leaving old code well alone if it doesn't appear
to impact the program. I, myself, have commented out many routines
and left inactive code for future reference in almost all the big
projects I've been involved with in the last twenty years. It is my

judgement that this code has been deliberately reactivated in order to necessitate the purging of the current system. I do not know who by. I do not know why, all I can assume is that now the code has surfaced, there is some kind of imminent operation that I have somehow triggered with this small event.

I'm told that my duties at Nightship are suspended as of this time, pending a review of the simulation by an independent team, but I have since found out that this is a lie and there is no team. What then, are they waiting for?

If you can examine this code and identify how it has been grafted into the program, bearing in mind your position at the CSI, you could possibly uncover when and by whom this action has taken place and even where its deployment might lead. Time is critical, as I'm sure you realise. Transmitting any sections of the code would not only be impossible but, as the recipient, would implicate you in this highly illegal act. I will have a window of hours, maybe minutes, to copy the simulation code and physically leave the campus with it before discovery.

I think we have worked together enough over the years for me to trust your instinct in receiving this information. Something is very wrong at Nightship and for such an important operation, it is the duty of those capable, to do something to ascertain the truth.

Please contact me regarding the original voice mail and indicate in some way that you understand the situation and are willing to meet me and discuss this within the next twenty four hours.

Be assured, you are the only person, that I trust, who can help me."

Whiting hit the screen with the tip of his finger and the email disappeared. The fuse was truly lit. He'd sent the email out to an anonymiser program that was still up, somewhere out there on the internet. If they forwarded it to Samantha Wilshire, at least she was clear, maybe not forever, but long enough. He'd had to use his field engineer's ID to buy an extra few hours of time, but he knew that it would all be traced back to him very quickly. He'd already dug too deeply into the affair to claim any kind of innocence. From somewhere within his less than courageous heart, he'd seen the executioner approaching and decided that the only thing left for him to do was run.

He brought up on screen the Free Your Mind app and readied himself. He looked around the tiny apartment one last time and through the door to the conservatory. A thousand reasons flooded his mind for not going ahead. They flooded out just as quickly and he turned back wearily to look at the logo.

"Phaedra? I have a document to store in the personal cab. Upload this."

He touched the icon and Phaedra replied in his ear.

"Uploading."

He'd read the notes a dozen times. It all seemed very easy and horribly insecure. As soon as the app was uploaded the icon sat for a moment and then faded into nothing. That was it. He had now committed the ultimate sin of the Global ID program. He sought to mask his identity. As the notes pointed out, the GLiD would show nothing untoward at any time but there was now a fundamental change to the way the unit operated. It would call its new home, somewhere out there on the internet. Assuming of course, that it still existed.

He didn't look back as he left the apartment. He knew that whatever happened in the next hours and days, for good or bad, he'd never see it again.

He chose a different workstation in a disused research lab and made the call out. In less than a minute he had bounced through the chain of proxy servers into the dense pack ice of the internet's uncertain darkness. He let the links guide him in to the silent beacon where he communicated with The_Gnome.

"Did you load the spice pile, Abe?"

"The app? Yes. Now do I get my information about Wilshire?"

"You need to leave a back door open for me Abe. When you leave the concentration camp, I'll forward you the dox out on the road."

"Hey, you could leave me high and dry out there!"

"Abe, you're such a tool. I could have royally fucked your GLiD after busting down the doors with an intruder program. But, we're negotiating here. Like gentlemen. Now, I want root access and your entire keychain with admin control. I won't use it til we've concluded our business on the outside. You have my word."

"Do I have a choice?"

"Right now you don't have much more than the rest of your life in prison. So, do it."

Whiting's face was stony with humiliation and fear. He had no intention of arguing. The logic, if that's what it was, had been worked out and agreed upon in the quiet of his apartment over hours of agonising and worry. He pulled up a keypad from the edge of the lightboard and tapped in a transfer code. His GLiD sent out the entire package.

Whiting sat for a moment, numbed and somewhat sick.

"I'm going to be leaving now."

"OK. I've got it."

The connection dropped immediately before Whiting could move. His contact was gone and he now had minutes to escape.

As he hurried from the lab corridor and out toward the main entrance, he could hear footsteps behind him.

He half turned as the Security Manager caught up with him.

"Hey, Whiting! Have you got something for me?"

Whiting broke into a trot.

"Yeah! I'm on it now. Give me an hour or so."

He was relieved to see that the Manager pulled up short and stood in the middle of the reception area watching him go.

The doors opened for him, and he felt the cool of the air conditioned atmosphere in the lobby. He realised with relief that his GLiD wasn't doing anything suspicious, and was sending out genuine data directly to the censors. He hoped that tracking him in the real world would be significantly more difficult.

Out on the main campus grounds, he had four minutes to get to a shuttle bus that would take him out to the station and from there beyond Nightship to London. He boarded the bus as it prepared to leave, caught sight of the scarabs and the hi-rise centre of Nightship's operations, and then it was out past the dormitories, the manufacturing sheds, the recreational areas of the township and on into the main station.

***

The Security Manager watched Whiting til he was out of sight and then spoke quietly into the air.

"He's heading for the shuttle area now. "

Friedland sat back in his chair watching the security camera footage of Whiting in the research lab.

"Good. Find out what he's been doing on that machine."

"Will do."

Friedland saw the Security Manager enter the lab with a technician and they began to fuss around the workstations. It didn't really matter, everything he needed was now in front of him.

"Get me a tunnel out. Board Level Encryption."

Friedland put in the call to Andrew Verrick who appeared on the screen full face, steel grey eyes twinkling with moment.

"Andrew, I'm afraid you won't be getting your sabotage story from our man."

"Our Individual of Interest?"

"Yes. He appears to be on the run. But we'll follow him."

Verrick smiled. A slow, lazy smile.

"Never mind. Do you have anything for us?"

Now Friedland smiled.

"A complete story! I've already forwarded it to you."

"Well, naturally, when we put it together, the editorial team will run it by you first. Just to make sure you haven't... included anything you didn't mean to."

"I'll stand by my report."

"I wouldn't expect anything else."

Verrick cancelled out the connection and his smile dropped.

"Supercilious bugger! But too late."

He was still in the Japanese room, hours after his meeting with Harry, and now relaxing in a green and gold kimono. There was a smell of incense in the air.

Around the screens stepped a young man, soft features and unfashionably long hair. He wore a short white robe and held a small glass phial in his hand.

Verrick's face lost its grim resolve, almost looking happy as he motioned to the seat beside him.

***

Whiting boarded the train at Nightship and it headed through the station tunnels and then out into the woodland toward the border. Phaedra spoke into his ear.

"You have a document pending download, Abraham."

"Who is the sender?"

"Adolf Hitler."

Whiting spluttered with indignation. How can these people spoof the identification system? It should be impossible!

"Yes, download it!"

He took the GLiD from his pocket as the train passed out through the Nightship border leaving behind the high wire fences and guard towers. Icons on the surface of the GLiD were already starting to fade out. A new symbol had appeared at the top of the screen. It looked like a radiating beacon. He'd never seen it before but he knew what it meant.

"Abraham? I... I can't see you."

"Phaedra?"

The voice quickly became a whisper.

"Abraham?"

Then it was gone. A coldness gripped him. He was now outside the monitoring capability of Nightship. He was in the middle of nothing and nowhere, his identity controlled from some dark site on the internet. As the train chattered on into the bleak countryside he started to feel a terrible creeping emptiness in his mind. He was isolated, vulnerable, confused and so alone that his body ached with the stress. He seemed to be catching a terrible virus.

By the time the train was entering the wastelands of north London, he had sat still long enough to appear calm and controlled. Two Nightship personnel who'd been watching him with guarded suspicion were now busied with their GLiD entertainments or screens of admin hovering above their laps in a thin blue glow.

Every so often his ear caught a buzz of static and then some random broadcast over the internet, as though searching for a receiver. He was sure it was communications traffic, though sometimes the local systems of the train cut in and the wi-fi points on gantries pipped with annoying regularity in one ear or the other.

His message from The_Gnome had been brief. It was Wilshire's address as requested and, incredibly, her access codes to the CSI compound south of the river. Whiting no longer doubted that they were real. His amazement was reserved for his own ignorance of the power that the hackers had over information of every kind. He remembered one of the scenes that flashed up in the loading screens to the proxy through which The_Gnome operated. It was a clip of video where a man with a towel round his neck turns past the camera to speak.

"The most valuable commodity I know of is information. Wouldn't you agree?"

As the train started to slow toward the station enclosure, Whiting couldn't rest in the silence. He pulled up a GPS screen and started to look for the controls. It was baffling. The interface seemed to have reverted to the default scheme, the typefaces were generic and colourless. The most worrying change was the complete lack of controlling logo that indicated which corporation he should belong to. He fumbled the GPS, asked for directions and received no answer. The screen showed routes that snaked through maps and settled on the station east of Watford. From here, he'd have to follow local instructions south, like holding out a hand into a thick fog.

The station platform was GLiD only and just a handful of Global IDs were on his train. He stepped behind a small group and followed them to the barrier where the Enforcement Officers were lazily waving scanners. He remembered to keep his head up for the recognition cameras and then realised that he'd taken no precautions with his appearance. It was too late, he felt the green wave of light cross his face and then the Officers were in front of him at the gate.

Behind their visors he couldn't tell if they were looking at him or past him. That was part of the unsettling test for passengers. Their body language might give them away to the cameras, but these low paid costumed security boys weren't paying attention and waved him through. Whiting had brief cause to thank The_Gnome for his guidance. As the paranoia calmed within him, he wondered if any of the other faces around him might also be operating on a cracked GLiD. He was out in the open, and suddenly anything was possible.

He'd called to Phaedra more than once during the journey, but there was no reply. He guessed why and, once out into the taxi ranks, he stopped in a shelter to retrieve the GLiD. He knew what he was going to find.

"Assistant? Visual."

In front of him appeared a horrible ghostly mannequin that he'd once known as Phaedra. It was the default avatar for a new ID deployment. It would be up to him to give it a name, choose a sex if he wanted it to have one, teach it his ways and preferences, sculpt its look and behaviour. It was something that GLiD users took years to refine. Even though he knew it wasn't real, he felt the terrible sadness of losing Phaedra, and in this lonely impersonal world, he wondered if he could survive without help.

"Audio comms only."

The digital cadaver disappeared and seemed to be waiting at his shoulder for instruction.

He pulled out a screen from the GLiD and arranged the route to the CSI campus in front of him.

"Guide me from here to the destination. Time: shuttle and taxi."

"One hour. Twenty minutes. Do you require section breakdowns?"

The voice was flat and tinny. A corpse that talked.

"No."

A terrible thought came over him. What if his local travel permits had already been revoked. He drew up a summary screen and naturally all his Nightship allowances had disappeared. There was, however, a new signed certificate that had appeared in the travel section along with a short note in the box underneath.

"You're going to need some bus fare, fuzzy face. Good luck."

Whiting almost choked with thanks. Out here, in nowhere, suddenly The_Gnome seemed like his only friend. Like a guide in the alien world beyond Nightship. How far he had fallen, so quickly and so easily. It was frighteningly prescient, what they said, 'there's no way back into the system and nobody survives on the outside'. It was the one thing from his induction at Nightship that stuck in his mind. At the time he'd happily vowed never to leave.

Yet, here he was.

***

Friedland took an elevator down from the executive offices and then chose to walk across the interconnect between two buildings. The glass tube was twenty floors up. The sparkle of lights faded up in the Nightship city complex and surrounded the transparent walkway. It made Friedland feel as though he were walking amongst the stars. A curious floating illusion, designed to disorientate, but sometimes thrilling to those who knew no fear.

A tone came from his GLiD and the Security Manager appeared, hovering in crackling blue at his side with a fringe of light around him.

"He has found a way to mask his identity since leaving Nightship."

"Last known location?"

"The train out. Once his signal was transferred from local sensors to the internet, we lost contact."

"What routes are available once his permit expires outside the station?"

"We have a best guess. He was due to meet a reporter from the Metropolitan. He may have gone up to Birmingham to meet him privately."

A vision of Verrick's lazy smile swept across Friedland's mind. Possible, but unlikely to trust in a reporter he'd never met.

"Any other guesses?"

"The only other line is down to London."

"Contacts there?"

"No one personal who would have a reason to protect him."

"Send out a detail to Birmingham, and one to London. As soon as the police get a lock on him, take over. Observation only."

"Yes, Sir."

The hologram blinked out and the lights of the city were returned to Friedland as he stood motionless amongst the stars.

***

The shuttle bus down through the clearance zone was stopped on an

110

overpass a mile from the fortifications. It was a standard checkpoint. If anyone had incorrect ID, they had nowhere to run to. Not for at least a mile, and the officers had a clear line of sight to drop anyone who failed to stop. The passengers filed out and across the meridian to the connecting bus on the other side.

They were scanned as they stepped down, and then hand-scanned onboard at the new one. Whiting tried to look nonchalant, a little bored by it. He let them see his full face and hoped that the sweat running into his eyes wouldn't register. He knew that his vital signs would be pumping overtime, he could never manage stress, but his blood pressure and heart rate alone would be screaming of his guilt.

An officer stepped in front of his path, and his head nodded up from the readings on the scanner and down from Whiting's stony face. Whiting had this idea to pretend he had some sort of flu symptoms and held up a handkerchief to cough into. The officer was having none of it and motioned him to leave the queue. Whiting's legs almost buckled as he stumbled to one side. Was this it? He assumed there was no point other than to quietly tell the truth and show no signs that he might be about to react violently to arrest. He put down the handkerchief.

"Excuse me, I think you ought to know..."

Suddenly, the passenger who'd been behind Whiting lashed out at the officer scanning him. He caught him at the base of the visor, sending his chin down onto his chest and the scanner tumbling to the ground. Immediately, the orderly line broke and bodies were running in all directions, some to take on the Enforcement Officers and others in a blind bid to escape. Officers at the other bus left their post and ran over drawing taser sticks and, once within range, launched bolts of electricity at the nearest body. Repeated cries to get down on the ground went unheeded and as Whiting shrank away from the violence he estimated six, maybe seven people were running down the overpass as the same number tried to fight the uniforms.

Whiting found himself behind the officers' lines and decided to head for the other bus. The body count was growing as the last passengers on the shuttle were caught in the crossfire and fell shouting with pain onto the road. Whiting joined other passengers cleared for the bus, nervously craning for a view, and he slipped behind them as one of the officers came back over to shoo them up the steps and onboard. Whiting made his way to the back and sat low in the seat, looking through the window at the carnage across the carriageway. In his mind's eye he could still see the guy who'd sat across the aisle from him on the bus. He was tall, thin and dry as a stick in his casual tweedy jacket and post-war clothing allowance trousers. He looked like some regular administrative type or an accountant. Why did he flip? And who were all the others running for their lives? It looked like something was getting closer and closer to going down and everyone, including Whiting, was jockeying for position.

The driver of the bus was escorted to his seat and an officer came down the aisle, scanning them all one more time. Whiting figured that everyone's levels were going to be sky high after the incident, and sure enough the officer just read the IDs and then nodded the driver to carry on.

They made their way off the rubble strewn interchange, leaving the officers to line up the prisoners and count the bodies. Whiting realised that his real ID would eventually be filed on a police incident record and from there, Nightship would know where he had been. Time had just got a little bit shorter.

***

The lights of the undertown hid many things in the darkness that they sought to dispel. Holograms had the power to appear, to look real and solid, but they couldn't project light forward. The brightness always fell away quickly and to Whiting's experienced eye they always looked too dark. Of course, to compensate, the saturation was turned up full, but then it looked even less real than before. Even as the depth of the darkness in the corners of the malls hid Whiting's face, other shapes would suddenly appear in front or beside him. Hooded figures of the street merchants, trading with each other, were looking for new customers in the shadows. They eyed the cringing figure with suspicion.

"Need IDs, man? You look like you need IDs. Come on, these are guaranteed. It's a whole new skin, man. Hey!"

Whiting's GLiD pipped briefly. He looked around unsure where it had come from. The damned thing was no longer tuned to talk directly into his ear. He hunched into a corner in the mall and tried to pull up a screen. There was nothing there. He was about to repocket the unit when he noticed a chattering, flashing symbol appear on the glass. He touched it. It was an old-fashioned written message, plain text in a window.

"Send this key here. Keeping Nightship busy for ya!"

An attachment arrow in the bottom corner moved in and out round a key symbol. Whiting had no choice. He knew he was near to the CSI compound as the great walls of the city were directly east. It was on

112

foot the rest of the way and he felt completely vulnerable.

He pushed the key symbol onto an outgoing tunnel and it disappeared with a default click. Then nothing.

He waited until his heart was thumping in his ears and he was whispering to himself.

"Oh come on, come on."

There was a crash above the bass heavy rumble of a food joint's sound system. It was the doors of a roller grill, big iron spiked shutters ripping apart. Whiting had already convinced himself it was an armoured truck coming out of security to get him. He was pressed so hard into the shadows of a grimy pillar that he was masking the call signal on his GLiD. He startled when he dabbed at the screen and a GPS map appeared before him, hovering like a giant window in front of his face. His assistant's dead voice said one word.

"Follow."

He brought the screen size down to fit in his hand and locked it to the top of the GLiD, then moved out from the pillar down the mall, looking back toward the sound of the grill. All was empty and dark, noises echoing like beasts in a jungle.

As he went, a ragged figure with an old style scanner called across the concrete to him.

"Hey! McAston! Want to buy some Dreemtime?"

Whiting ignored it and hurried along.

The figure appeared again, from behind a stanchion right in front of him. He had a grimy, unshaven face and dark brown teeth hidden in the shadows of his lined jowl. A Russian snow hat was pulled down to his brow.

"Come on McAston. You look like you need a bit of friendly. Where you off? Don't go!"

Whiting's voice was worn thin.

"Leave me alone. I don't want anything."

The figure advanced on him, long heavy trench coat flowing out and his eyes staring bravely into Whiting's face.

"Come on McAston, you're ex-army. Doing well, I bet. Help out a buddy."

Whiting was confused by the mistaken identity and repelled by the rancid breath of the shambling corpse stumbling into him. In a panic, Whiting pushed his inquisitor in the chest and there was a moment of pause. He thought that maybe a knife would appear and end his misery right there, or he'd just be mugged, beaten and left for dead.

To his surprise, the antagonist seemed to fold up before him with a loud wheeze and fell back against the wall, the net scanner falling from his grip and clattering on the slabs. In the sickly yellow reflection of neon on concrete, Whiting saw the snow hat slip off and the man's bald head gleamed with sweat. It looked as though at least a third of his skull was missing, as though scooped away by the metal fingers of a lightning predator and the gaping hole had been clumsily grafted closed.

The man was dazed, calling softly under failing breath.

"McAston. Don't go. Don't leave me."

Whiting was appalled and stumbled into the semi-darkness toward jumping shadows on a distant corner, where muffled music came from unseen shop fronts.

He leaned up against a concrete stairwell to review the GPS map. The location was seventy five feet higher and a mile to the south. The stairs led up to the street. He could see the building frontages against the dark purple sky and feel the sting of rain slanting down onto his face.

He was trotting up the stairs, stumbling on trash and frightened by the unlit corners in deep shadow. Before he'd made it to the street, the fatigue of the day was bearing heavily upon him. His feet ached, his body was sick and almost all hope had gone. As he turned into the street at the top of the stairs, he fell into the arms of two well-dressed individuals, faces half obscured under wide brimmed hats like old time feds. Whiting tried to find his breath.

"I... er, sorry."

"That's all right, mate. Mind how you go."

With Whiting back on his feet, the two men carried on their way, heels clicking on the wet pavement. Whiting brought up the GLiD and the GPS map bounced up before him. He needed to cross the street and head between two giant frontages. Looking up, he could see the sky through the upper windows. This whole place was being demolished. His heart sank when the emergency lighting, strung between the lamp posts showed that the alley up ahead was indeed very narrow, and very dark.

Whiting summoned up his final reserves of energy, slipped the GLiD back into his pocket and started to run into the dark mouth of the alley.

He tripped forward more than once, something slimy underfoot, or brick rubble and trash scattered as though from an exploding bomb. He stayed in the middle between the parallax of the rooftops and strained his eyes forward into the dark. A helicopter overhead danced search beams along the alley and to Whiting's relief, the dot of light at the end was a large station coming into view. His way to the end was clear. It was almost in a state of exhausted collapse that Whiting emerged, staring up at huge video screens in a terminus full of people. The calm robotic tones of the station announcers cut in and echoed along the platforms. Enforcement Officers scanned him through the turnstile and he almost fell up the steps into the light.

Amongst the holograms and the blaring advertisements of the news channels he felt safe to openly consult his map. He mingled with commuters on a GLiD only platform, ignoring the looks at his dishevelled appearance as he dug into his pocket.

A hand fell on his arm and he tensed visibly.

"Good evening, Mister Laslo. This way please."

A station hostess in her green uniform and hi-visibility fluorescent jacket was smiling at him with an impatient humour. He was standing almost directly underneath a scanner and was only just getting used to the proxy IDs.

"Er, yes. Thank you."

She guided him down the concourse and off through to the offices. His mouth dried with the unasked questions. Was he being arrested or helped? They took an elevator up a floor to a smart executive restaurant and as he stepped out, the hostess motioned security.

"This is Mister Laslo. Table 49."

The security guard, dressed as a floor waiter, nodded and the hostess was gone.

Whiting no longer cared where he would end up. He felt a minor glimmer of relief at the civilised surroundings of an executive lounge. It was washed with quiet music, an all GLiD environment where individuals could relax because they were safely monitored at all times. The street had been every bit as bad as he'd heard. At least now he was in some sort of shelter.

Table 49 was a booth in a central island of the vast restaurant floor. It conferred a little privacy that the shifting, overlit patterns of the ceiling projections denied to tables out in the open.

Whiting mumbled his thanks to the guard, who disappeared away behind him. He found his way through the diners, some of whose intimate conversation was broken by the sweaty tramp in rumpled clothing.

The booth appeared to be empty so Whiting slid onto the bench at one side of the table, looking furtively around him.

"Good God Abraham, what the hell happened?"

Whiting still had the energy to jump nervously and in doing so, the cutlery clattered on the table as his knee came up. From out of the shadow came a face he recognised. She had short blond hair and, right now, the face of an angel. She wore the short-sleeved jacket of a business suit and a tie dragged down from her open collar.

"Oh God. Samantha, thank you so much..."

Whiting shocked himself by starting to sob as he spoke and he couldn't finish the sentence. He breathed deeply, but it came out in a kind of juddering motion.

From across the other side of the table she took his shoulder and guided him further along into the booth.

"OK, calm down. It seems you've got a lot to tell me."

She poured water and pushed him the glass.

"And by the look of things, it could take some time."

***

"We think we've lost him at this time, Sir."

The Security Manager looked down, waiting for Friedland to react.

"How?"

"Well, he seems to have kept off the main lines. Wherever he's gone, there are no direct links back to the police and army databases at this time."

Friedland's displeasure was obvious.

The Security Manager tried to offer something.

"We could put out an all points... put it in government hands."

Friedland's anger had him speaking his thoughts.

"No. It's too soon. We need this to be live television. A shoot out in the street and a body to put on display. It has to be seen to be done!"

"I'll double the search teams."

"Do it!"

The Security Manager left Friedland and walked quickly through the adjoining offices. He was getting nervous. He'd not been given the opportunity to draw Friedland's attention to a report, circulating at lower levels, that there was an intrusion into Nightship's systems currently in progress. It had just been raised from Threat Level One to Two.

Friedland looked out into the night. He was losing his place at the table on this one. But it was a live action, the pre-cursor to the final operation and in the stirring chaos, there would be points scored and points lost. He saw Verrick's lazy smile again as the moon slipped behind the clouds.

***

116

By the time Whiting had bumbled his way through the gist of his story and backed his GLiD archive onto a strange device that Wilshire had produced, he'd also eaten a little and was starting to feel calmer.

Wilshire had her own questions.

"Abraham, first, who the hell is your friend, 'the gnome'?"

"He's not my friend. Just some asshole on the internet who sold me this masking software."

Whiting checked himself, remembering the travel certificate and the heads up to Wilshire, without which he'd still be nowhere. He groaned.

"I guess he's not such an asshole."

"He seems to me to be a smart guy. He got us together - somehow. You couldn't come to the CSI campus though, so this meet was my doing."

She leaned in closer.

"Abraham, I've checked out what you told me before, and I think you're probably right. It's a set up for somebody's benefit. But if it's strictly between Nightship and the secret service, I have nowhere much to go with it, unless you count the news organisations."

Whiting dabbed at his face with a serviette and shrugged his shoulder. "Personally, I don't. I was due to be interviewed by some clown called Heath from the Metropolitan tomorrow, and no doubt he was going to tell me that..."

"Heath? Clayton Heath?"

"Yeah. I think that's his name."

Samantha Wilshire sat back a little in her bench seat and spoke quietly.

"Well, that Clayton Heath was going to be Bolstrode's marketing man, back in college."

"Really? I didn't realise you even knew him."

"Yeah. That clown is an ex-boyfriend."

Whiting almost managed a laugh. Wilshire knew there was little time to lose. She slid out from the booth looking up toward the bars and reception area.

"Abraham, you stay here, I have to find Rose, you know the hostess? She's on my team, I sent her out to pick you up. She will find you somewhere here in the station hotel to hole up while we figure out what to do."

Wilshire headed out across the restaurant to find Rose. She was nowhere to be seen. Looking through the big plate glass windows

117

down onto the station concourse there were a dozen hostesses in the right uniform but she couldn't be sure who they were.

Wilshire made for the elevator and squeezed in as two people got out and the doors started to close. She ran out onto the platforms and looked through the herds of shift changers and CSI technical staff. At last she caught sight of Rose and started running toward her, calling her name.

Rose turned in the distance, saw Wilshire, and made her excuses to the passenger with her, before trotting away down the platform, looking back over her shoulder as she picked up pace.

Wilshire couldn't understand it. Rose was running from her as though she was running from the devil. And then something twigged. Wilshire turned back, pushing through the crowds and the queues, back into the building. She couldn't wait for the lift, so she ran round the stairwells that climbed up the outside of the elevator shaft and opened the door back into the restaurant.

Back at Table 49, Abraham was sitting looking at his plate of half-eaten food. There was a small red hole above his left ear and a thick line of red running down his cheek. His GLiD had fallen onto the bench beside him. It was entirely blank.

11

Heath reached out for his drink, eyes closed against the sun and fingers crawling across the cool flagstones. He could hear a murmur of wildlife in the forest beyond and a faint sigh of waves on the shore. His fingers collided with the warmth of skin. He opened one eye to look up and see Cerise, stood over him, one leg cocked forward and her body gleaming with a lightly perfumed oil. Against the deep blue of tropical sky she was a naked, bronzed goddess. As she knelt and brought her head down close to his, he opened the other eye. She was quite perfect, a face filled with character and natural expression, far removed from the distortion of surgery and the nervous flavours of mind control. Her smile was real.

They had been making love for hours out on the deck. Far enough from the main house to be private, but close to the beach and the pool house bar. Each time he lay exhausted in her arms he had lapsed into an amphetamine sleep where spots of sun played through the branches of date palms and banana. It was a dreamily detailed pattern, like a warm defocused kaleidoscope playing over his eyelids. All the while his revving ego was fed with dreams of conquest. Heath the great hero, Heath the success, Heath the victor and, with each childish image of fist-pumping, sweat-flecked machismo, his unleashed adrenalin was tweaked and the neurotransmitter levels were raised in accordance with his subscription.

The new Cerise looked down at him, long hair loose around her face and eyes that matched the blue of the sky.

"Everyone's here, Clayton. Are you coming up to the house?"

Cerise helped him shower in the pool house. Time was slowed to accommodate a little fooling around, and finally she dressed him in a thick white robe and draped hefty gold jewellery around his neck. He admired himself in the dressing room's full length mirror. This was Heath as he imagined himself. The one man who could out-think a robot army, the killer intellect who dominated the great elites and had them invited to his Colombian mansion where he would dispense wisdom and largesse.

He walked the long gravel drive up to the terrace of the big house. It was Spanish colonial style, interlocked on many levels with orange roofs and colonnades, punctuated with courtyards and balconies. His private army had the perimeter secure, way back beyond the forests and along the clifftops. Cerise walked alongside him in a pale blue, figure-hugging wraparound and long heels. The scene was set, the night only just beginning.

Heath's taxi was right on cue, as every day. He was finding it uncomfortable, sitting so upright all the time, so he experimented with slouching on a slant with his feet propped up on the food dispenser. It was still no good and he kicked at it with growing petulance.

Mimi was pissing him off and he had decided that he was going to change her appearance to something more like the new Cerise. He liked the pale blue dress too. That might have to make an appearance. He let her ramble through his calls and email and use the little informal interjections, but he was tired of that kind of woman now, fawning and mindless, humorously teasing and ever ready to please. She had to go.

The taxi got within a block of the white concrete concourse of the Metropolitan building. The feeder lane to the taxi ranks at the front had been closed off and it was foot traffic only from here. Heath baled out and strolled up the middle. It was the size of a football field and lined with lights and grid lines. They showed the pedestrians where to stand at night when the great holographic lightshow of Metropolitan News was broadcast to the masses. It was the iconic aerial shot of every main news bulletin and, as a major city centre plaza, was permanently populated with dozens of GLiD carrying professionals.

Heath was wondering how today's unusual cloud pattern, that resembled Venetian blinds, was able to split the sunlight into a faint rainbow of pink, purple and orange. That couldn't be anything to do with man-made pollution, the American volcano or the ongoing problems in Japan.

"Hey, mind where you're going!"

Heath was walking straight into the path of a protesting pedestrian. He tutted and moved around them, then suddenly stopped dead and looked back.

"Holy shit! Samantha. What are you doing here?"

"I just needed to be sworn at by an old boyfriend."

"Well, it's a shock. You didn't tell me you were in town. Hey, come up to my office, I'll show you around."

Samantha stayed exactly where she was.

"Yeah. I heard about your, er... promotion. Seems the board have warmed to you after all."

"Hard graft. Integrity. Teamwork..."

"Yep. All things you still need to work on. I'll look at your super-villain control complex another time if that's OK, I actually came to see you about something more important."

"You came up to Birmingham just to see me? Hey, have you got something I can use?"

"Let's find out."

She took Heath by the arm and led him to one of the busier on-ramps of the Metropolitan concourse and sat on a painted concrete bench at the side. Heath looked baffled.

"Here? It's not very private."

"Exactly. But it's more private than being inside the building."

"Our conversation will still be cached somewhere."

"Yeah, I know, I worked on the Speech-Data algorithm for government collection and storage from Global ID."

"Just sayin'."

Samantha had cause to wonder, one more time, what she ever saw in Clayton Heath. Boyish confidence had only been masking distorted ego, and curiosity had created a skin over his inability to calculate depth. She wondered if he had moved forward to any degree.

"Remember when you were hell bent on being a flash salesman back in college?"

"Entrepreneur."

"Sorry. Flash salesman 'entrepreneur'. You were going to host the seminars for me and Reid and present some products to industry."

"Sure."

"Remember Bolstrode?"

"Yeah, of course, you know I do. He was your guru. Head of the Faculty. Big nuts professor with a half-baked libertarian agenda."

Samantha shook her head, a slight look of incredulity on her face.

"This job suits you, Heath. It really does. You reduce everything to a video caption and it's all totally distorted. You knew Everett Bolstrode as well as me. He was a great man, a real visionary. He helped us develop our first anti-intrusion programs and build our case for keeping the old internet unregulated."

"He was an anarchist!"

"You fell out with him because he saw through you. You were everything that was wrong with our ideas. You wanted to sell programs to the government that would control people's lives."

Heath tapped at the GLiD in his pocket.

"Well, they went ahead and did it anyway!"

"That's right, Boy Wonder. That's why there's no on-off switch on a

GLiD. Ever wondered about that?"

Heath backtracked.

"Look, we seem to have this same argument every time we meet. I can't believe you miss it so much you came all the way from London just to remind me how a crappy college company start-up failed to... start up."

Samantha stood up.

"Let's go and take a walk."

"Well, I would love to take some more abuse, but I have a morning meeting."

"At Nightship? No you don't."

Heath's look was frozen.

"Your contact was murdered at my dinner table last night."

***

The Executive level news report made it clear that the body taken from the table at the North Central Station restaurant was that of Abraham Whiting, Senior Project Simulation Specialist at Nightship Systems, cause of death to be confirmed. Who he was, how he died and why he was there dining alone, wouldn't be released to the public media until some time tomorrow.

Friedland could feel the situation slipping away beneath him. His own men had never caught up with Whiting's whereabouts. That he was in London was not surprising, but the North Central Station was the local waypoint for very high level workers who lived off campus and commuted daily to the Cyber Security Institute. His contacts at CSI were working on possible liaisons, but they were naturally evasive. He wouldn't hear anything before the affair had gone public. It was largely academic what had happened and who had been responsible. This whole thread was, well... a dead end. Unless Whiting's death could be spun through doubt or conspiracy or innuendo, then Nightship's upper hand in offering legitimate control of the Random Sentry administration would be lost. But of course, doubt, conspiracy and innuendo were commodities controlled by the news media. The MIs had the BBCE. The only corporation mouthpiece now was the Metropolitan, and Verrick's fellow directors were in charge of that narrative.

Friedland's limousine had brought him through the Nightship perimeter just as a security lockdown was kicking in. The guards at the high fencing on the outer road had sent out their own ATRs to patrol the area and once Friedland had passed through, the whole township was sealed.

Claxons were sounding on the outside of the labs and the red flashing bulkhead lights indicated no-go zones. Friedland had the limousine stop at Security Control and he waved his way past the armed sentries who stepped out to meet him.

"Just what the hell is going on?"

The Head of Security, his military uniform still half buttoned, guided Friedland to a laboratory schematic on the giant plexi-wall screen.

"We've just had another scarab go down. Both one and two are offline, the Research Centre is under attack and the testing labs have taken big damage."

"Why have I not been kept informed? How can a cyber attack be unstoppable? Shut down all unnecessary tunnels. Get a UN emergency request out, I want a GSC1 now. We need to lose the internet."

"Yes, Sir."

Friedland's fury was still rising. He grabbed an analyst who was shovelling multiple screens through his finger tips and almost shook the information from him.

"How are they going from building to building? Why can't we shut them out?"

"Er... they seem to have the root access to all the keyed security, Sir. They've got hold of enough keys to run riot and cover their tracks as they go. We're just chasing them round the system, following the destruction!"

Friedland turned away to look at the schematic, red flags appearing and even screens scorching out and dying in the Security Centre itself.

"Whiting! He's given them access. I didn't think the little worm had it in him."

A controlled calm came over him and he almost smiled.

"Well, well. Cover your tracks, but we know where you bastards are from. You're about to get a visit, and then you'll know the meaning of destruction."

***

Heath waited for the certificates to drop in to his GLiD and, when they came through, he was gratified to see that Harry's promise of unlimited travel was good.

His destination was taking him west to the strategic development town of Telford, close enough to the frontline of the insurgency. He'd seen the documentary about how the demarcation line of the old A5 had been a frontier of resistance over a thousand years before when the Vikings were held separate from the Saxons. There was something about the push of progress that always faltered upward of this area. They said even the Romans never fully took the North, only occupied it for a while. The onward march of corporate law was hitting similar boundaries. There were few campus towns north of here, the furthest being Glasgow, and that was under military command.

His train was manned, in each carriage, by a complement of regular army. They looked up with vague disgust at the dumb advertisements and tin pot music that hovered in the prestigious GLiD carriages. These were aimed at executives with serious privilege and the entire country wasn't yet comfortable with the return to the worst excesses of consumerism for an overpaid few.

Heath concentrated on the background research that Mimi was queueing up after getting the brief from Samantha. He remembered Kelvin Reid as a dysfunctional geek who had seen Heath as a know-nothing extrovert and definitely not worthy to join their team. At the time he took it that Reid had a secret crush on Samantha and, thinking back, Heath may well have gloried in the juvenile conquest of a woman. It wasn't so cool when Samantha dumped him and Heath in turn dumped the computer tech course to join the piranha squad in Journalism. The Metropolitan sponsored the course and encouraged all the students to be forward, brash, pushy little hatchet men and women, just like the heroes of the opinion-led media who sometimes visited the seminars. Heath fitted right in and since that time everyone, including his future colleagues knew him, affectionately or not, as an arsehole.

Reid, on the other hand, aced everything at college and was offered a job with the old Intel corporation. He took his programs and research ideas with him while Samantha played it safe and went with an offer from the Cyber Security Institute. Heath reckoned the CSI liked the look of her work and figured that her presence on a committee in front of MPs would sweeten their messages. History showed that he was right, but for the wrong reasons. Long after she'd forgiven his immaturity and kept in valuable professional touch, she'd been the power behind Heath's modest success on the Metropolitan news floor. She helped with technical background that he could never have put together and gave a modicum of accuracy to his wayward opinion slots.

What happened to Reid? No one really knew or, at least, no one was saying. He disappeared some years previously, having been a star of the Intel team that wrote for the new Quantum generation of chips. Leave of absence said Intel. A breakdown, said his colleagues. Samantha said she didn't know either way, but if anyone knew how the Bolstrode program had ended up in government firmware, it would be Reid.

Instead, Samantha gave Heath the whereabouts of Everett Bolstrode himself, the only one who might have a clue about his protégé Reid. She'd kept in touch for a while after he'd been ousted from his post on a number of ludicrous charges that thinly veiled the real reason. He had started to actively fall foul of the college authorities and their government led policies on the strictly political direction of higher education. Notions of equality had long since passed through the barriers of sex and race, and the juggernaut of 'right thinking' had enveloped political opinion. In the turmoil of war and the catastrophe of epidemic disease, a man with a following of young educated minds, who criticised the government, was considered seditious and potentially an intellectual terrorist. He was arrested on charges of threatening to undermine the war effort. Finally, emails and phone transcripts were produced to show he was colluding with undesirable forces, if not the enemy itself, and he was sentenced to twenty years in the correctional system. Like a lot of valuably educated people who entered the penal system, he didn't stay locked up in a cell. He was put to work in industry where his talents could be used to repay his debts while he underwent social readjustment and political re-education It was all to make a better man of him.

Heath stepped off the train at the Telford Business Town development station. The town claimed to be 'the birthplace of industry' and had certainly grown since the end of the war to accommodate dozens of smaller corporate entities in tightly controlled compounds. Bolstrode had been seconded to an obscure manufacturer called Itania Industries and Mimi's research showed Itania to be part of the vertical supply chain for Zura, the German aerospace company who were now investing heavily in the United Kingdom.

Heath was met at the station by an Itania taxi and taken imperiously through the gates like a visiting dignitary. The private contractors that Itania used were dressed in a beige uniform with the yellow and black helmets of Zura. Their chest rigs were loaded with ammunition for their heavy duty machine pistols. They snapped to attention for every taxi that cruised through their checkpoints.

From the impressively advanced reception area, Heath was taken on an electric cart by his escort guard. They travelled through the large ultra-modern complex of offices, workshops, laboratories and what he guessed were seven storey dormitories for the workforce. Like so many compounds, it seemed that only the most important people were allowed off the site.

He emerged in a block of glass-walled offices above a factory floor. Down below, robots managed an assembly line that incorporated giant compression chambers and steel tunnels fed by pipes that disappeared up into the roof space. In the sterility of the lab's production area, banks of status lights blinked in changing patterns. Heath had never seen anything like this before and he let out a low whistle of approval as they marched past the observation windows.

"Good of you to look me up, Clayton."

Heath turned to see a familiar face, shockingly aged since the last time they'd met. He wore a lab coat and plastic clean room trousers.

"Hello, Everett. Thank you for agreeing to see me."

They shook hands and Bolstrode seemed surprised at the courtesy.

"Well, I don't get to approve my own appointments, but it seems the Metropolitan has some influence. As for me, I would definitely have agreed to see you. You look well."

"Er.. so do you."

Bolstrode didn't smile. His face was lined with stress and his hair was snowy white. He was a little more stooped in the shoulders than Heath remembered. The confidence and courage of his old delivery was long gone.

"This your office?"

Bolstrode pretended to look around it.

"Yes, I suppose it is. Take a seat."

"Thanks. I guess you're wondering how I found you."

"No. Not really. If Sam hadn't told you I'm sure you could have put in a request. The Metropolitan has long fingers. It's more a question of why."

"Sam says she hasn't talked to you for a long time."

"That's right. The more I get involved in this, the less communication I'm allowed with the outside world."

Heath jerked a thumb behind him toward the factory.

"What exactly are you involved in?"

Bolstrode stood up and motioned Heath to an observation window on the opposite side of the office.

"Couldn't tell you if I knew. Compartmentalisation is pretty tight. But there are shops like these with laser drills putting holes in things and cutting up steel."

Heath watched the sparks jump as metal sheets were fed under the drill and thin jets of light darted with pinpoint accuracy at their targets.

"Never had you down as a welder, Everett."

Bolstrode took Heath across the room to look down at a hi-tech chamber in silver and white. He pointed down to a line carrying three foot long curved silver plates suspended from a conveyor.

"We're finishing baffle plates."

"For what?"

"Well, it's got to be engine parts. Turbines of some kind."

"OK, so what's the mystery?"

"Well, whatever they are, they're not regular engine parts. I produce and control the algos for a deep pressure particle coating that seals every unit."

"You mean some sort of protective layer?"

"Oh no. This is way more delicate and exacting than a paint shop! These particles are at the molecular level, strung across the plates at accuracies measured in the sub atomic range. The failure rate has to be zero. That's less than the machines can manage by themselves."

"Wow. Secret process. You're a man of many talents."

"Yes, well, don't forget I came from an industry background when the universities fell short of qualified staff. Anyway, it's secret enough that I'll never know what it's about and therefore can still talk to people like you."

Heath watched the plates being lined up outside the chamber.

"Maybe it's for the military mechs or drones. We keep hearing about new advances on the battlefield every day."

"There's millions of these things, Clayton. Enough for every man, woman and child left on this planet to have their own fleet of drones. But it's way beyond military spec and way beyond their needs."

"Doesn't your boss tell you anything?"

Bolstrode pointed at a panel of lights across the corridor.

"That's my boss."

"Jesus. I only ever saw street cleaners and garbage men taking orders from a machine!"

Heath glanced at Bolstrode's top pocket and then down at the bracelet round his wrist.

"You don't have Global ID, do you?"

Bolstrode went back to sit down.

"You should have guessed before. Remember, I'm a prisoner on secondment, but it's still not compulsory. Yet."

He held up his wrist.

"I'm tagged like an animal, but I'm still a human being."

Heath felt old arguments rising.

"Everett, implanted chips are progress. Every day more people are having it done. Tags, RFID, they're just not secure."

"Oh I know about that. I saw the story you ran with the kidnappers who cut the RFID tattoos off the little girl's arm. Encouraged a lot of people to have their kids done, as well as themselves."

Heath spread his hands.

"It was a reasonable decision."

Bolstrode smiled.

"Was it even a real news story, or one of your cartoons?"

"What does it matter? Sometimes you have to brainwash people a little bit to make them see sense."

"Clayton... does it ever occur to you that technology can be used to either empower people or to control them? My 'boss' there is the only ideal GLiD carrier. Input and output are obeyed instantaneously, without clumsy thoughts to misinterpret. The programmer doesn't have to second guess responses or suspect personal agendas. It's a machine obeying a program. Like the machine that generates your world in the Dreemfeelds. Nothing can go wrong there, because there is only you to command the AI. That's your ideal world. Well, we're in someone else's world here and they want us all to obey without question. Our thoughts are their thoughts..."

Heath waved it away.

"Everett, you haven't changed! I guess the reorientation class is a hoot!"

"Clayton, you still feel you're invested in this, but you're not. We're all disposable."

"Then why are you still alive? You're not the only computer 'genius' who can spray paint an engine manifold!"

Bolstrode looked around as though trying to find a new direction to take the conversation.

"Clayton, it all still goes right over your head, doesn't it? I'm alive because I'm more useful that way... at the moment."

He lifted the wrist with the bracelet.

"I'm not kept in line with this. It doesn't control my actions. The threat to the remnants of my family keeps me in line. As far as I know they are alive, they have food vouchers and a pigeon hole apartment in one of the container cities. They can be disappeared at any time and so can I, but there are also still some jobs that AI can't handle."

Heath was looking down at the floor. He knew he'd overstepped the mark. Bolstrode took it a little slower.

"Remember when the latest fad was for AI in the courts? Gave the legal system a chance to leave its responsibilities behind and let the logic of the law be interpreted by a computer. The JusticeBots I think your media were calling them. They tried to carry it over to the frontline in the war and reinterpret mass murder as justice. What happened next? Well, the JusticeBots thought *everyone* should die, regardless, because every human is intrinsically capable of failure and logic dictates that if you haven't broken the law yet, you will. Eventually."

"Yeah, I remember that. Fucked up idea."

"Well, I guess that shook up the powers that be. By whom I mean the very, very few whose agreements dictate the direction of life for the rest of us. The thought that they might be held to account by something of their own creation, however far down the line, would have been just too much. Sometimes, Clayton, it's human fallibility itself that forces us to do the right things."

Heath decided to brighten up.

"Well, thank you Professor! As though proof were needed, I should have paid more attention in your classes."

"Amen!"

"Like Kelvin Reid, maybe. What happened to him, Everett?"

"Reid? Brilliant. Went on to the Quantum teams at Intel."

"After that?"

"Well... maybe he paid too much attention in my classes. Wouldn't take the security chip, if you remember. He developed his own ideas around dangerous themes like liberty and personal freedom. When the legal system was testing AI and then the Global ID Pro scheme was introduced, I think he ducked out of Intel before he had to take the chip. That's my reading of it anyway."

"Ducked out where?"

"No idea. Maybe you should ask his wife."

"Wife? I didn't know he was married."

"Yes. Nice girl called Deena. Of course, she's technically his widow now because he hasn't been seen for over three years, so officially the plague got him."

"D'you think he's dead?"

"Ask her Clayton. I know where she used to live and people aren't moving around much at the moment, so it stands a chance you'll find her."

"Thanks. I will."

"Don't have paper and pens anymore so I have to email it to you. Can Santa's little helper pick it up for you?"

"Sure. Mimi? Can you get this?"

"I am connected Clayton. Just waiting for it to be sent."

Bolstrode couldn't hear the reply. He smiled.

"Mimi? She sounds interesting. What does she look like?"

"Mimi. Visual."

The hologram came up and hovered, from head to knee in front of Heath.

Bolstrode approved.

"Thought so. She looks a lot like Samantha, doesn't she?"

12

"In a shock move this morning, the Home Office announced a temporary re-enactment of the Emergency Powers Act across the United Kingdom in order to contain the outbreak of multiple threats to national security.

"The Home Secretary, Jadalgupta Bhindi, in defending the first countrywide use of the Act since the outbreak of war said it was 'regrettable but necessary' following the flare-up of violence and terrorist extremism in northern England. Curfews in Manchester, Liverpool, Sheffield, Leeds and Newcastle will be in force from six p.m. to six a.m. every day. The Home Secretary has announced a zero tolerance approach from the army and police, for those not observing the curfew. With selective travel restrictions in place and checkpoints at major road junctions manned by United Nations peacekeepers, the government hopes to contain the spread of violence. The aim is to save lives without forcing direct confrontation with the terrorists.

"The Home Secretary also mentioned in a special briefing to the news media that concerns had been raised about militant groups in the West Midlands. While not directly involved in the northern conflict, anarchist cells were, instead, supplying arms and ammunition to the insurgents through the 'inadequately-manned checkpoint system'. Ongoing raids by police on suspected terrorist cells in the Midlands will be stepped up under the new implementation of the Emergency Powers Act. We are advised that this will include arrest and detention without charge and the use of deadly force for those resisting arrest.

"In the South of England, a co-ordinated series of cyber attacks on government datacentres has spread to the UK administration's chain of technology companies and infrastructure suppliers. Unconfirmed reports of an intrusion into Nightship Systems' headquarters at Bedford follow a lockdown of the campus and a full overnight internet blackout. An assessment of the damage is ongoing and there has been no comment from Nightship so far about the loss of any confidential data or the compromise of essential systems. While the situation at Nightship is said to be 'under control', further attacks on the Sussex and Hampshire Area datacentres are still hindering vital services. In an unusual step, local council administrators are encouraging those with new allocations of food vouchers to stock up in case of an interruption to the distribution system, as a result of the attacks."

Mimi had kept up a constant newsfeed about the troop movements and travel lockdown that was undoubtedly now taking place. To reach this God-forsaken scene of decay and dissolution in south Birmingham, Heath had sat in stationery trains for hours, becoming gradually less patient with the first class snacks and drinks and the constant gibbering of the advertising holograms. He could mute them, but he couldn't stop them diving down into his face, gurning, waving and shaking their cartoon arses to get his attention. It told Heath a lot about his fellow passengers as the smart adverts read the preferences from people's IDs, or pestered a returning customer, by altering the content to attract their attention. Heath's strangely alien hula girls with overwide hips, were a line of little Asian boys for a nonchalant viewer across the aisle. Someone else clearly liked their females large which nowadays was a suitable rarity to pique the interest.

Heath had taken the time to fill out his report on Bolstrode and forward it directly to Harry as requested. His free movement was predicated on the forwarding of all files, interviews and gathered data back to the Metropolitan. It was known as keeping the receipts to claim expenses.

By the time Heath was walking through the processing centre in Stourbridge the day was almost over. As the shadows lengthened the whole area became a stark wasteland, all sight of the old streets and shop fronts disappearing into hollow darkness.

Mimi got him to the residential camp and then through the high wire and the muddy tracks of alleyways between the containers. He found the south entrance and pressed on through to a broad avenue of old Edwardian semi-detached houses that rose up the hill. Some of the rooms were lit with the pale yellow of paraffin lamps, burning who knows what, or standard issue LED battery lights. It had been a long time since there had been mains power.

"She's not at home, Clayton."

Heath had left the few residents, who'd been watching him with suspicion, back on the road and in the camp. This was strangely deserted.

"Where the hell is everybody?"

"The distribution point at Stourbridge Four is surrounded by three thousand two hundred people, approximately. They are being issued with essential supplies to twice the value of their entitlement. There is an eighty one percent chance that Deena Reid will be there, assuming that she is not already dead."

Mimi always added that to location logic. Heath would often quietly chant along with it. Life expectancy had become an ephemeral commodity in the years since the war and the plague.

"Let's go there."

"Sure, Clayton."

The distribution point was the gutted shell of an old supermarket. The escorted trucks came in through the heavily guarded back yard and pallets of food packs wheeled themselves out through the front where the contractors called the mob singly through a rank of temporary turnstiles.

Heath pulled his coat around him in the grey gloom and started to slip between the milling crowds of dishevelled and miserable residents. Megaphones called names and numbers and tried to organise them into lines. Arc lights swung across the sea of humanity, watching for disturbances that could be pinpointed and resolved with a crackle of taser sticks.

"They've caught your GLiD, Clayton. They're watching you."

"Good."

Some of the residents were dressed in the boiler suits of council administration, a few hi-vis jackets of undoubtedly family men in charge of young family members. They pushed and jostled as though their entitlement was paramount.

Heath had his head down into his collar, partly to become more anonymous and partly to hide the drifting smell of unwashed clothes on stale bodies. He scoped left and right, fixing on faces as they came into the light of the arc lamps up at the turnstiles.

"Stay on the outside of the people, Clayton. She will look to slip through the thinnest part of the crowd."

Heath patrolled both sides of the shifting masses making sure Mimi could see as many faces as possible. It was hopeless. Eventually, Heath gave up and walked up to the armed distributors. They had his Global ID on the scanner and were surprisingly courteous.

"Evening, Mister Heath. What can I do for you?"

"I'm looking for someone. Can you tell me if they've already been through?"

"Name?"

"Deena Reid. Female. Twenty seven years old."

"What sort of ID?"

"Just a card."

"Wait here a minute."

The contractor let his scanner swing from his belt and shouldering his weapon, slipped behind the lines and headed for the turnstiles.

Heath kept looking, but he was back in a few seconds.

"She's not been through. But she's local, so she'll have to come through in the next few hours or she'll be going hungry. This is the last drop for a week."

"A week? I thought it was every day."

The contractor thought he might have said too much.

"Ah well. May be a different team, I don't know. Hold on..."

The contractor cupped his hand to his earpiece and concentrated for a moment.

"Looks like we've got her on face rec. Do you want to come through?"

Heath went behind the lines and saw through the open doors of the gutted supermarket. It was piled high with pallets of rations being offloaded in the back. Low loader pallet trucks were beetling about between the aisles. They were processing people out front as fast as possible and the grateful public were scuttling away laden with boxes, paranoid that there might be muggers in the many shadows.

"Can I see her back here?"

"Yeah. Sure."

A minute later and the contractor came back holding the arm of a young, frightened woman. She was dark like her profile, looking shorter, half Indian Heath reckoned, her eyes now wide with expectations of the unknown. The contractor let her go and motioned that he was returning to his position.

"If you need anything, shout me."

"Sure."

Heath stood in the shadow of the old supermarket portico as the pallets came out to the turnstiles. Deena Reid looked at him with trepidation. Heath tried a smile.

"No. I'm not the police."

"I know. I can tell."

Heath could also tell she wasn't going to warm to him any time soon.

"My name's Clayton Heath, I'm a journalist. I want to talk to you about Kelvin."

She looked away, like it was an old request.

"He left years ago. I haven't seen him and I don't know where he is. OK?"

"OK. That's... pretty clear cut. Can I at least talk about when the two of you were together?"

She didn't look particularly keen. Heath nodded at a pallet of boxes on its way past.

"I'll buy you dinner?"

She was getting cold standing in the doorway, the rain was just starting.

"OK. I suppose so."

Heath guided her to the contractor who'd found her.

"Hey, can you sort out her consignment for me now?"

The contractor was starting to think Heath was asking for a lot of favours.

"Yeah. I should think so, Mister Heath."

"OK. Wait a minute."

Heath turned to Deena.

"Give me your card."

As she did so, Heath withdrew the GLiD and put the card to its back.

"Mimi. Transfer a couple of days worth of food vouchers onto this card."

"OK Clayton."

He handed her back the card and the contractor pointed the way to the distribution point. Clayton tried one more blag.

"Hey look, thanks for the help. I don't suppose, er... you have any local taxi concession here, I mean she's got a lot to carry and I don't think she'll make it all the way home."

The contractor tutted and then sighed.

"Yeah. We've got a personnel carrier. You can have one trip in that."

As they loaded the back of the taxi, Deena couldn't hide the pleasure of her good fortune.

"I've never seen this much supplies. Not since I was a kid and the supermarkets were rammed."

After all the years of heavy rationing, Heath was surprised by the amount they were being given. With his additional gift also being doubled, Deena was set for, what looked like, several weeks.

She'd also never been in a taxi. Shuttle bus yes, but taxis were always beyond her means. Like most people who had survived the war and the plague, she had no real job, just government subsistence and continual assessment for places in the new factories.

Her home was a section on the ground floor of an old house on the avenue. She had a walled-off area of a living room through which the family on the other side could be heard arguing in some language she couldn't understand. She lived and slept in that room. There was a toilet and shower cubicle off the corridor in an understairs cupboard. The stairs were boxed off and belonged to another apartment.

Cooking was done on a wartime tabletop electrapak stove near the door. Compared to the container cities, this was pretty desirable.

They sat in the living space with mugs of tea. Some LED lights were softened with scarves to tone down the glare on the peeling walls. She'd hung pictures as best she could, made some rough curtains and arranged her few possessions wherever they'd go. It was all slightly better than surviving. Heath tried to be upbeat.

"Kelvin was in college with me. We worked together on some projects."

"I don't remember him mentioning you."

"We weren't always that close, but he was a brilliant student. How did you meet him?"

Deena felt the old questions starting to surface.

"I was a researcher at Intel. It was quite an open company in those days, everyone knew everyone on the site."

"It was a UK campus, right?"

"Yes. Not like these big cities they're building now."

"When was the last time you saw him?"

Here were the old questions.

"I don't know, it's so long ago now that I can't exactly remember the last time. I think he just never came back to the apartment one night, so maybe the last time was that morning when we both went in."

"No note, no email."

"Nothing."

"Do you think he's still alive?"

"Maybe."

Her face softened.

"A lot of people got lifted from places like Intel, but they turned up in court or police custody. Or some of them eventually got released. The police had nothing to talk to Kelvin about."

"There was mention of a nervous breakdown. He was pretty intense, as I recall."

She smiled sadly.

"No. Kelvin wasn't suicidal, depressive, psychotic, on drugs or any of those things."

"So that would be just a covering story?"

"Well, it came from the psychological evaluation reports that we all had. They told him he had 'dangerous thoughts'. That sort of thing. He was very libertarian, believed in technology as a means for people to free themselves and he wasn't happy with too much control being exercised by the old corporations or Wall Street or the banking system."

Heath heard an echo in his mind.

"It can either be used to empower you, or control you."

"Yeah. That's the sort of thing he used to say. They didn't like that, so when he went missing they made out he was some sort of unhinged anarchist nut."

Mimi was whispering quietly in Heath's ear.

"She's lying, Clayton."

Heath drank at his tea.

"So, Deena, why aren't you working? You could easily get a good job with your background."

She looked him up and down briefly.

"There's no way I'd be tagged. I'm waiting for the whole stupid idea to fail and we can get back to being just people again."

Heath glanced at the boxes of supplies piled high.

"It brings a lot of benefits, Deena. It's the future."

She shook her head with a tut of contempt.

"You can't have worked that closely with Kelvin when you were in college together. He would never have agreed with that."

"But you had RFID at Intel."

"Yeah, but it wasn't so... invasive. I don't want something I can't remove. Kelvin knew how to defeat all that automated ID stuff anyway. He used to say that for every billion dollar initiative there was a two dollar hack."

"Yeah. We actually worked on defeat mechanisms and anti-intrusion, privacy programs. Like Bolstrode."

Something rang a bell in Deena's mind.

"That was the name of his professor. He liked him."

"I know. I saw him today. He told me where I might find you."

"I don't know how. It's been a long time."

Mimi was back.

"She's telling the truth, now Clayton."

"People can be found. I could find Kelvin."

She looked down into her tea.

"He probably doesn't want to be found."

"Well, I think we have to find him. I think his work is going to be used for something that nobody ever voted for and it'll affect you, me and everyone we know."

"How?"

"Stuff he worked on with Everett Bolstrode in college which Kelvin then took to Intel. Somehow, it was stolen by the MIs and is now being used to create a... situation."

"Is that what the Emergency Powers thing is about?"

Saying it out load seemed to give it validity in Heath's mind, where before it had seemed like a mistake or a stupid conspiracy theory.

"Yeah. That's exactly what it's about."

***

As midnight rolled in, the distribution point was closed and the trucks took away the turnstiles, the palletbots and the arc lights. As they were sealing up the old supermarket, an army jeep with floodlights on the bush bar circled into the empty car park.

There was a friendly exchange between soldiers and food distribution contractors before the area of the town started to take on a different tone. Soldiers were moving in, blocking off streets at crossroads, building high temporary walls that no one on foot could see over. Signs were being hung on fences. There were timetables of shuttle buses to the station and directions to roads that had not been closed. As the job was done, the trucks and jeeps were moving on and a smattering of local police checkpoints were left to set up their huts and crowd towers. While the residents slept, there was a whine of megaphones being tested in the streets, slung from the top of street lights, echoing through the rain. The police had rolled out their armoured crowd control vehicles, quickly repainted from their army field colours and renamed Civil Enforcement. By dawn, a one way maze of streets from residential areas to the stations and processing points was taking shape in towns all across the country.

***

Heath was helping Deena to look through her collection of small suitcases and sports bags that were all she'd taken when the evacuations began. She'd never felt the need to unpack memories of the past and so, apart from her clothes, the bags and cases had been stashed in the space behind her sofa bed. She unzipped a holdall.

"Kelvin was a real back-up freak. He used to make multiple copies of everything, in all different media. I think he moved it around. That old three two one thing we were all supposed to do. Three copies, two different media, at least one off site. I never knew where they went."

"Did he store it up there too?"

Deena looked at Heath and his raised finger and she smiled.

"Kelvin thought the cloud was the stupidest idea ever. You wouldn't even know where it had gone, never mind how you could get it back! That's what he said."

Among the family stuff she had found an envelope of photographs in

138

cardboard frames. She looked briefly and handed them to Heath.

"Kelvin in college. Are there any of you in here to prove who you are?"

Heath sifted through them. There was Reid, slightly unkempt hair, glasses, the look of a rabbit in headlights. He was posing with a bunch of other sickly-looking computer kids. Heath recognised a few of the names written in pen along the bottom of the frame. Then there was one Kelvin had taken with Samantha when they were working together. It was titled The Everett Bolstrode Team. Heath felt a moment of poignancy to once again be looking at Samantha's angelic face, youthful and confident, the way he remembered her. A wave of sudden loss passed through his mind and he felt disorientated for a moment. He quickly passed on to another picture. It was Reid, back in his room at the halls, sat at his desk and holding the front paws of the janitor's cat up toward his computer. The caption read: 'Mouser's on the case!'.

"Oh shit!"

"What?"

"Can I have a copy of this picture?"

"Yes, I suppose so."

Heath put it down on the arm of the chair and took the GLiD from his pocket.

"Mimi. Get a shot of this. Include the frame."

"OK Clayton. Do you want to upload the datafile as well?"

"What datafile?"

"I'm picking up RFID from the photograph."

"Er... wait."

Deena hadn't heard Mimi whispering in Heath's ear, she'd been too busy digging through the holdall to hear Heath's mumbling.

"What's the matter?"

Heath slid the photograph out of the frame, turned it over and held it up to the light.

"I think this photo was produced on a repro printer. He embedded a drive in it. I remember printing drives myself. Mimi, scan this at hi-res and show me the RFID drive."

"OK Clayton."

From the screen of his GLiD, Heath pulled out a scan which hovered in the air as he blew it up.

"Mimi, increase the contrast."

The picture became harsh and grainy. There, between the fibres of the photo paper were the unmistakable spirals of an RFID matrix.

"Wow. He backed up into a picture. Of course, in those days there would have been no GLiDs to detect it."

Deena was surprised but vindicated.

"I didn't know it was there. Can you read it?"

Heath stopped to think.

"Probably... but then so can everyone else."

If he uploaded it to the GLiD, Harry would be able to share it straight away. Heath wanted time. He had an idea.

"Mimi, open me a tunnel. Confidential encryption to a diplomatic bag. Use Isobel Prine's key. Direct transfer. No local copy."

"It's open, Clayton."

"OK. Upload this RFID drive."

"It's done."

Heath sat there in silence for a moment, waiting to see if Mimi could find any more drives among the photographs. She couldn't. He was starting to feel that something was coming full circle in his mind. Within a single day he had come within the orbit of his old college contacts, all of them trying to tell him something that he didn't want to hear. There was nothing direct, just suggestions to distort his worldview. It was as though they could see the dozing monster standing directly behind and tied to him by the electronic leash of the GLiD. They had no intention of waking it with the wrong words or ideas, it was up to Heath himself to listen. On his shoulder sat the silent witness, Mimi, recording everything and storing it for later review. Personal actions have personal consequences, he remembered telling the new recruits. Because that's what he was told the day he was supplied with a GLiD.

Deena put down her bag of paraphernalia.

"Hey look, do you want to eat something? It's not like we're short of food."

"Yeah. Sure."

Heath stayed in his distracted state while Deena unpacked a box over by the cooker. She looked out through the window and down into the darkness of the street where a mix of vehicles had converged in a pool of headlights.

"Uh-oh. This doesn't look good."

"What's going on?"

Heath was straight over to the window, peering through the makeshift curtain. He caught the drone of helicopters and sure enough the dancing beams of several searchlights were converging on the convoy.

"I'm going to get a closer look. Lock the door after me."

Heath was out and down the steps onto the driveway. He only planned to get close enough to pick up some Global IDs and find out from Mimi what the local transport was doing, but the search beams of the helicopters were highlighting portable guard towers. New rows of chain link and razor wire disappeared back into the darkness.

He pulled up a screen and could see army and police IDs moving down the road and more following.

He was about to tell Mimi to get him some transport out of there and back home before getting caught in a drill when a pencil beam from the back of a spotter truck caught him full in the face. A megaphone cut through the glare.

"Would you step down here please, Sir?"

Heath dropped the hologram and it vanished. He held up both hands to indicate compliance and walked down the crumbling tarmac to the pavement. They'd have his ID. He'd be fine.

A sound from far away suddenly got closer. Shouts amid gunfire, a crash of hardware from beyond the perimeter fencing. An army unit swung into the road on a truck and the roar of a helicopter gunship came over the rooftops, opening up on targets that only the infrared could see. Even before Heath could dive behind the stump of a garden wall, a battle zone had appeared. The helicopter was circling in an ever tighter course and the gunner seemed to be loosing volleys of fire into the air at random. As it lurched to one side over the houses a spray of fire cut across the spotter truck and came rushing up the pavement in front of Heath. He felt the chips of stone jump around him and the smell of scorched metal.

"Holy shit! What are they doing!"

He shuffled further behind the wall, finding dead shrubs and windblown garbage. A roar of voices was getting closer, threaded with commands from megaphones far and near. The helicopter spiralled back over the rooftop and an army truck came hurtling forward through the darkness.

A pattering sound grew around him and the sound of rock bouncing and skating along the pavement. The army spotter truck moved forward and in its place came a heavily armoured crowd control vehicle.

Troops had fanned out from the truck and taken up positions in the corners of the houses. Heath thought he could still get out of this, telling Mimi to forward his location again to all GLiD receivers along with a full profile.

"Received but not responding."

"What's the fucking matter with them?"

He wanted to stand up, hands raised and shout, but when the automatic fire whistled over his head, he thought again and hunkered down.

He could tell without seeing anything that there was a riot coming towards him. The army had the weapons if not the numbers, and Heath suspected that if this was like the insurgency reports, then both sides would have night vision and some form of scanning.

He suddenly wished he'd never come outside. Curtains and blackouts had twitched all down the street as the riot grew. All the bottom windows were securely shuttered and, for Heath, there was no way to get back to Deena's door.

He wanted to get out of the line of fire and ended up in a zig-zag course, scrambling over rubble and along darkened paths. He stood up, back to a gable-end wall round the corner of the main street in time to see the black outlines of the mob. They had commandeered a taxi that spearheaded the charge. There were a dozen dancing lights of Molotov cocktails and a constant shower of bricks and stones that rattled on the tarmac, long before they reached the troops. The megaphone was warning them one last time, but even before that warning had finished, the crowd control vehicle had sounded a klaxon in two short blasts.

The crowd scattered as an intense microwave beam caught them in its searing heat. The front of the taxi crumpled and started to smoke. Then, a supply of Molotovs in the back exploded in a fountain of chemical fire. Screams filled the night air as bodies twitched and rolled, pouring smoke as they tried to run. The flames of the taxi lit dark bundles that lay in the road, a smell of acrid burning rising in the night air. The klaxon sounded again and the crowd started to shrink further away to safety.

Heath had been mesmerised by the scene. He'd never been this close to an enforcement operation and seen flesh cooked like meat on a skewer.

He never heard the soft footsteps that stopped right next to him.

He turned and, in the soft orange light that flickered in the distance, he saw a big figure looking down at him, a good head and shoulders taller. The face was partially hidden by old-style flying goggles. The figure had a child-like half grin on his big face as he spoke.

"Hello."

Heath was prompted to say hello, but as he opened his mouth, a huge fist caught him full on and the world dissolved into silence.

13

"This morning, Britain awakes to the first nationwide homeland military action since the war. Troops are sent in, across the length and breadth of the mainland, to secure railway stations, supply depots and civil amenities from the attack by rebel insurgents.

"The Prime Minister, Sarion Dundas, is preparing to address the nation from Downing Street as the full picture becomes clearer. Britain, once again, stands on the edge of national conflict as vital services are interrupted and innocent lives are caught in a deadly crossfire.

"Over now to Downing Street where Mister Dundas is beginning to speak."

"The government's primary concern is to secure the function of the internet around which so much of the country's infrastructure is based. Any prolonged outage would mean that trains and buses will not run, food and medicine will not be delivered, power stations will fail, communications will break down and the normal functioning of the country would cease.

"United Nations troops are helping our overstretched army regulars, civilian police force and their Enforcement Officers to protect vital installations and ensure continuation of vital supplies to distribution points. But, the time has undoubtedly come when we, as one nation, are simply compelled to embrace a once and for all solution to ensure that the events, once again unfolding around us, cannot go on indefinitely. Our problem has always been that those who would seek to harm this country and our way of life have been able to hide anonymously within the internet system. They are taking no responsibility for their actions, having no checks and balances levied against their radicalised hate speech. A failure by us to act, and curb this lawlessness, means they find themselves able to attack and adversely affect those services and systems that maintain the country and serve its people.

"I have therefore mandated our security services to begin a co-ordinated program to weed out those insurgents whose identity is not verified by the Global ID standard, remove them from our society and to detain them in a safe place where they can do no more harm and their useful future can be determined.

"I am asking every right thinking citizen in this country to work with our police forces, and our international help, and to positively demonstrate that those right thinking citizens are not a part of the

problem, but a part of the solution to securing our country's defences and way of life.

"I have spoken before, many times, about the benefit to everybody of adopting the Global Identification strategy. Global ID finally brings everybody into the jobs market. We have all seen the freedoms that it offers to professionals of all backgrounds as they go about their business, increase their prosperity, expand their opportunities and sleep safely at night in the knowledge that they and their loved ones are protected. I think that all these things are vital to the progress and well-being of any civilised country. Therefore, at this time, I have decided that as this crisis passes and we set about building a better future with guaranteed security for all, we shall prioritise on this new system those who take up Global ID in the immediate future. They will be first on the list for new housing, new careers as well as all those current benefits such as travel, food, insurances and freedom of movement.

"For those people, the future is bright. For all those who choose to remain a part of the problem, let me be clear, there is no future. Without Global ID, ultimately there will be no place in society, no allocation of the resources shared amongst the rest of us, and only the darkest suspicions for the reasons behind the desire to remain hidden within the shadows that we seek to illuminate.

"This crisis will pass. I promise you that. We have the resources to be effective, the manpower to cope and the will to succeed. During these unprecedented times, when we must all dig in together, I urge you to stay calm, stay focused and to join me in the struggle for a new beginning."

Heath woke up coughing. It was shaking him awake and every time his head moved, pain circled his skull like a knife trying to peel his brain. There were noises flicking from ear to ear, chopped up phrases and the machine noise of a receiver trying to filter a special frequency from the sea of garbage. There was light through his eyelids and a giant throbbing in his lower face. He couldn't even swear. Just a groan as he breathed uneasily in and out. There were voices somewhere close by.

"As long as I don't have to do the long words."

"No, we can go with the descriptions, and I'll take just six out of nine."

"Six!"

"I think that's very reasonable. It's two thirds of the total."

"Oh, OK."

As the voices became clearer, Heath thought they were in the room with him. They sounded strange to his ears.

"Go. Give me six."

"Umm, leaves!"

"Yes."

"Flowers!"

"OK. That's two."

"Stems!"

"Yep."

There was a pause.

"I'm stuck."

"Think under the ground."

"Oh. Tubers! Roots!"

"Come on. One more!"

Heath managed to get an eye open and a square of light burnt it shut again. As he gradually became accustomed to the pain his vision stabilised and he was looking at weak sun through a skylight.

"Bulbs!"

"OK. That's six. Any more?"

"Hey!"

"Just asking!"

He turned to the sound of the voices. At the foot of an old wooden bed, next to his, sat a little girl with big bunches of hair sprouting from above her ears. Her T shirt hung over her jeans with the slogan 'Fear Me' in big letters. She held a large tablet computer in her hands and was angling it towards a five foot cartoon rabbit that stood at her shoulder. It wore a red waistcoat and small round glasses. It was pointing at the tablet.

"You might have got fruit and seeds!"

As it came into focus, Heath realised he probably wasn't dreaming. He coughed again and managed to speak.

"Who the hell are you and what am I doing here?"

The little girl's head flicked up in a swirl of hair bunches. Her eyes widened.

"Oh crap! He's awake!"

She dropped the tablet, slid off the bed and ran for the door.

"Magnus! Bomber! He's awake! He's woke up!"

The rabbit looked at Heath and then the departing girl. He had a worried look on his face. His slightly vague, old man voice tried to sound authoritative.

"Well, hmm, I hope you're not going to be disruptive. I mean, we like to keep things informal, but we have to maintain a little discipline..."

Barging through the door at the end of the dingy bedroom came a line of very large, very useful-looking characters. Their long hair and beards framed unsmiling weather-beaten features. They wore a lot of broken leather, the partial remnants of uniforms too singed and torn to be identified but from somewhere they'd got hold of the latest army issue battlefield boots.

Heath stayed still as they surrounded the bed. One of them tossed the tablet to the little girl behind him and the rabbit blinked out and was gone.

Heath looked up at the group, some of them with arms folded, as they glared scornfully down at his sickly body.

Heath tried a weak smile.

"It's OK fellas. I'm not going to be disruptive."

When they got Heath out of the house, he was marched, one on each arm, down a covered passageway that smelt of oil and diesel. Heath felt the fear and nausea rising in his stomach.

"Are you going to kill me?"

The guards said nothing and were joined by others as they came outside into an industrial yard. It was lined with old machinery that had been partially dismantled. The walls of the yard were high with racking loaded down by components from the stripped machines. It stretched away round a corner where an old JCB was chewing up motor panels and aluminium fencing. They stood Heath where he could look up at the racks of dirty rusting pistons and chassis piled one over another like breakfast waffles. The pain in the middle of his forehead and the sickness in his gut was more than fear. He couldn't hear anything. His GLiD was saying nothing. He wasn't even sure which pocket it was in. Most worryingly, the internet was silent.

Finally, someone of his own height and build approached. He had a long black goatee, shorter hair than the warders and the same uniform of leather, scorched battledress and boots. The new stranger glanced up at the racks.

"Hard to believe they're about to ban metal, isn't it?"

Heath had to try hard to organise his wandering thoughts.

"Who is? Who's banning metal?"

"TPTB, old pal."

"Why?"

"Oooh, it's dangerous. You could hurt yourself, so no citizen-employees will be allowed metal. Only plastic. Of, course agriculture and industry can still apply for licences..."

"Can they?"

"Oh yeah, and the military. But, seeing as we're killing each other by remote control these days, it probably comes under industry. Good, isn't it?"

Heath was a few questions behind.

"What's TPTB?"

The stranger stroked his beard.

"Bloody hell, it must be like living in a deep, dark hole."

The little girl appeared at Heath's elbow and looked up into his face. She spoke with gravitas.

"The Powers That Be!"

The warders had loosened their grip, but stood ready to catch Heath if he flopped over. Heath needed to know.

"Are you gonna kill me?"

"No, mate. We leave that sort of thing to the respectable people in suits. We're the cavalry and this is Jacky's breaking yard."

"Jacky?"

"Yeah. He won't have crossed your radar. He's one of the last guys in town still running a business and trying to keep people fed or out of the way of the cops and their chemicals."

The stranger with the goatee studied the side of Heath's face with a look of sympathetic consideration.

"That's one hell of a bruise you got there."

Heath remembered.

"Yeah. Somebody hit me."

The stranger looked at Heath's guard.

"Bit hard that one, Bomber."

Heath slightly turned and recognised the flying goggles, now pushed up into his hair. The big man looked down at Heath with sad eyes.

"Sorry."

At the top of a construction, twenty feet up in the middle of the yard, a door was built into the end of a container. A figure called down the winding wooden stairwell.

"Hey Bug! Jacky's got a few!"

Bug graciously waved Heath along.

"Come on. Jacky's got fingers in a few pies, so he might have something to help you."

A group of young children had gathered to watch the prisoner make the long walk toward the yard's offices. Bug walked alongside.

"You don't see any of them in your city compounds either, do you?"

"No. The state nurseries take all the children."

Bug sneered as they climbed the steps.

"Yeah, just keep telling yourself that. And life expectancy has come down low enough to clear the streets of them pesky old wrinklies too."

From the top of the stairs, Heath could see out over the racking walls and make out a road through fields. It stretched away into the gloom toward the grey shapes of a town. He felt marginally better for the fresh wind in his face.

At the top, the big door scraped open wider and he walked into a large yard office, made up of several containers welded together. It was dark enough and dirty enough to be a working environment. But, a cluster of old fashioned screens were fanned out around the main desk where maps and charts were trapped under piles of, what Heath assumed to be, books. More of the street gang were gathered, pointing at the maps and scrolling an illuminated tile while watching the screen. They stopped and looked at Heath, then moved back to stand either side of the big chair. In it sat a man with a short smoky white beard, glasses and an old French Navy cap slung on the back of his head. The old guy let Heath look around for a moment.

"Hi. I'm Jack. Welcome to the machines."

Heath didn't know what he was talking about. Jack waved it away.

"Never mind. Here. You'll be wondering where this is."

He scooted Heath's GLiD across the desk.

"Go ahead. Pick it up."

Heath took it and instantly, the swirling nausea in his gut started to fade. The smooth glossy screen, however, was totally black.

"What have you done?"

"We gave you a little something to help you with the cold turkey. Don't worry about your soul-stealer. Your girlfriend's still in there. But we had to just temporarily split you two up, or she'll be out there telling everyone where you are."

"And where the hell am I?"

Jack leaned back and intertwined his fingers.

"You're in my dam yard! I didn't want you, but you were heading straight into a full scale riot of turkeys waking up on Christmas morning. You'd be sharing a plastic box with the rest of them if we'd left you."

"Sorry. I don't get it."

"We've known about you for a couple of days. You're easy enough to follow. You fucked up our chance to get Deena out last night. If we'd called round with you there, you'd have been ringing your bloody cowbell for help."

"Deena Reid? Why?"

Jack pointed past Heath's shoulder.

"Tell him."

"Hello Clayton."

Heath turned to the voice and a shaggy figure in a combat jacket and tinted glasses came into the light.

"Kelvin? What the hell happened to you? Have you been out here all this time? You've been working in a scrapyard? Does Deena know you're here?"

Reid held up a hand for Heath to calm down.

"OK, take it easy. No, I don't work here. I came down when the shit hit the fan and Jack said they were bringing you in. I've been in touch with Deena on and off, but couldn't get to her. She's been a face in the cities for a while. But it was time to pull her out now that the big crunch is here. It's over for anyone left inside the city limit."

"What do you mean over?"

"This is the endgame. We can tap government communications pretty easily, and follow the plan."

Jack cleared his throat and with both their attention on him, waved them out of the door.

"Kelvin. Take him. Show him, if it'll do any good. Personally, I think you're wasting your time."

"OK. Thanks Jack."

Kelvin took Heath by the arm and led him back outside into the light as the group round the desk went back to their maps.

"Hey, don't mind Jack. He's lost a lot of people to the security state over the years. He just wanted to see what a fully paid up member of the fantasy factory looked like."

"Fantasy factory?"

"Yeah. The media. Disneyworld in suits? You spin the Global ID shit for the government."

Heath tried to smile.

"Oh you mean the TTPBs?"

"You learn nothing, do you? Look, the transnationals have been lobbying to change the definition of national citizenship for years. So that only microchipped sheep count as people, and even then they're just disposable employees. Everything and everyone else is going to be a wild animal to be hunted down."

Heath staggered down the steps into the yard.

"Is this what it's all about? Kelvin, we're in the middle of a national security event. It's action against terrorism, not action against you and me."

"False flags, Clayton. The terrorists are an invention of the state to provide a context for their agenda. They rely on useful idiots like you to propagate myths in the media and create a narrative that can be used to exterminate their enemies and justify the laws that keep people under their control."

Heath was feeling better all the time.

"You don't change. Isn't this the same shit you were pushing in college?"

Reid's shoulders drooped a little. He put a hand in Heath's chest to stop him and turned to the minders with a small apology in his voice.

"OK guys. I'll, er... look after him from here."

Reid led the way back into the building and the maze of reconstructed passageways and laboratories. Heath figured that the yard had been an old car park of a council building, since turned over to the demolition contractors. Noticeboards were still in position on the walls, signs spoke of council chambers and meeting rooms. As his nausea cleared, he could feel the questions rising in his mind.

"Why can't I hear the internet, Kelvin?"

"Your GLiD's down, like Jack said. Just temporarily, unless you er... want to rejoin the human race, that is?"

"They'll know I'm offline. They'll come for me."

"Actually, no they won't. Right now the Metropolitan datacentres are swapping out servers for a whole new set of clothes. There'll be big holes in the Global ID network for about twenty four hours. Kind of a bonus, really. For you, that is."

They turned into a room crowded with computer paraphernalia from years past. Bunches of old cables, carefully wound, hung in overlapping rows on pegboards. Piles of drives and old server chassis rose up from the floor. In a well-lit semicircular console near the middle of the chaos sat a young boy, maybe fifteen, with long, blond hair in a pony tail. He had an elaborate array of old flat screen 2D monitors around him. He took out an earpiece and pointed a finger at Reid.

"Hey Tinfoil, my man."

"Clayton. This is The_Gnome. He took the call from Abe Whiting at Nightship."

Heath shocked himself awake.

"Whiting? The Bolstrode thing? Your cat virus!"

Reid smiled.

"Yeah, I heard all about that. Old code. Totally useless. But proof if it was needed that they'll use anything and anyone to spin a story."

"I suppose you know I was due to meet him..."

The_Gnome interrupted.

"...before he was popped by the MI."

"Maybe. You're all very well informed, even for hackers."

Reid positioned Heath where he could see the big screen in front of the jumble on The_Gnome's desk.

"Better informed than you, my friend, if you think that Bolstrode was anything more than an excuse. Have we got that other little diversion?"

A feed from the Metropolitan came up on the screen and The_Gnome cued up Heath's last broadcast. It cut in toward the end.

"...the robots that build other robots that build the factories for yet other robots to manufacture our products are simply taking orders from the internet. The machines we sent out to protect our freedoms against the aggression of the eastern axis, now keep us safe at home..."

Reid was blowing air between his teeth like venting steam.

"Congratulations Clayton, you can't tell the difference between machines and people. Now that you're a little bit of both..."

The_Gnome turned up the volume.

"...the voice of protest today is just one man alone. He is known to you and me as The User. He is not the demon of your dreams, but a product of our age. He is one of us, a face in the crowd..."

The_Gnome and Reid looked at each other. The_Gnome spoke first.

"Doesn't he know?"

Reid smiled.

"He's probably the only one."

The_Gnome motioned Heath closer to the monitor and tapped around on his keyboard. Heath tried to revive his old confidence with a smart remark.

"You can't run to a lightboard then?"

The_Gnome kept tapping while he replied.

"You can't encrypt as you type on a lightboard. They only have one character set, the rest is done in the cloud. With the old-style analogue boards you can send it out end to end with no intercepts. Thought you'd know that. Tinfoil said you were at college together."

"Er... we only did the same courses for a short while."

The_Gnome nodded sagely.

"That's right. You went over to the dark side. OK. Come and meet The User."

The monitor blinked onto an encrypted carrier connection and a table of questions and topics appeared in the grid. The_Gnome highlighted one at random and a stream of text started to flow up the screen. It was cut into sentences and paragraphs, a rapid conversation with links and referrals, a picture or an illustration. Reid pushed Clayton in toward it, encouraging him to read.

"Welcome to the darknet."

The topic on screen revolved around Secorp, a name Heath recognised from the news floor and something else called The Tin Man. He tried to read it as it scrolled up.

It was circular logic. Secorp needed a target to aim for, and they were willing to create it. The secret service needed a really big event to consolidate government support for their program and they used Secorp to make it happen.

The thread wound on. Comments interrupted comments, sometimes hysterical in tone, often with poor alternative spellings. Sometimes they were trailing off into something else before being brought back into line by the bold type of someone calling themselves an administrator.

Heath's eyes flicked down the separate posts. Next to the time and date, all the commenters were called US3R.

The_Gnome hit a button on the edge of the monitor.

"Let's hear it."

The sound faded up, an artificial voice speaking the words on the screen.

He opened a new tab and then another thread of conversation. A similar voice started to intone the message from the new US3R over the top.

"It's easy to do what you're told - especially when they are holding a gun to your head. It's comforting not to be terrified all the time, to just give in and accept somebody else's will."

There was footage of soldiers, somewhere out on the smoking, wrecked edges of a town dragging women and screaming children away from bodies that lay smouldering in the rubble. Snatches of music and voice over from video footage cut through and around the voices.

Another thread centred around digital news compositing. Footage of Sarion Dundas at a rally of ecstatic party faithful was, as Heath knew, a simple fake. It disturbed him to hear so much criticism on the commentary of something that they'd all been persuaded at the time was the right thing to do. It was created as a positive and necessary act of illustrating support and unity for the government.

"There is no appreciable difference between what you see and what you create! It's now just a matter of what you believe. The real war was a war of faith, and the losers were all the people who did what they were told."

It sounded somehow different, standing in a room with people who were only expected to believe the words of a television broadcast.

A small crowd of curious crew had heard the cacophony of robotic voices coming from The_Gnome's stockroom and pushed in to hear what was new. A couple of the little kids snuck to the front to look at Heath. Another thread opened and more voices piled in. It was an old video of a near riot as a union speaker laid into the smartly suited executives who sat impassionately in a row on a dais. Behind them was the giant slogan 'Progress!'.

"We're trying to stop the carnage, you fucking cretins! If idiots like you woke up to the destruction brought to us all by corporations like yours, you'd have been begging people like me to get you out of this mess years ago!"

It was getting difficult to hear individual voices, but Heath could see the point. The_Gnome turned it down to a background bubbling of noise and left it to Reid to explain.

"See Clayton, all those years ago when you thought you were so much smarter than the rest of us and quit science for opinion, you started to rely on other people for facts you weren't allowed to question. I've seen the broadcasts you've written and your cut and paste hit pieces. It's the same bullshit as the BBCE and every other alphabet mouthpiece, just rewritten by a different hack. They took your ego and made you look a fool. The internet you miss so badly is just the worthless mind control of the corporations who've claimed ownership of all the content. The real world has to find its way around on the back of a shitty signal between a comsat and a stockbroker's drug dealer. Well, I'm The User, he's The User, everyone in this room is The User. Anyone who gets onto a carrier is The User. The few millions left around the world who aren't plugged into a GLiD are The User! We're the virus that they want to contain and wipe out."

Heath held up a finger for quiet. Something was clearing in his mind, but it was fraught with confusion and conflict.

"Have you... talked to Samantha?"

Reid shrugged.

"Frequently."

"She never mentioned..."

"She wouldn't. Anything anyone says to you is recorded for later. Any current keywords shoots you to the top of the list for revision. She took one hell of a chance just coming to see you. Clayton, face it, only people like you, so heavily locked down and desensitized by the system, wouldn't have a clue what was really going on. Because ironically, it's you who makes the news. You are responsible for writing tomorrow's history. And it's all bullshit! Like all your pampered, preening colleagues, you're an overpaid stooge. A convincing patsy."

***

Heath ate a meal with the crew of the yard and their children in one of the abandoned offices. They sat round an old boardroom table on some office chairs and were served up a thick soup in bowls with chunks of bread. Bug pointed at the bowl with his spoon.

"Not your usual synthetic crap, eh Heath? This is real chicken, real vegetables."

Heath pushed it around. It did smell weird, but it was a long time since he'd had a meal and it felt good to eat, now that his system was returning to near normal.

His hosts gave the silent sulking Heath a crash course in news from the darknet. The northern uprising was not so much armed rebels overthrowing the forces of law and order, as families banding together to keep their homes and not be brought inside the city limit checkpoints. The snipers were an invention, as were the beheadings and the indiscriminate rape. As Heath was having confirmed, the falsification of the news began a lot higher up than the 'persuader' videos that he was helping to create. Those credits to an 'unnamed source' or the 'unconfirmed reports' around which he was building a case were only the sickly shadows of a much deeper and more compelling story. The intelligence reports from the field had never seen the outside of an office since they were created at the Ministry.

A network of resistance, however, was strung throughout the big city ghettos, reporting on conditions, manpower and security. From the factories and the farms, maintenance workers, cleaners and servants were using any terminal or device they could find to hop past the information firewalls and out onto the darknet. It was a constant flow of anonymous information that was reposted around the boards in the hope that it would be received before the monitoring services intercepted and deleted it.

A big topic among the Users was the next generation of machines. Automation had been creeping steadily forward year on year, but the feeling was that soon these machines would maintain and repair themselves, and then replicate spontaneously as required. Once the maintenance people were no longer needed, then the last links between man and machine would be gone. A new player would be in town.

"What's going to happen to Deena?"

Reid sat across the table staring into a mug of coffee.

"Some of the guys are going in again tonight. She's smart, she'll stay out of the way until we get her. As long as she doesn't board any trains."

"Oh. Does she have travel allowance?"

"Of course not. She wouldn't go voluntarily. It'd be a one way trip. But you can travel, of course. If you're convincing about your time off the grid, they'll have no way to fill in the missing hours. Once you're back online they'll be able to find you, though, so if you really insist on going back to the evil empire, it'll have to be soon."

Heath's mind was caught in the indecision. It was so much easier to think when Mimi was making the suggestions.

"I have no choice, if what you say is true. I need to talk to Samantha and I have to report in to my boss. "

Reid grunted.

"You need to have a long conversation with yourself first."

***

Heath rested that afternoon. The nausea had now passed but the headaches remained. He lay on the bed staring at the blank face of the GLiD. This was his passport, his currency, his identity. He started to realise how little was left without it. Almost as though he ceased to exist. He thought of his colleagues at the Metropolitan. An image of Isobel Prine passed across his stuttering mind.

He slept on and off for an hour before being awoken by Reid.

"You got to go, Clayton. There's news from down south at another reclamation depot. There seems to be some sort of factory shut down going on and folks are being questioned. They lost the signal to their man Hokey, and he never hangs up!"

Reid got Heath back into his reporter's coat.

"You're going to have to be OK to travel."

Heath was subdued.

"I feel like shit."

"Yeah, well, I wish it was all just guilt, but I reckon your body's taking a beating from that uncontrolled zapper in your head."

Reid took him to the main gates where the big trucks rolled in. It was getting darker, though here on the outskirts the sky didn't seem to have such a vicious film of purple.

"We've got you a lift as far as the city interchange. Lay low until your GLiD kicks in. Don't worry, it will. Oh, and er... I put you an Easter egg on there. You might want to thank me later."

"Hey Kelvin. That reminds me. When I was at Deena's I found an RFID drive printed into a photo. What was on it?"

Reid looked vaguely puzzled.

"No idea."

"It was in a picture of you at college with Mouser the cat."

"Man, that does sound like college days! Well, it won't be anything important. Just a back-up from some drive, probably. I made a lot of them."

Heath was disappointed.

"Yeah. Deena said. Thought it might be something relevant. Look, I'm sorry I screwed up your operation last night. Hope you get her out tonight."

"I hope *both* of you get out. You're crazy for going back. There's still a chance to break free out here. I can fix it."

"I may have compromised someone. I have to put it right if I can."

"Wow. A glimmer of humanity."

The driver dropped Heath a mile before the first checkpoint. It was the first warm night of the year and the haze over the distant city was a familiar, low deep maroon fog.

He waited at the side of the road, sat up against the sandbags that weighted down a sign that warned of authorisation required up ahead. A flood of army lorries passed on the road he'd just come down and all returned to silent night breezes for another hour.

Just as he felt that sleep was coming, a soft tone came from the GLiD in his hand. The screen showed a small green diode in the top corner, steadily blinking.

The Global ID logo faded up in pale blue and slowly icons started to populate the screen. Heath felt a rush of chemistry in his blood and the headache immediately started to fade.

14

"The government has ordered a temporary shutdown of all non-vital social services, including the distribution of home supplies, access to interactive social media television, and the movement of hospital patients from home care to clinics.

"The Ministry for Roads and Transport have insisted that trains and shuttle buses will continue to run and urge all passengers to comply with officials at stations to ensure that services continue to function.

"All air traffic has been grounded for a period of seventy two hours to allow necessary work on Air Traffic Control systems to be completed. The last charter flight out of British airspace flew members of the Royal household out to join the King and Queen and the Royal family at their retreat in Switzerland.

"The Ministry of Defence has denied an allegation from the back bench MP and former Prime Ministerial candidate, Mace Rebley, that the Ministry has colluded with the Prime Minister and his Cabinet to relocate abroad during the crisis under a special protection order from the secret services.

"The Prime Minister himself has said on several occasions that the entire governmental apparatus of Great Britain will remain in place in London to 'administer the needs of the country and if necessary to pass emergency legislation to protect our way of life.'"

Another squad of police were being issued with new taser sticks and small arms. The pistols were hi-mag signature pieces, locked to the individual GLiD, activated by the proximity of the hand chip and loaded with exploding tips. The rules were for discretionary fire. The officers spoke little to each other, strapping on the riot gear, stab-proof padding and ammunition pouches. They carried their helmets and taser sticks, shuffling into lines and boarding the armoured personnel carriers.

Once out on the road they sat in communal silence, listening to their own personal orders whispered into their ears. Their grim feelings of foreboding for what they were about to do were regulated by the GLiD's tiny pulsings to the brain and the constant repetition of keywords in the orders. The robotic whisperings subconsciously triggered their conditioning programs that had been fed to them during the last sleep break. Even that wouldn't be enough for the day ahead and before they had reached the drop points, a signal was sent to all personnel. They reached into the first aid pouches on their knee pockets and took out plastic ampoules. Over the next minute each man snapped the top, inserted it as far into a nostril as needed to form a seal and then inhaled the contents vigorously.

As the ramp of the APC was lowered, the police squad filed out, black visors on the helmets now hiding any expression that was left, and they sprang into lines, ready to follow the orders as they were broadcast.

* * *

The Metropolitan building was in turmoil, the internet still partial and highly unreliable. Since halfway through the night shift, whole floors of the building had been plunging into darkness. Systems were resetting, then power was restored and employees sat frozen with the lack of orders from their rebooting GLiDs. Only the broadcast floors and live studios had kept power throughout. They were buoyed up by the emergency generators and a major concentration of security staff and engineers. They had no control over the internet which continued to stutter and freeze, adding drama to the emergency broadcasts that showed on the big screens across the cities. Sometimes, when a main city square was blacked out and all around was darkness, the only light was from the screen. It was sixty feet wide and high up on the side of a building, fed by the council's promise to maintain its power in every crisis. People could see it from their apartments and dormitories, patrols stopped to gaze up through the fine drizzle as the calm, synthetic delivery of the news holograms was betrayed by the freezing and stuttering of reception. The broadcasters repeated urging for everyone to remain calm could take several minutes to jerk its way through the static. Cycling colours of a broken transmission and the occasional notices would coldly announce that the feed could not be found.

By daybreak the power was restored at the Metropolitan and the confusion was multiplied by the new shift, dribbling in late from the sporadic transport that was still running out in the streets. Tensions were high as the expectation of instant information was no longer there. Colleagues had to be sought out and spoken to, lists had to be hand written on a text document or made with anything that came to hand now that pens were no longer around. Meeting deadlines passed in the confusion of sparsely populated conference areas, and the work of the day was never started.

Harry barged through the corridors of the editorial floors, shoving the meandering crowd aside. In his fury he commandeered a lift, pushing everybody out just so he didn't have to listen to the idiotic questions

159

and lack of decision from near useless minions. He kept his hand near the emergency stop button in case the programming in the lift started to fail. He was not going to get caught between two floors and, if necessary, would cancel the ride and try and find the stairs.

The lift made it and Harry found himself up in the special operations area, above even the senior editing suites. His GLiD was unlocking doors for him as he went and once inside the short corridor to a silent and highly confidential meeting room, he took out the handset and watched the security status changing on its face. It was showing the highest corporate security clearance that the Metropolitan could provide.

In the meeting room was a representative from Compliance, along with a legal adviser and Harry's two Asian hit men from the graphics division.

"Aren't we being joined by a director?"

Harry had almost named Verrick, but checked himself at the last moment. The suit from Legal was unmoved by the question.

"At this stage we are simply confirming the situation. When we are in agreement it can be escalated."

Harry took a seat opposite the unsmiling Asians.

"I see. Dirty work first."

The woman from Compliance cricked her neck slightly as though uncomfortable with Harry's informality. Her voice was suitably cold.

"I think we'd all be happier if you'd kept our suspect closer to home. Building a case against him before he has been apprehended is hardly watertight."

Harry could afford to be positive and almost smiled.

"We have him. That is, he's back on the grid. He came back up sometime before dawn, not far from his last known meeting. We've already fast tracked his transport and as soon as it picks him up he'll be on his way back in. He suspects nothing."

"Make sure he doesn't. What we have here should be comprehensive enough for our purposes, especially when you have forwarded to us the transcripts of his latest interactions."

"I understand. I think you'll be satisfied with what you see."

Harry looked to the compositors.

"Could you run the security video, please?"

One of the comps pulled up a lightboard and from the dark projection circle in the middle of the table came a rotating hologram of a busy station scene. Harry narrated as the crowds were pulled and pushed by the Enforcement Officers into lines.

"A week ago. The day that he began his promotion to Editorial. At the first opportunity, he deliberately cancelled out his taxi upgrade to ride a second class train in to work. Seemed to choose a particular station and, well... you'll see why. It took us a couple of days to requisition the CCTV, but you can see him coming onto the platform and heading through the passengers to a location where we now know he was due to meet his contact.

As you can see, it's some serious low life, nobody that a person in his position would normally ever want to deal with. It's no doubt a disposable courier that the real contacts will remove to cover their tracks. They exchange a few words and then it's here that you see him pass something over."

The suit from Legal was having trouble seeing exactly what it was.

"Do you have that any clearer? Can we tell unequivocally what it was?"

Harry motioned to the comp.

"Yeah. If we look at it from another angle it becomes quite clear."

The video changed to a different camera and between the milling bodies, and as the footage zoomed in, what appeared to be the hand of Clayton Heath could clearly be seen passing a GLiD to the small white hand of the girl.

"Being state transport CCTV imagery, we're clear in the courts from any accusation of creating it from scratch. We had to, er... enhance it a little to make it clearer, but now you can see there's no doubt. We think that he's the source of the previous generation handsets that have been going missing over a period of time and been channelled into the hands of terrorists. In this case, moving him from his previous role seems to have led him to be careless."

Compliance and Legal looked at each other. Compliance spoke first.

"If this is what it looks like and the GLiD archives back up his location at the time, then there is ample evidence just from this footage to take action."

Harry was happy.

"Oh, I think you'll find this is just the tipping point. Once the systems are back up we'll be helping the police to take his apartment to pieces. We have most of the transcripts from his interactions right up to yesterday's shutdown fiasco. We just need to build a case from the results. It's open and shut really."

Compliance was keen to proceed.

"We need him to be under arrest immediately or this situation is not fully contained. I suggest a police escort to bring him in."

Legal set down his GLiD on the table, documents disappearing into nothing as he did so. He squinted into the looping hologram where the girl was slipping the handset beneath her clothes.

"Bring him in alive? If he has time to make a statement that is contrary to the evidence, it would lead to major delays in bringing any case to a hearing and beyond that to a satisfactory resolution. Something which, under the present chaotic circumstances would not serve. The cause of the problem, as I understand it, needs to be resolved at the same time as the problem itself."

He looked briefly at Harry.

"*That* would be an open and shut case."

Harry came back straight away, cueing the comps with a waved finger.

"We have anticipated that. This will be the breaking report. We're keeping it until a point where we need to stop delivering bad news and start to turn the tide by making people feel positive about the future."

The screen came up and a synthetic newscaster appeared in front of a picture of Heath taken from the personnel records. They listened to the blank, emotionless delivery.

"In a statement just released by the office of the West Midlands' Chief Constable, armed officers have arrested a journalist from the Metropolitan News Service. It is in connection with the cyber terror attacks that have crippled services and brought misery to people all across the country. In an unusual move, the arrested man has been named as junior sub-editor, Clayton Heath, a recently promoted research journalist. He was detained after a special Home Office warrant was issued in conjunction with the special privileges granted under the Emergency Powers Act. At this point there is no statement of the exact charges that have been brought against Clayton Heath. But, the Metropolitan understands from unnamed sources that recent broadcasts, written by him, may have been used as a covert recruiting tool and springboard for the cyber attacks that are still rocking the country. Heath, a failed computer technology graduate with a history of running foul of authorities and colleagues, managed to join the Metropolitan six years ago as a researcher. More on this breaking news in the main bulletin on the hour."

Harry leaned in.

"Of course, if Heath were to, er... make a break for it, his termination would be ample proof of guilt. No?"

All eyes were on Legal now. He gathered the handset and slid it into his jacket pocket.

"We may need this to be put out sooner rather than later. I hope the main bulletin is already prepared and with Broadcast."

"It is being approved now, along with the web story and support."

Legal was on his feet and Compliance swiftly followed.

"I think you'll find it's going to be run very soon."

***

Isobel Prine had handed over her keys to Data Security and Compliance shortly after the brown outs and breakdowns started to dog the Metropolitan building.

Within minutes she had been brought into a security office to be questioned by a Compliance team. She was wide-eyed with bafflement.

"I have absolutely no idea! I mean, I'd been asking for project assignment for the whole week, that's a fact. I didn't think that was unreasonable as Heath and me had been on the same team for years. He told me over and over it wouldn't be happening without an official team formation. Of course, that's the rules, so I knew that..."

The Compliance Officer looked up from the report sheet hovering in the air before him.

"But you still gave him a key to your project area?"

Isobel kept holding her breath.

"Well, I thought it would just remind him to include me when the time came. It's like a calling card, you know?"

Compliance wasn't impressed.

"No. Not really. Records clearly show that a data transfer was made last night, and yet this morning there is nothing in your diplomatic bag. How do you explain that?"

"Maybe it was interrupted in the power cuts? Or the server drive was brought down."

"There were no power cuts at that time. But I grant you there may be issues with servers at this time. *Temporary* issues with servers."

Isobel was turning quite pink in the cheeks. Compliance checked a small graph jittering in real time at the side of his report sheet.

"Miss Prine, could you please breathe normally. Contrary to the myths on the news floor, holding your breath will not impact on the results of a lie detector."

She exhaled quickly, trying to make it look like a puff of disgust.

"I was not holding my breath! But I do kind of start to hyperventilate a little when I am being bullied and accused of..."

"You're not being bullied, Miss Prine. This is a simple question and

163

answer session and I would like you to calm down and co-operate with a serious investigation."

"Well, I will if I just know what it's about."

She held her breath again.

"Miss Prine. Whatever the data was, and according to the transfer record it was substantial, it seemed to disappear during the exact same time that the Metropolitan's own monitoring service was taken offline. That's a coincidence."

Isobel nodded.

"That is a coincidence!"

"Please don't hold your breath, Miss Prine."

"Well if I'm nervous, and it makes no difference anyway, why can't I..."

"At this point I have to inform you that if there is anything you know that you are not telling us, when we find out it will not only seriously impact on your career, but under the unfolding circumstances may also become a police matter under aiding and abetting the execution of terrorism."

Isobel exhaled violently again.

"Terrorism! That's crazy."

"That's a fact. You will be called in again during your next shift, or if there are further developments, during your downtime. Transport may be sent for you. Please be ready. OK. That's all."

The Compliance officer closed out his screen and waved her away.

She stood up and another member of the team held the door for her. He smiled sympathetically as he nodded to the half-lit corridors beyond and the milling technicians.

"Don't worry. We'll be back to normal soon."

She looked at him with big eyes.

"Yeah? Don't hold your breath!"

***

As the small jet broke the cover of the clouds, the pilot spoke to his passenger through the intercom.

"We are now in Swiss airspace and will shortly be entering a holding pattern above Geneva Airport. Estimated time of arrival and landing is twenty five minutes. Weather is overcast but clearing with a temperature of thirteen point one Celsius."

Andrew Verrick touched the button display along the bezel of the porthole and the glass turned from a foggy grey to clear. Through the haze he could see the retreating shapes of the French mountains and far below the dark blot of Lake Geneva appearing on the horizon. He dabbed the button again hard and the glass faded back to an inky black. In front of him was a large executive desk with a hovering array of screens stacked in a fan for him to select. His line to Nightship Systems was reporting on the commissioning of new servers at the nation's datacentres. A video feed showed units being removed from a corridor of racks and deliberately smashed into a recycling caddy. The new racks were a cool, shiny black front panel adorned with the Global Identification logo. As they were powered up a steadily blinking green diode appeared. Down the side of the feed an overlaid map with constantly changing waterfalls of numbers updated and changed shape.

Verrick brought up the raw news footage from the Metropolitan editing suites as it was coming in. As usual, when there was high drama to broadcast and the effects were designed to be emotionally, rather than intelligently experienced, the screen was being cut into several feeds with multiple commentaries to choose from. It was untreated video and would be heavily augmented with 3D when it could be fitted into the narrative. A helicopter view showed the barricaded streets packed with crowds being herded forward by police lines. The central core of people were pushing forward while the fringes were busy with scattered figures trying to climb the shuttering and wriggling on the razor wire as police caught them with taser sticks. Within the broken drone of helicopter blades, the megaphones on the watch towers urged people on to the ramps that led down to waiting carriages at the station. Another feed showed an interior of a gutted factory that had been painted up white with large colour coded squares high up on the walls. Down below, the herd were filling sectioned off pens that narrowed into turnstiles. From the gantries, technicians in masks were regulating a flow of air conditioning down onto the crowd adjusting a mix of the sedative and soporific Sordax into the tubes slung from the ceiling. Young adults and parents clung with their gaunt elderly family members, but frightened faces fell into step at the command of the tannoy. They shuffled past black clad and helmeted lines of commandos in full gas masks.

Through the turnstiles, the families were clinically, and sometimes tearfully, separated into individual bodies with cards and papers, then ushered through the plastic ribbon sheeting into a bright white corridor of overlit cubicles. Each was manned by masked angels with brilliant gowns and white rubber gloves, who took the dazed and compliant citizens toward a heavily reinforced chair with a head plate and straps.

Verrick had seen enough of miserable rabble in the rough adaptations of the old meat processing plants, though he felt a thrill of power in witnessing subjugation backed by the threat of slaughter. Sometimes, he was repulsed by the hordes of dirty mindless biomass, and only the visions of twentieth century concentration camps with their silent footage of bulldozed bodies could calm his anger. In more personal moments he favoured the corruption and submission of somebody young and frightened, extracted from the herd to be brought before him, cleaned and prepared, and utterly helpless.

As his mind drifted back to the screens, he brought up an altogether different vision. Watermarked with Dreemfeelds in one corner, the sparkling, oversaturated video capture showed Clayton Heath, bedecked in ludicrous gold chains and ingots, or affected in a wide brimmed hat that tilted over one eye. He watched himself, robed in white against a marbled hall, an incongruous jumble of classical antiquity and movie star trash culture. He was, of course, being pleasured by a group of slender young women in their fashionable strips of revealing clothing, faces flawlessly painted and hair in elaborate designs. Around him were the open beaches and hot blue skies of an endless tropical paradise. He was instantly changing locations or partners as his mind flickered between possibilities. There would be grand fireplaces in baronial halls and then the deck of a luxurious yacht.

Verrick was disgusted. The fantasies of immaturity were the legacy of this great technology. The only redeeming feature was that underlings could be so easily kept in their place with just the promises of infantile pornographic gratification. As long as they thought no further outside their stereotyped twitchings, they could never question what was being done to them or how they were being used. Verrick did pause the Dreemfeeld for a moment once the scene had instantly become the news floor of the Metropolitan building and Heath was greedily stripping the figure of a young journalist. He was pushing her back on the desk and hiking her skirt and running his tongue up the inside of her cocked leg as she pointed her naked toes into the air. Verrick finally smiled.

***

The television had come on automatically after the latest power cut and was beaming out from the wall of the tiny living room. The Metropolitan, The BBCE and SkyGlobal were all filling the channels with exuberant news of the joyful fight back against terrorism by the

166

ordinary people of the country as they queued in their thousands to take up Global ID. They swapped footage of interviewees who were all in agreement that the time had come to patriotically get behind the government, that they had been reassured by friends and family who had already made the transition, that the fantastic rewards on offer were just too good to miss. The footage showed orderly queues of smiling adults, waving to the camera as it dollied past the lines, accompanied by swirling triumphant music. Even the holographic newsreaders had fixed grins and the twinkle of a digital tear in their eyes.

Isobel Prine barely noticed any of it. Her mind was troubled by the turn of events overnight. Yet another fire drill that guided the staff into exit positions. Then came more power cuts, whole floors blinking out, emergency lighting fading up in a gloomy blue. There was another momentary loss of identity through the stumbling internet. Shortly after, came a notice from Security that the datacentres were coming back online. All information traffic, professional and personal, would have to be scanned and reviewed before release back to the workstations. It was a bit of luck.

She took one last look out of her apartment window at the spreading green landscape of Cannon Hill Park. Jeeps in the far distance, like black ants busied at the outer rim of their territory. They meandered around guard towers and disappeared out toward the barricades.

She waved a hand at the screen and the sound died back to a bare murmur. A small wall mounted bookshelf held the paraphernalia of childhood, a photograph of parents and mementos of the past. She slid out a diminutive old tablet computer, the white plastic yellowing where the edges had caught the daylight. She took a small slate, half the size of an old credit card, from the top pocket of her jacket and laid them both on the low coffee table. She sat on her sofa and faced the pictures on the television. It seemed to be showing an old new year's eve celebration with cheering crowds and fireworks as they welcomed the time to come. Prine made a mild swatting motion with her palm and the television dimmed to standby, replaced by a small red Metropolitan globe standing out from the wall and slowly revolving.

The old tablet was manually operated and she glanced her fingers over the slowly booting device trying to find the projection slider and then the local link protocol. Eventually, it worked. The maximum resolution of the projection that appeared above the tablet's face gave her a sickly off white panel somewhere over eighteen inches wide and a foot high. A message was simply stated in the middle of the screen. No connection to the internet can be found. She slipped the slate onto the surface and let four corners of light locate it on the tablet. New controls appeared and she accessed the drive.

For an hour she scanned the contents. There were movies, old internet television documentaries, texts of scanned books and news footage from many years ago in a blurry, two dimensional delivery. The documents talked of things she'd never heard about, like regional wars in Africa and the Middle East that were fought over broken trade agreements and the issuance of international loans. There were ideas that America had once sought to push east to the borders of Russia and China using European integration as a platform for covert aggression. It wasn't the history that was broadcast on television today. She read about the American CIA using proxy armies to try and topple foreign regimes. There was a convoluted documentary about a cartel of private banks funding terrorism through the City of London. She followed the file links to a batch of documents and memos about a place called Porton Down and another called Fort Detrick. They seemed to be discussing the use of biological warfare to induce crisis that would tip the balance in time of war. From there, she stumbled into a trove of documents that had been ripped from servers, scanned, screen grabbed and resurrected from basic text. She was looking at alphabetical lists of military projects, inception dates and annotations. There were thousands of operation names, collected under subheadings and their degree of national security classification. With curiosity bounding she scrolled through the lists and finally searched for the latest inception dates. It took her to a place in the table called Random Snow. She glanced up the list at the annotations, dead links to departments and personnel, enigmatic locations and titbits of description. She looked down the list again at the nondescript names. Random Scope, Search, Seed, Sentry, Shock, Signal, Silence and Sister. Only one entry had no links and an above top secret classification. It was called Random Skies.

She returned to the root of the drive and dug into a new vein of documents. Transcriptions of police scanner data, voice communications, GPS locations, lists of people's names in columns for detention or transport. It slowly dawned on Prine that there was enough information on the drive to keep her entertained and intrigued for weeks, maybe months. As she shut down the tablet, she thanked her good fortune that journalistic instinct had caused her to copy the upload at her desk as soon as she accessed the root and realised the nature of the material. OK, all the journalists had illegal external drives, it was just the way it was when you wanted to protect your crumbs of information. But, this time, when the internet first went down and panic began on the news floor, she saw a chance and killed the data in her file cache, preventing propagation to the official Metropolitan backups. With her heart beating wildly, she convinced herself it was the perfect crime and, by the time the internet came back up, the slate was in her pocket and she could deny all knowledge of the original download. The big question that occupied her mind was, why would Heath send her banned, and what looked like classified, material when possession of such would probably terminate both their careers? He had some explaining to do.

***

Clayton Heath was walking toward the noise of the crowd in the rubble of a south Birmingham suburb. He had a travel certificate for a train into the central compound where he was due to meet his taxi that would take him in to the Metropolitan. He was spotted a way off by a contractor in full battle dress with a scanner clipped to the side of his automatic rifle.

"Hey you! Heath! Get over here now."

The voice had a thick American accent. In reply, Heath waved an arm and weaved his way around the piles of reclamation and the mountain of concrete waste to approach the gunman. He kept his hands out of his pockets as he got up close.

"Have you read my ticket? I need the next train in to Central."

The gunman was unmoved.

"You're in a restricted area. You got a ticket for that, too?"

"I came in at the checkpoint a mile or so back. No one said anything about restricted areas. Just read me and let me through."

"Yeah, well that's your pussy-ass British army. Where you coming in from?"

Heath was losing patience.

"That's none of your fucking business. I'm a Metropolitan employee and that's all you need to know. Now, where's my train?"

The gunman stood frozen for a moment, considering his next move.

"Well?"

Finally, the contractor heard a word in his ear and shifted his position to point further on.

"You picked a hell of a time to be wandering in the redev. Follow round to that shuttering where the dozers are parked up. I'm passing you on to the controllers in the run. They'll get you to the train."

It was only when the crowd noise had grown in size to that of a near riot that Heath was struck by the jittering paranoia of the American contractor that he left prowling in the rubble. As he came into view of the crowd controllers at the top of the fifteen foot barricades, they waved him on with the barrels of machine pistols. He joined the station concourse overlooking the street below.

The crowd were a ragbag of unemployed from the social housing dormitories, shift workers still in their yellow safety vests and ID bracelets, or old people stumbling in the drifting tide. They were being herded into the railway station. Those on the inside of the crowd moving slowly and unwillingly on. At the outer edges, the younger fitter men were trying to push back against the UN troops who barked their orders through megaphones. When contact became inevitable, the taser sticks flashed and tempers on all sides grew a little shorter.

Heath was marched along the parapet to enter the station with a guard, having established that there was a particular seat already booked in his name on the next train out. He kept one eye on the growing dissent down below. The disturbance flared into direct conflict as a taser stick was pulled into the crowd and the soldier with it. For a moment it sounded like the cry of victory, but without further warning the crack of automatic weapons rang out and the shouts turned to screams as a swathe of bodies fell back in the crowd.

Heath was open-mouthed with shock. Taser sticks had always been enough in the past. Something else seemed to be driving the frenzy amongst the population. As he reached the steps down onto the platforms he looked to the back of the human tide and could see in the distance a massive crowd control truck bringing up the rear. It had deployed a square metal dish above the personnel compartment, giving it the appearance of a giant green grey peacock with a solid convex parabola for a tail. The crowd were being pushed forward by the microwave emissions from the truck's dish that threatened to incinerate any who hung around within range for too long.

In the darkness under the station roof Heath was urged along the platform by his guard. Across the tracks was the familiar sight of Enforcement Officers separating the passengers into lines. One of the screens high on the gantry between the stairwells and motionless escalators was flashing simple black words on a white background. Phrases that had once also been distributed during drills, on cards and in phone text messages, had now taken on the mantle of stark orders: LINE UP, BOARD CARRIAGES, STAY CALM. It was the same drill he'd heard a thousand times before, when passengers groaned with tiresome necessity and drew on their reserves of wartime patience. But now the situation was undoubtedly for real.

Panicking people were spilling onto the platforms too quickly to be processed. There was, at first, unease amongst the officers as they tried to coordinate with the troops herding the cattle forward. People were pushing barriers out of the way and jumping down onto the tracks, thinking that this might be a way out. A contingent of soldiers appeared and in the few seconds it took them to realise that there would be nowhere to put the overflow, they opened fire and bodies twitched and folded up, falling across the tracks. The crowd screamed and pulled away from the edge as Heath's guard hurriedly pushed him on beyond the unfolding chaos.

Turning into a tunnel toward the north bound platforms, Heath could just about hear Mimi in his ear. She was telling him about voicemail that was finally being forwarded from the Metropolitan servers. Heath's adrenalin was pumping, his mind racing forward with the unfolding story and the conflict in his mind. He was barely listening to her as she reminded him of the calls that had been listed as urgent. Harry Toliver, Isobel Prine, Samantha Wilshire were all names that registered as vital to contact. Did he want to hear them? In his impatience, Heath found himself shouting to be heard above the tannoy and the rolling echo of the riot some way back.

"Reply to all. Calls acknowledged. I'm waiting for transport. Will respond in due course!"

Up ahead was a short train on an empty platform, fully lit and waiting for passengers. The guard waved him forward.

"Wait at the barrier. There's a delay on the pings, but it'll pass you through in a couple of minutes. Front carriage!"

The guard was getting further orders.

"Looks like you're an important guy! Leaves as soon as you're aboard. You've got a whole train to yourself!"

Heath waited at the barrier watching the lights on the turnstile. His ear caught the sound of heavy machinery deep in the station as box cars moved forward into position, doors rolling back. Along the opposite platform a team of soldiers were pushing big black plastic coffins toward the tunnel. High above in the roof space, a huge television screen for waiting passengers was broadcasting public service announcements.

He stood waiting for the turnstile and studied his GLiD. He was about to reply to Isobel Prine when another message was forwarded from

Samantha. On an impulse, he took it and her voice cut in straight away.

"...been recalled to CSI with no further details. Clayton, you're being invited to a very special party. Suggest you make a long detour if you don't want to end up late like my dinner guest. I can meet up with you and our mutual friends at your last destination when the trains are back to normal. Watch the news for details."

The voice disappeared and left Heath with a series of chopped up phrases going through his mind and not much to connect them. Then his eye caught the television screen. It was now showing footage of another station in another town. It was the unmistakeable pulsing autofocus of a CCTV feed boring into the heaving platform and highlighting a familiar figure in a long, dark coat. Heath recognised himself, a somewhat smarter and more focused figure from another time. The CCTV started to slowmo and a helpful red circle showed Heath's hand sliding a handset to the elfin girl he briefly remembered. His picture appeared in a side window like a police mugshot. It had been digitally altered to make him look ugly, blank and psychotic, like the many targets he'd requested to be 'treated' in his own stories. He couldn't hear the commentary above the station noise.

"Mimi. Give me the audio from the Metropolitan newsfeed."

The sound connected to his ear.

"...seen as the results of his handiwork plunged the travel system into disarray. His arrest at the station came moments after a police officer was shot dead in the course of his duty. Even before this crisis is resolved, questions are already being asked about how a disgruntled employee and failed computer graduate could get away with terrorist activities in such a controlled environment as a national news broadcasting network. Given the amount of pieces he wrote about cyber terrorism and public enemy number one, The User, questions must be asked. Was he effectively given too much freedom to misinform both the public and his employers about the depths of his involvement with the criminal underworld? Was he so brazen and so overconfident that he felt he could implicate himself to the entire viewing public and get away with it?"

The pictures had changed back to the documentary that Heath had made. His grotesquely altered picture was superimposed on the screen with a quote: 'He is The User. He is the demon of your dreams. He is one of us, a face in the crowd. He may be someone close to you. You may be looking at him now.'

A crisis moment swept over Heath's mind. It was a mistake. It was part of the shutdown problems, it was a bad dream. It was anything but true. Mimi was speaking quietly into his ear.

"Clayton. Stay here and wait for the Enforcement Officers to guide you safely onto the train. Place the handset in your pocket and hold out your hands. Do not move when they approach."

Heath dropped the GLiD into his pocket, eyes barely moving from the screen that had frozen his picture and put up his name fifteen feet wide in the air above the platform. A thousand thoughts dropped into his mind. A sort of dull sickness rose in his stomach as the words of Kelvin Reid came back to him. '...you thought you were so much smarter than the rest of us... you started to rely on other people for facts you weren't allowed to question. I've seen the broadcasts you've written and your cut and paste hit pieces. It's the same bullshit as the BBCE and every other alphabet mouthpiece... ironically, it's you who makes the news. You are responsible for writing tomorrow's history. And it's all bullshit. Like your pampered, preening colleagues, you're an overpaid stooge. A convincing patsy.'

Mimi kept cutting in over his thoughts.

"Stay calm, Clayton. Don't move. Wait for help."

Samantha's voicemail rang out in his mind, '...suggest you make a long detour if you don't want to end up late like my dinner guest.'

She was talking about Whiting and Whiting was dead. The picture was finally becoming clear.

Heath swung his head round, blood thumping in his ears and sickness rising from his stomach to his eyeballs. From the far end of the platform he could see the Enforcement Officers being routed back through the platform tunnels toward the increasing clamour of the crowd. A ragged figure came skidding round the corner, running in his direction. In an echo of gunfire the running man pitched forward and sprawled on the concrete leaving Heath in the line of fire from a contractor's raised rifle.

They looked at each other for a moment, the gunman caught between the sight of Heath at the turnstile and his face high up on the television screen.

"Don't move, Heath! You're under arrest."

Heath raised his hands in the air, hardly breathing, as gunfire sounded in the tunnels and a mob broke through at the far end of the platform. The contractor swung round and opened up at random. Heath ignored Mimi's calm demands for him to stay with his hands raised and when he noticed that the lights were green and his personnel picture had appeared on the turnstile screen, he pushed through and ran for the train. The door seals relaxed and as they slid apart, Heath ran into the empty train. Back on the platform, an automatic rifle had been taken from a fallen soldier and in the confusion and carnage, escaping citizens were trying to force the doors of the other carriages. Bullets shattered windows and allowed others to dive head first through onto the train.

The doors shut behind Heath and the train's program made an automated announcement through the tannoy, half lost in the gunfire and screams. The carriages started to move, swaying and bumping into a rhythm as the platform started to slide by. Heath stayed in a front seat, head well down as a window shattered somewhere close by sending cubes of glass skittering down the aisle. He felt the darkness of a tunnel dimming the carriage, pocked with the muzzle flashes of automatic weapons further down the train. He nodded his head upwards during a break in the noise and caught sight of a soldier's full face helmet looking at him through the dividing windows between the carriages. This was the only Global ID carriage so there was no connecting door to the rest of the train. If Heath was a marked man, then his stalker would have to shoot out the windows and climb across the carriage links or wait until an emergency call brought them to a halt.

As the train started to pick up speed through the outside rail yard, Heath felt a buffeting wind in his face and caught the chatter of the train on the track over the retreating gunfire. He dodged his head up again and saw the visors of soldiers in the next carriage. Clearly the opposition was gone. In a mad moment he saw the blown out window across the aisle and as the train started its characteristic whine of acceleration he stood up, scrambled over the seat and launched himself out through the disintegrating glass.

15

"The act being passed in this chamber is an acknowledgement of the right of the state to take custody of all people and all property into a trust for the benefit of another because some event, state of affairs or condition has prevented them from claiming their status as living, competent and present before a registered authority. The state thus becomes a trustee of all lands, property and goods until such time as a person comes forth to reclaim those titles and is thus recompensed by the state.

"The identity of a person is that which has been created and owned by the government and represents a share of the state's total assets. The identity itself is a legal construct represented by the name, number and unique characteristics of a Global Identity certification, wholly and only comprised of the legal concepts contained within the requirements of a Global Identity registration.

"Claim upon the goods held in trust is to be made by representation to the court's authorities in lieu of the state, by a Globally Identified person and no other, these other being considered legally dead and lost beyond the reach of the State.

"Upon successful petition to the courts, a Beneficiary is declared and the title of goods held in trust is granted to that Beneficiary. The trust, transferred by virtue of decree is thus a temporary and not permanent trust entitling the Beneficiary only to equitable title and use of the goods, rather than legal title and therefore ownership of the goods. The trust remains within the Court's judgement for the duration of the Beneficiary's life or until the necessary future sequestration of the goods by an act of the State.

"Wherein all Global Identity is certified legal within Corporate City States, underwritten by the Crown Capital City of London Corporation, otherwise known as the Crown Corporation, the person so identified shall present their status as living and their claim upon the benefit of lands, properties and goods held in trust by the state.

"That this right of the state should take effect from this day forth, pertaining to those persons already Globally Identified and during the lifetime of the Globally Identified person, and those who formally petition to be Globally Identified hereafter, and to those who will be inducted naturally into the Global Identification system from birth.

"In passing this Act through the chamber, it is acknowledged that all goods held in trust are private trusts or Fide Commissary Trusts administered by commissioners, which may be private corporations

Dovi Abarlev looked out of the fourteenth floor window and down onto the intersection of roads below. Between the colourful red rooves of the trams, taxis linked and wound behind a mix of limousines and delivery wagons. A hot spring sun was burning off the cloud and the breath of warmer weather blew through the streets of Basel.

"Your meeting room is prepared. Guests are arriving."

Abarlev turned to face Schakt, the banker.

"Thank you, Ephraim. When they are all here, I would like you to sit in please."

"Of course."

Schakt nodded his head in a reflexive bow and left the room. Abarlev looked around at the decor in his new office. A curious mix of walnut antique and the new post war frameless glass technology that burst into form through interactions of light and sound. He felt as though he was straddling the old and the new like a bridge that would guide the human flow into the future. He had offices in London, New York, Tel Aviv and Moscow, but somehow a place in the capital of the emerging new world was especially satisfying.

The meeting room was carefully preserved in the guise of its original purpose in the nineteen thirties. The long, slim boardroom table was built to seat many more people than Abarlev's meeting. There would have been heads of new and old central banks around the world coming together to co-ordinate their countries' aims and their places in a global technocratic future. With their advisers and aides excused, the capstones of individual pyramids of power would form a layer of something much bigger, a new interlocked foundation for what was to come.

Abarlev waited until the guests were seated and the tall double doors had been quietly closed behind them. He sat at the head of the table and addressed the familiar faces now waiting on his pronouncements.

"Welcome, my friends, to this final meeting of the Quorum Group. It has been solely through the agreements of the people in this room that the events unfolding in Britain could take place at all. The conclusion

176

of our business will form the basis of a roadmap for the other failing states of Europe and the future rebuilding of the greater continents around the world. We have conquered and so we must now consolidate.

"In Britain, right now, the purging of the system is underway. Under the cover of the Emergency Powers Act, new laws are being swiftly implemented in the parliamentary houses that will soon allow us to assess the full and final extent of available and required manpower and resources. The City of London is preparing a new Domesday Book, if you will, to ascertain the potential revenue of a fully audited population. This isolated island nation is, once again, to be a microcosm of the wider world. The first industrial revolution was aproof of concept. The success of this second revolution will turn it into a proving ground for further projects. But that will be addressed by other groups. Our work is almost done and we will be moving on. Mister Verrick has coordinated the media coverage of the unfolding events with the other broadcast media in Britain and I hope that when the time comes he will be able to count on all our support for a new role as the chairman of the Metropolitan service."

Verrick smiled and nodded his approval, feeling he might add a little more to his CV.

"Thank you, Dovi. I came here via Geneva following a meeting with our President. Until such time as it becomes prudent to step in, it is generally agreed that my current role is most beneficial to the ongoing operation, where I can oversee the tying up of loose ends. But I'm sure I shall be... passing the hat round in future, soliciting votes."

"Indeed, Andrew. There is some degree of realignment to take place. For instance, the question has already been raised about the legality of the forced relocations. In order to curtail any awkward investigations into the possibly heavy handed administration of the public at this time, there will be changes of leadership and also the identity of some of the mercenary forces employed on the ground. We are also able to invoke international security laws to classify much of the military action undertaken by the United Nations on behalf of the British Services. There is a separate legal process for the imminent removal of political opposition to the new framework, which I'm told has quickly passed through the Royal Courts and been acknowledged by the respective Ministries. We need not concern ourselves with that here. It is the primary function of General Rishek to marry the political and military agendas of the British leadership into a cohesive and functioning engine."

Rishek sat stone faced. They all understood the function of the hatchet man. Abarlev relaxed a little.

"For my part, I expect to encompass further duties, positioned primarily here in Switzerland. The company we called Secorp will disappear back into the imagination from whence it came and gradually all traces of its record in Random Sentry will be erased. It will be important for the future to see that the steps we have taken were based on a solid and unswerving logic that history will find glorious and beautiful, and that any opposition was never going to be effective."

There were sage nods around the table.

Schakt half raised his hand, dithering with a question that became a statement.

"Er, talking of opposition, there are no projections for the time and cost of dealing with the dissenting public."

Abarlev tried to look as though he was considering, but he had no more time for diplomacy.

"The audit will reflect that we have acquired as many as possible. The dissenters will be executed. Any who fall through the net and escape will be managed as animals are in the wild."

An awkward silence followed where nobody moved and Abarlev wanted to move on.

"If there are no more observations, I will take all your reports in turn. By signing off your parts in the operation we will have concluded the major strategic elements. At that point, there will only be minor details that need to be chased down and resolved."

***

Heath followed the train tracks from a distance, dodging through the roofless shells of houses and staying close in to the remaining factory walls and abandoned tin sheds. Mimi was driving him crazy, refusing to stay on silent and cutting in with emergency messages from Harry Toliver demanding reports on why he was no longer on the train and telling him where the nearest checkpoint was located. Heath replied to nothing, keeping his commands to Mimi short and unrevealing. He knew that the GLiD was reporting back his every move and gradually, as the evidence of his flight through the city became evident, more agencies would be taking an interest in the rogue face on the emergency news bulletins.

He felt unnaturally thirsty and his head swam with nausea. Every time Mimi focused his attention on the GLiD, he felt a fresh wave of debilitating dizziness sweep across him, knocking him off balance. Climbing through the mud and rubble of a spoil heap he dropped the handset and it clattered over the twisted remains of a chain link fence and skidded under some concrete posts laid on the ground. Immediately Mimi was overriding the mute status, a sound was growing in his ears and his heart started pounding in his chest. He felt the uncontrollable urge to scramble down the heap to the fencing posts, falling hard as he did and rolling the last few feet to a stop. The pain started to subside and Mimi quietened down. He knew he must be within reach, and hidden in the shadow of the spoil heap, he groped in the shallow muddy hole beneath the posts for the handset. His fingers brushed over broken glass and scraped painfully along unseen points of jagged metal. He found the smooth surface of the GLiD and dragged it back out to where he lay. It was wet and scuffed, but the screen was unbroken and shone a kaleidoscopic array of red warnings and emergency notices through the clots and smears of mud.

As Heath struggled to his feet, Mimi appeared in her default head and shoulders guise, the picture above the GLiD stuttering and jumping. She was agitated to the point where her flickering expressions couldn't match the urgency of the instructions being relayed by Toliver.

"A patrol has been notified of your position and is coming to get you. Do not move from your current location unless instructed to do so!"

The pain was growing milder and his vision had stabilised. He sat on the heap, cold and muddied, thinking maybe this was the way it should be. He was tired, unused to exertion, and Mimi's voice had lowered a few tones to the soothing velvet purr that he'd spent so long refining. As he sat listening for the call of a megaphone across the wasteland and Mimi's image shone out like a beacon for the troops to follow, he wondered how he'd ever let himself fall into this trap. He tried to chase it back in his mind but there was no pivotal moment, no bad deal that was struck, just a blind blundering and unquestioning acceptance of official stories. A journalist had no option. To question was deviance, to harbour alternative thoughts was disloyal. But where there was acceptance without resistance, then how comforting was the calm reassurance that someone else was dealing with the dissonant horrors of the world.

The more these insinuations wound through his head like a disembodied voice, the more calm and narcotic were his thoughts. When he caught the sound of engines in the distance, brought by on a turning breeze, he almost smiled with relief. Something more than Mimi's platitudes were soothing him into a trance, spreading warmth where he was chilled and cocooning his mind in sleep. Yes, they were definitely engines. He would stand up and make himself visible. Stand up, Clayton.

As he pushed himself off the ground he caught the winding tone of the siren as operatives were deployed in the distance. He was almost vertical, gripping the GLiD as mud dried around his fingers when, in an instant, the screen blanked. He stared for a second. Then came the pain. It was like the radiating streaks of agony from a bullet in his chest, but he had felt no impact. He half fell back onto the rubble feeling sickness and searing pain sweep across his body. The hand holding the GLiD was oozing blood and every move was a new sting of shredded nerve endings.

"Clayton?"

"Yes?"

"Where are you, Clayton?"

"I don't know."

Mimi had vanished but the groaning voice was in his ear. She was confused. Then he knew, the internet had gone down.

He could hear voices now, and they were close by. Their comms were down too and they had to call to each other for positions. As his heart raced and the pain returned, Heath knew he had to run.

He kept low, dodging behind the gutted factory units and in between the bulldozers and trucks in the yards. He had no compass, no idea of direction, just an overwhelming desire to be as far away as possible from the sound of the voices. He couldn't run, but he could lope like a wounded animal, every step jarring his bones and catching burning cold breath in his chest. He found himself crossing a road, seeing an open gate and staggering up into the blank wastes of another industrial estate, guided by an unseen hand.

Mimi was trying to cut in with her usual repetitive regularity, but the sound of the blood pumping in his head was drowning out all but a few robotic snatches of her voice. He had no sense of time, how long he'd been staggering along. Whenever he thought there was a dead end up ahead, he found a turning down an alley, through a yard, across a patch of grass down by a canal, along some crumbling Victorian walls or back up onto a new level.

Amidst all the grey and the brown and the twisted metal roots of old industry, his eye caught a splash of colour. It was the frontage of an old café, quickly abandoned, the metal shutter only half down. It had bright No Messin' Cola signs outside and garish pictures of fast food. His thirst returned with the thought of fresh water and, looking back only once to listen for voices or footsteps, he slowed to a stop by the half hidden front door.

The shutter was jammed down over the broken pane, and Heath failed to shift it with his free hand. Painfully, he unwrapped his fingers from the GLiD and let it drop into the torn pocket of his coat. With the heels of his hands under the shutter he pushed up with his legs and felt it give. It moved a foot in one sudden jerk and almost toppled Heath forward into the glass. He stepped back and kicked at the big broken pane. It fell in with a crash and he tapped in the longest shards that remained with the sole of his shoe.

Inside the café, bistro tables and chairs had been hurriedly stacked and when the power went, the kitchen had been abandoned and the place half closed. There were other signs of struggle, glass smashed across the floor and broken furniture. Heath stood in front of a darkened vending machine. He could see cans and plastic tubes of drink inside. Without any qualifying thought, he picked up the metal leg of a broken bench and jabbed it as hard as he could at the perspex front. It cracked immediately, and after a few more desperate smashes, he broke a hole that could be easily extended. Reaching through, he took the nearest tube of orange drink and leaned against the machine, allowing the sweet fizzy liquid to regenerate the taste buds in his mouth. Swallowing was painful, but totally necessary, his body seemed to be crying out for moisture.

Heath swept the chairs off a table, righted one and sat down with his drink. Instinctively he reached for the GLiD and gingerly laid it on the table in front of him.

"Mimi? What's going on?"

"Claaayton... it's time to get up."

"I can't get up. I need to rest."

Mimi appeared in front of him, a strange mishmash of clothes and styles pulled from his local preferences. Without the internet, she was all but useless as a source of knowledge. She was agitated and looked around with a half smile and a nervous grimace juddering across her face.

"No, Clayton, you neeeed to get up. You're here."

"Where? Where am I?"

"Looook. I have something for you."

She turned and indicated the wall ahead. There was a large advertising poster with chocolate eggs bursting with cartoon chicks

181

and rabbits.

"Happy Easter, Claaaayton."

"Easter?"

"I have an Easter egg for you but you have to be... a gooood boy."

A vision of Kelvin Reid flashed through his mind.

"I put you an Easter egg on there."

Mimi was awkwardly speaking his words. She tried to laugh and look happy, but she was in the voodoo grip of another program.

The green diode suddenly pipped into life and the internet started to come back up. Icons faded into view like watery ripples and they shimmered with the broken voices of Mimi and Reid.

"You might want to thaaank me later."

"Kelvin? What the fuck is happening?"

The calm voice of a narrator in a tutorial movie cut in.

"Any kind of factory, machine shop or hobbyist will do that uses Computer Guided Miniature Tip technology. The program will identify a compatible machine with its RFID signature."

"RFID?"

Something connected in his mind. Heath noticed a weak blue light appear on one side of the GLiD. He waved it around and the blue light tracked around the screen.

Mimi cut back in but with Kelvin Reid's urgent voice.

"Stay here Clayton. Let them find you. They're on their way."

Heath pushed himself up from the table and staggered out into the estate.

The GLiD was fading in and out as Reid's voice passed between his ears.

"It's all right. Help is coming!"

Heath's will was breaking down under the pressure. He fought to stay focused.

"No! You're not Reid! I'm not listening!"

Heath pointed the GLiD forward and stumbled in the direction of the light. As he went, the screen became a radar, picking up the signals that machines used to find each other, or to look for the internet. Each machine's unique identity flowed around the directional dot and seemed to be rejected in favour of another.

The narrator was back.

"Allow the handset to settle. Each of the target markers will be identified in three dimensional space..."

The radar blips took him more than once into the tin walls of a factory unit. He followed them round and tried to find a way through, figuring that these dots were a half mile or so behind the building. A small orange dot permeated the blue and the name L4P-1X was his only clue to the name and purpose of the machine.

The narrator seemed to skip back.

"Good. This model is in the database. Now follow these simple set-up instructions."

As Heath followed the light forward, he came to an open door and a dark corridor beyond. As he checked the GLiD again he heard shouts in the distance. They were calling his name. They knew where he was and he suddenly realised that some of those blue dots were most likely the GLiDs of his pursuers, and he'd been actively moving toward them.

Mimi had reappeared next to Heath and though the screen was a regular size, her face was blown up to fill the square of light, an angry red ranting face that had more than a hint of Harry Toliver in the features. Whatever she was shouting was subsumed by the calm delivery of the narrator whose instructions had long since befuddled Heath's mind.

The L4P-1X had been joined by a slew of other orange dots and the GLiD was collecting information on them. Heath ran into the corridor and pushed through the half open heavy security door of a machine shop. The factory was still lit, the machines on standby. The place had been cleared in a hurry. In a jigsaw puzzle moment of lucidity, Heath wondered how many of the baying herd in the station might have been shipped there from these machines when the troops came.

The GLiD was taking Heath forward to a rank of automated fabricators. He stopped in front of a rig that looked slightly familiar. It was similar to the standard laser drills he'd seen at Itania.

"Position the head carefully between the handle grips. Listen to the recurring marker tones and when the tone is continuous, the computer will have located the subdermal implant."

Heath recoiled in revulsion. He'd heard all about this. The horror stories, the disasters, but the narrator's voice was soothing and calm.

"Modern implants, no larger than a grain of rice, are implanted in a shallow scraping of the skull so that bone will naturally grow over it, protecting it from damage or forcible removal."

"Oh shit!"

Heath heard voices outside, then the metal side door crashed back. He turned, shoving Mimi's huge laughing face out of the way. They were coming. The nausea rose in his stomach and his rubbery legs were barely capable of supporting his unbalanced frame. He threw away

183

the screen of Mimi's face and like a desperate child, looked for a dark space under the rollers of the assembly line.

He scooted backwards on the floor underneath the conveyor and pressed himself into the cowling of an engine drive at the turn of the rollers. He knew they'd find him. It was inevitable.

He saw the shadows of their legs first and then the big army boots. Three soldiers at least, maybe four, there could be dozens pouring through the building. They stopped in front of the conveyor. He could hear the continuous tone of their scanner now that it was within arms reach of his chip. Heath saw no reason why they shouldn't kill him there and then.

One of them squatted down and peered under the conveyor at the sweating, sobbing, torn figure struggling to keep a distorted, mad hologram from continuously reappearing at his side.

***

To the obvious satisfaction of the delegation from the MIs, the City of London was a place of calm and order. Business continued with a clockwork predictability. Even the big screens that were wrapped around the corners of buildings at significant junctions seemed to have little to report of the chaos in the suburbs. The big story was Chinese investment, the deals with the Heng Corporation and the benefits of its new city status in southern England. Advertisements played outside the footage, pushing for better deals on spending the comms allowance, or discounted health insurance in exchange for medical experimentation.

The City's servers never failed, and the lights stayed on within that comfortable bubble. No one felt the need to be concerned by the altogether expected news that hundreds of thousands of casual workers were finally opting to join the modern world and register for Global ID. Had the Prime Minister not said on endless occasions that where there was unity there was strength? Surely, uniting the country had been the dream of politicians since a parliament was first formed. Today, as usual, the trains were running on time.

The purges began in the elegant squares and avenues of the political class. The small fleet of armed mercenaries, headed by the black limousines of the MI, swept unhindered through every barrier, gates unlocked by magic and apartment foyers obligingly swinging open. The leader of His Majesty's nominal opposition was first invited, and then dragged, from his fine house, while every dissenting voice in the party was taken at gunpoint from his apartment and loaded into the waiting vehicles.

High ranking military officers who may, or may not, have voiced constitutional concerns about the abduction and processing of citizens were detained by the military police and taken to join their families. Two High Court judges committed suicide rather than face an inevitable arrest and were found in their beds, one with his wife motionless beside him and the other in the arms of his dead gentleman friend.

The convoys moved in and out of the City limits all day. They ferried their prisoners to relocation camps from where they would disappear into the fog of news reports. Sometimes 'unnamed sources' would be quoted and later in the week the news media 'would learn' of the prisoners' indeterminate fate during those busy news days when viewers could be suitably distracted.

Further down the system, the purge had to be more discrete. Too many eyes of people who were not privy to grim reality would see colleagues and bosses marched into the dark jaws of a waiting truck. For those with particularly sensitive contacts, there was neither the time nor the will to concoct a soothing and plausible cover story. These problem people were just liabilities.

Friedland's security manager felt a lingering sense of relief as the lights of the Nightship campus came back up. Like a clean-up team after a fire or flood, the roads were criss-crossed with emergency vehicles and groups of technical staff filing into buildings to plan the return to normal business. He took a message from a perimeter team to sign off the surveillance equipment that watched no-man's land and was picked up by a crew in a personnel carrier. They stopped out in the woods to check an old guard tower that bristled with dead sensors. As the security manager looked up into the unseeing eyes of the cameras, one of the team drew his pistol and blew a hole through the back of the unsuspecting man's head.

Harry Toliver sat relaxed in the middle of his long, expensive, low backed white sofa, a drink in his hand and a view through his apartment window of the Metropolitan building in the near distance. He'd been expecting Andrew Verrick, but he was now out of the country. Instead, Harry was debriefing the whole Heath affair to a young, slightly effeminate man with long hair and more than a hint of make-up around his eyes.

"Yeah. So there it is, Heath is dead. Resisting arrest while trying to escape through the redev. They'll bring him in and we'll finally have some pictures to go with the cautionary tale of domestic terror. Sure there's been some holes in it, but, like all the best crimes from the top level of government, they never stand up to much scrutiny."

The young man nodded and shifted slightly in his chair across from Harry. His voice was light and frail.

"Yes. Not very credible upon dissection. We always have to rely on the media to brainwash us with an official story."

Harry raised his glass, clinking with ice.

"Well, you know what they say about those who can't remember the past."

"Or perhaps... history is written by the winners."

Harry's smile dropped. The young man's last twitch had materialised the long black snout of a silenced pistol and in a moment of realisation, two slugs hit the centre of Harry's white shirt and a bloom of red began to crawl. The glass kicked back and bounced away, Harry died eyes open and fixed on the white edifice of the tombstone that rose above the city skyline.

Mohammed al-Degri, under house arrest since his resignation, had been at his study desk all morning reviewing the sketchy chapters of a memoir that he hoped would tell the truth about his premiership. About how vulnerable honesty can be and how good intentions could be so quickly undermined. He'd thought for so long that after the war and the H61K outbreak that the internecine battles were over, the shadow government of secret agencies was redundant and the country was truly clearing up the mess that the previous century had left behind. But of course, it was really just another move on the grand chessboard and if he didn't report it, there may not be enough people left to verify the truth.

When his wife brought him tea in the mid-morning, he was slumped across the desk, face twisted in pain by the massive heart attack that had killed him. She was so horrified, she dithered and stared, dropped the cup and finally ran wailing from the room. She never noticed the figure retreating from the French windows, sliding in between the voluminous rhododendron bushes and disappearing back to report that another loose end had been resolved.

***

Heath stared at the face before him, now lit by the pale LEDs of the machine's console.

"Heath. You're an even bigger plonker than Kelvin Reid."

"Bug?"

"Come on out of there. We've only got a few minutes!"

Heath had lost most of the motor function in his arms and legs. He was dizzy and felt the constant need to pee. He let them stand him up

186

and he smiled punch drunk at Bug's goatee. He recognised the flying goggles wrapped round the big face of Bomber, who grinned idiotically back at Heath. Bug got between them.

"Concentrate! You do everything Hokey says, got it?"

Heath was struggling with Mimi's overamped babbling in his ear but he heard enough to look round at a little half caste lad with gingery dreadlocks like a pineapple top with a smudge of beard under his chin.

Hokey was loosening the mounts on the laser cutter and barely noted Heath's grunt of greeting.

Bomber held Heath steady while Bug helped Hokey try to move the kit into position. He kept an eye on Mimi and knew that Heath would be hearing multiple voices in his head. He kept up a monologue to try and keep Heath focused.

"I told Reid and that fucking gnome that the stupid program was a death sentence. Failure rate hundred per cent when you try and do it alone. He knew you were too straight, and probably too stupid, to use a foxer. So we came after you and Reid tried to get us all together. Dam, how do you live with that bloody thing?"

Mimi was dodging around Heath, moving through angry, officious, or pleading. Sometimes a growling robotic voice was reciting email into his ear or quoting from irrelevant documents and regulations.

Hokey shook his head and tugged hard at the laser mounts.

"We ain't got enough room, I can't get the mount horizontal. It's an L4P, they're not made for it!"

Bug looked at Heath with a face of accusation.

"Bloody hell, between you and Reid you couldn't even find a decent machine."

Heath was gibbering to protest his innocence and Mimi was trying to hover between them.

"Hoke! Get this fucker up high as you can. Bomber! Put him on."

Heath was lifted effortlessly onto the conveyor and lay face up underneath the drill, a look of mute horror on his face. The GLiD slipped out of his pocket and clattered over the rollers. The laser hissed into life and began to charge. Mimi had overridden her sound and vision parameters and was cycling through garish colours and shouting so loud that Heath was swinging his head from side to side.

"Clayton Heath, your formal termination of employment from the Metropolitan International News Service is herewith delivered. All insurances, travel permits, food vouchers, carbon credits and the due privileges of your employment are revoked and cancelled... The

Management disavow all knowledge of actions undertaken that may be..."

Bomber retrieved the GLiD and handed it to Bug. Hokey got Heath's head between the side guides on the conveyor and tightened them so Heath was stuck, staring up at the point of the laser drill. Hokey furiously scratched at the side of his head and neck.

"You OK, Hoke?"

"Yeah. It's bad today."

Bug waved the GLiD over Heath's face.

"Come on, wake up! You need to hold this."

"What are you going to do to me?"

"I'm gonna zap all those nasty little thoughts in your head."

"Oh God no!"

"Shut up and don't move."

Bug put the GLiD in Heath's hand. It happily chattered to the laser and let Bug tap in the permissions to acquire its target on the drill's keypad. The laser buzzed its safety warning and an orange hazard light revolved in its plastic cupola.

A red spot of light slid down the side of Heath's nose and as it worked its way up, Mimi became judge and jury.

"You may not remove data from the premises... you may not communicate the intellectual property of the company to any other employee of the Metropolitan International News Service unless otherwise instructed to do so..."

Bug waited til the drill stopped moving.

"Ready, Hoke?"

"Just about."

"You may not use the internet for non-company related business..."

"Do it!"

Hokey had the control pendant in his hand and let his thumb hover over the pulse button. Heath was wide eyed and breathing in short gasps, the red dot fixed over the top of his forehead.

"You may not bring your own food onto the premises, including teabags..."

Hokey touched the button and a short crack of sound joined with a spark of light. Heath gasped and a wisp of smoke rose and disappeared into the air above his head. Mimi wept and her voice disappeared.

Bug grabbed the GLiD and nodded to Bomber.

"Get his hand up!"

Bomber pulled Heath's hand up over his head and held it palm down on the conveyor. Hokey pushed the mount forward and Bug acquired the second target. Mimi's silent and ghostly image was that of a crying angel fading into nothing. She reached forward to touch Heath's outstretched hand. Bug nodded his head.

"Go!"

Hokey watched the dot between Heath's thumb and forefinger, then hit the button.

Heath screamed as the last connection to the GLiD was broken and pain flooded his body, mingling with the silence and emptiness, floating free into infinite space. But his true horror was the absolute terminal experience of being entirely alone within himself.

16

"It's now Day Three of the fight back against domestic terrorism on the British mainland. Last night Prime Minister Sarion Dundas addressed the nation to announce a further two week extension of the Emergency Powers Act which has brought martial law to the streets of the UK. During this time, parliament will complete the framework for a new all party government in advance of a proposed general election that has been postponed until later in the year. While parliament is, effectively, in recess a joint operation to manage the country through the crisis has been co-ordinated through the British Military Command structure, headed by Sir Derry Thornelow. A spokesman for the government confirmed that Sir Derry's job was to 'get Britain's essential services moving, to keep the lights on, to make the countryside safe and restore order to the towns and cities.'

"In our main night time bulletin we'll be charting the progress of the UN forces who have stood between the army and the northern insurgents during weeks of bitter conflict and bloodshed. As the vast majority of the British public have now opted for enrolment into the Global ID scheme, we look at those who have chosen not to register and the risks that they pose to their families, children and loved ones, as well as the wider community. They will join the likes of criminal hackers and political dissidents in re-education centres where the government hope that a national scheme of care and rehabilitation will successfully reduce the risk posed by, what are being called 'progress deniers'.

"Tonight also, we'll be showing the Metropolitan special investigation into the career and final downfall of the self-styled hacker terrorist who became Public Enemy Number One, known to the intelligence community as The User. We reveal how Clayton Heath, a low-level employee here at the Metropolitan, was unmasked by a special security team, and then secretly monitored for a year as he gave away his underworld contacts and unwittingly furnished the authorities with details of his deadly intentions. Heath was shot dead at a South Birmingham railway station during an armed stand-off with police and army marksmen as he attempted to escape from justice. We look at the lessons learned from the systemic abuse of the security system and its toll of human lives. We ask how future governments can work with businesses and institutions to ensure that murderous individuals like Clayton Heath and his network of accomplices, would never again be allowed to cause the kind of

chaos and misery that brought the country to a standstill during this year of 2032."

Samantha Wilshire had been summoned before an executive committee of her employers at the Cyber Security Institute. It was shortly after the grimly altered prison style mugshots of Clayton Heath had begun to be shown every few minutes on every channel. They were like a constantly recycling thought that would burn itself into public memory.

A contact alert had drawn pitifully few friends of Heath in for questioning, but Wilshire's travel permits and GLiD record told the story. She chose not to attend the committee's meeting and, when her Global ID was located in a down elevator heading for the CSI private taxi ranks, a security squad was sent to bring her back. They followed her on the scanner and saw that she'd diverted into the women only washrooms by the foyer. A female officer was sent in, taser stick unclipped at the belt. Her scanner showed that the third cubicle in a long line was her target.

The officer slipped the scanner onto her belt and drew her taser stick, standing one foot forward to the cubicle door.

"Wilshire! You are under arrest. Do not resist!"

She levelled her boot at the lock and smashed the flimsy door off its hinges. There was a short scream from inside and the officer found herself looking at an old Chinese ancillary worker from the motor pool, legs raised where she'd fallen back in shock, her bloomers stretched between her feet like bunting.

***

Andrew Verrick relaxed into the leather seat of the long, black limousine that drove through the quiet streets of the City of London. Beside him was Friedland who had been saying little, choosing instead to listen to Verrick's quietly assured tones.

"We both had loose ends to tie up, and I think you'll agree, neither of us have lost anything of great value."

"I lost a trusted security manager, Andrew. Very loyal and hard to replace."

"He knew enough about your escaping decoy to leave you very exposed, and nobody's that loyal."

"We all value our spies on the shop floor."

"Indeed. But they must always be replaceable."

"Have you replaced Toliver?"

Verrick allowed a slight smirk to cross his face.

"As a spy? Not yet. But I have a face in mind. She's not squeaky clean and I think it'll pay to bring her up through the company and keep her close to me."

They both watched the streets slide by, flickering in the holographic glow of a giant stock ticker that wrapped around the corner and lost itself in the sharp glass and concrete constructions of the city. Verrick motioned through the window.

"Do you know what this is up ahead?"

"Yes, it's the MI5 building."

Verrick nodded.

"Did you know I'm in the service?"

This time Friedland smiled.

"I'm not surprised. The media is riddled with MIs."

"Look. Nightship is still at least nominally American, but your chairman wouldn't have to know if you did a little work for us from time to time. Jolly good rates of pay."

Friedland remained unimpressed.

"Well, seeing as you trump my every move, and seem to know what I'm reporting, then maybe it's not an unreasonable request."

The limousine pulled through an arch into a heavily armed checkpoint.

"Reporting? Oh, you mean like the location of those little buggers who brought down your building? Well, let's just say they've got a lot more scrap to deal with now."

***

Heath was being pushed along by Bomber through the rubble banks that had sagged into the streets. They had created a wavering and well-trodden path through the ribs of the city suburb.

Bug had gone on ahead to scout for security, but all was quiet. He climbed down from a blown-out window and picked his way back.

"Nothing. It's like they're not even looking for anyone. We could be clear back to the van."

He inspected Heath's vacant expression and the almost comical med bandage that Bomber had cocked over the laser burn on his head. They'd abandoned the remains of Heath's coat in the factory, but even his jacket and shirt were ripped through to the bare shoulder and he was streaked in mud, oil and sweat.

"You're a fucking mess, mate."

Heath heard the voice but couldn't place it. The world was a funny, quiet place and everything seemed new and indistinct. Every view was like a quick painting of a captured reality. Every noise was a fascinating detail.

Bug turned to Hokey.

"I hope you didn't boil his brain."

"Well, whatever it is, it seems to be an improvement."

Bomber laughed with a short, low chuckle and Bug nodded them forward.

Bug's customised vehicle was an old petrol pick-up truck, the roof stripped off and the sides reinforced with thick welded sheets of steel. Rudimentary shields protected the wheels from being shot out and a big cow catcher on the front came to a suitable point low to the ground. It was hidden in a big double garage next to a once grand house that was now just a shell awaiting removal. Bug slid behind the wheel and pushed an ignition button with his thumb. The engine roared and blew a plume of diesel smoke into the back of the garage. Bug blew a kiss to the plastic Barbie doll mascot that swung from the top of the windscreen and gunned the engine onto the street.

With the passengers sat low in the back behind the shields, Bug lost no time bumping through the edge of the clearance zone and out into the lanes. He'd found one of the many holes in the perimeter security where a vehicle could slip in and out of the restricted parts of town. It was through the back gates and across the grounds of an old stately home that stood in the distance. The windows had been bricked up and formal gardens left to become overgrown. One day no doubt, Bug thought, that'll be some big wheel's reward for services rendered to the regime. Until then, the army wouldn't be allowed near it, pissing in the hallways and using the garden stoneware for target practice.

Bug pulled across the A road, knowing that it would be patrolled at intervals and then he stuck with the back lanes, staring forward into the encroaching undergrowth and never looking back.

It was mid afternoon when they skirted the silent streets of another town and pulled up at a safe distance from the clutch of army vehicles that had gathered from all directions. They were focused on the high metal walls of the scrapyard, down the service road from the dual carriageway. A billowing cloud of demonic black soot was rising from the yard. A bulldozer was dragging down a section of wall through which could be seen the orange glow of flames and a raging heat that boiled out new smoke into the ever expanding column above.

They watched it burn for a few minutes, until Hokey felt able to speak.

"That's what they did to our place, too."

The spell was broken, and Bug sat back down in the driver's seat, a thousand thoughts in his mind and a terrible weight in his heart.

"That's what they're doing to every place. Time for us to go."

He fired up the engine and put his foot to the floor.

**

The helicopter slowly rose from five hundred feet until it started to reach the gloom of the hanging sky, then it started a long wide turn. It was tilting to one side to allow the passengers in the back a view of the ground. The gold livery on the side that spelt ZURA against the matt black of the body made it look like a predatory wasp choosing its target. The head of security pointed to town buildings in the distance.

"From the main campus to the treeline below will be no-man's land. The main city skirt will rise here, a hundred and seventy five feet at the highest point. It will house workshops, hangars and security space at every quarter of a mile, and over a thousand mechs in total."

Hanser nodded with approval.

"Good. Does that include surveillance drones?"

"Absolutely not. You have a separate licence for up to five thousand armed response drones and permission to secure and surveil up to eight miles from the skirt. Of course, the first mile is mined as far as the perimeter warning."

"A killing floor, as it were."

"If you like. Nobody could make it across to the skirt. Every inch is covered."

"Excellent."

Hanser turned to the architect.

"The main campus will be functioning as Zura UK by the autumn. I need to know how long before we are self-reliant and I can dispense with the government's mercenary army."

The architect tried to look reasonable.

"If we have the manpower and the machinery, the skirt could be closed within four years."

"I can bring as much manpower as you need right now. I have bought licences for an extra thirty thousand Global IDs from the Ministry of Employment. The workers will start to be delivered as soon as their implants are bedded in and they are fully processed. Once the manual work is done, you will have all the automated construction that you see in your inventory."

The helicopter's path took them over low hills and up into the mist.

194

The architect moved a holographic model around on the table between him and Hanser.

"Right now, we're over the first foundations of the main skirt. A half mile stretch across solid rock."

Hanser looked down and could see a geometric, grey expanse in the earth, gently curving into the distance. The tendrils of service roads curled away to the main highway. He was not happy.

"It will take too long. We do not have the luxury of four years. And then there is the question of the dome."

The architect felt he had found a loophole.

"Well, the technology that will construct and maintain the dome is still in the experimental stages. It must be finalised before we complete the design of the skirt."

Hanser looked at him as if he were a worm.

"Do your job, architect. We have no choice."

He jerked his thumb at the mist through the window.

"You'll be glad of a roof over your head soon enough."

The helicopter had turned in toward the town where construction scaffolding, bulldozers and half constructed roads were manned by dozens of crew. Their yellow helmets were moving industriously, like a thousand specimens of pond life under Hanser's microscope.

* * *

The spring rain was coming in as the first shades of evening darkened the hills. Bug finally relented and turned on the big old round frog eye lamps above the cow catcher. A pool of light painted the broken tarmac of the lanes. Hokey was trying to raise somebody on an old walkie-talkie, but all he got was static.

They came to a main road and all eyes scanned the road for patrols. It was still strangely quiet. Bug bounced the pick-up across the road and they started to climb into the foothills of the Welsh mountains.

Heath had been slowly coming round and now sat with one hand holding onto the side of the truck. His head was up and looking around, taking in the hillsides and their barely lit hamlets. The villages cowered under the latticework of a velvet sky scarred with angry black stripes of night cloud.

Hokey was enjoying the air, lightly scratching at his neck. Heath watched him for a minute.

"You got fleas?"

"No man. Caught a whiff of the gas when they were clearing people out south of the river."

"What gas?"

195

Hokey shook his head at the dumb question.

"The London Plague? Remember? They blamed it on the Afghan Flu."

Heath left it. Everything was new to him today.

Higher they climbed, leaving the last village and pushing past the hill farms. They had been cordoned with miles of razor wire. In the outbuildings sat dozing farmhands with Thermos flasks and loaded shotguns.

Hokey jumped when the walkie-talkie gave a little metallic cough. He raised it up and pressed the button.

" 'Ello? Billy? Moo? Anyone there?"

A small child's voice cut in through excited breaths.

"Um, what's the password?"

"I don't bloody know! We haven't got one. Get Billy."

"Oh OK."

Hokey tutted and waited til a gruff voice broke through.

"Who's that?"

"It's the tooth fairy! Who do you think it is? We're coming in. Bug, Bomber and Hokey plus one. Don't fucking shoot!"

"Hmm."

The climb into the hills had narrowed the road into a single lane. Trees either side were turning black as the sun started its descent to the horizon. Bug reached the crest of a hill and took a sudden turn left into the verge. They drove through a half hidden gateway and down onto a shallow plain that was still bright with late afternoon light. He stopped in front of a high old stone barn, the engine running, and waited for figures to emerge from the shadows. Rifle barrels slanted into the air from where they were slung across their backs and ammo belts hung crossed in front of their leather jackets.

Only Hokey was smiling as he jumped down off the back of the van, stretching and deep breathing.

"Alright Bill?"

"Come on, get inside."

Bomber helped Heath off the van and they trooped inside the barn. It was much bigger inside than it looked. The main room had a gallery and wooden stairs and there were corridors off the back. Near one wall was a multilayered perspex booth and inside it was a shiny silver drum kit.

Heath noticed guitars around the walls, cables and stands. Up at the top in a gallery was a wide window through to a room full of recording equipment.

The figure of Old Jacky appeared on the steps from the control room.

"Welcome to Soundhenge. The last redoubt."

As the main room of the recording studio filled with people from the kitchen and the bedrooms, all coming to see the new arrival, Kelvin Reid appeared with Deena and Heath felt a first twinge of emotion.

"Kelvin, I... thank you."

"You didn't make it easy, did you?"

Heath shook his hand and as he relaxed, took Deena's hand.

A voice beside him was familiar.

"What the hell happened to you?"

He turned to see Samantha, smartly dressed in black SWAT gear complete with military cap.

Heath's renewed energy faded immediately and he hugged her, breathing in short gasps and, for the first time in countless years, feeling an emotion all of his own.

She helped him stand back on his feet and she moved the grubby med bandage off his head, wincing at the burned skin and small eruption of clotted blood. She held up his hand, unwinding the dressing and seeing a similar sight.

"Jesus. What a state."

Heath was confused for a moment. Her hand was unblemished. He moved the cap back on her head and there was no mark.

"Are you still... connected?"

She shook her head and smiled.

"Clayton. Remember, I worked on these things at CSI. I learned a few secrets. How do you think politicians and corporate heads get to do what they do? You can turn them off. Nobody drills holes in their heads anymore."

Hokey slipped away with a cosmetic throat clearance and Bug stroked his goatee thoughtfully. Only Bomber thought it was funny.

That night the old college trio sat in the recreation room of Jacky's remote country studio and caught up with the missing years. Reid had been the conscience of the group. He was the first to decide that his chosen career was ultimately not in the best interests of all those people who bought into the technology. They innocently relied upon the explicit benefits that were sold above all else. They didn't consider the consequences.

Samantha Wilshire had seen every innovation, every collaboration and presentation of her work used as a basis for further control and manipulation by consecutive governments. At no point did they consider the safety and guardianship of personal freedoms in an open society. The truth came to her slowly and when she found Reid out there on the internet, anonymised to all but the few who knew him, she started to look for the way out.

Heath, being the worst kind of salesman, had always believed his own script. It took the sight of his distorted criminal's face on a newsflash in a railway station to jolt him awake from the fantasy world where images on a screen are passed off as reality.

The three stood briefly outside. They watched stars struggle through the night clouds and looked toward the hills, beyond which the towns and cities were coming back online and a new way of life was emerging.

Samantha saw Heath begin to shiver.

"You didn't come dressed for the country, did you? Admittedly, I had to borrow an outfit..."

Heath was barely listening.

"I wonder what happened to Bolstrode?"

Reid's apprehension spoke for them all.

"He's smart. He'll still be around. He once said that if we've learned anything about the injustice of holocausts and massacres, it's that it only takes an agreement of the few to affect the many. There aren't a lot of people left outside the grid. I wonder if there's enough."

Printed in Great Britain
by Amazon